CARRIE'S LEGACY

L.W. KING

This book is for my dad, my inspiration.

CONTENTS

I would like to thank my lovely family, for having patience and understanding while I was writing this book.

To my long-suffering husband, I will be eternally grateful for the freedom and praise.

To Hollie for all the encouragement and becoming so engrossed that she got lost in the story!

To my children, whose unique and quirky personalities inspire me every day!

CHAPTER 1

She stared out of the small cottage window; the earlier heavy snowfall which covered the ground made her shiver... Not that snow in January was strange or unusual. Times, however, were strange.

As a child she was afraid of people, well, people that were not her immediate family anyway. Her mum, dad, Auntie Peggy and Uncle Bill were the only things that she trusted along with nature, of course. She never trusted her sister Jade or brother Billy, they both made it clear that they didn't like her. The rose bushes in her small front garden were her best friends, as too were the trees that lined the bottom of the hill next to where she lived and the many animals that she encountered.

"Do you remember when you were five and I read your palm?" a thick Scottish accent said, making her jump.

"Peggy! I was miles away. You scared me half to death," she said, smiling as she turned to face her. Peggy was always such a welcome sight. Always there to help and guide. "Of course, I remember it, you and Uncle Bill were sleeping in our living room on the sofa bed. I used to love sneaking down to listen to your stories about Bonnie Scotland,

and dragons and fairies, such happy times," she said with a sigh.

"Aye, lassie, they were." Peggy sighed too.

She turned again and Peggy had gone. She went to the fire and added some more logs. Rubbing her hands together to keep them warm, she told herself that a cup of tea would warm them.

As she sat in the chair in front of the fire cradling the cup for warmth she began to think back to when she was a small child. Happy days. Ever since the day that Peggy had read her palm she was intrigued with the occult and the supernatural. She knew she was different to other children. While all the other girls in the street were out playing with their dolls and prams, she would take herself up the hill with nature, sitting in the trees, talking to them.

Her memory took her back to one morning she got up and heard voices coming from the kitchen. She waited behind the door when she heard her name mentioned.

"We should do something. There must be a reason she does it every night," she heard her dad say in his broad cockney accent.

"We can't take her to the doctor, he'll think we're barmy!" said her mum, not so cockney but still with a London accent.

"Last night was dangerous, if the front door had been locked who knows what could've happened!"

She walked into the kitchen and looked at her dad. "What happens every night and why is it dangerous?" she asked innocently.

"Nothing, love, we were talking about someone up the road. Weren't we, Bob?" her mum said and glared at her dad.

"No, sweetheart, we were talking about you," Dad said, giving her a comforting smile.

"Bob, honestly! I was trying to protect her," said her mum whilst scowling and shaking her head.

"She could hear us. She isn't bloody stupid, Mags." He pulled her in for a hug while her mum was drying the breakfast dishes.

Em looked up into her dad's big brown eyes. "What do I do every night, Dad?" she asked, knowing that those big brown eyes could not lie to her.

"Well, darling, for the past year, you have been sleepwalking."

She laughed. "People can't walk if they are asleep, silly."

"Well, my darling, they can, and you do," he said, hugging her tighter.

"So, what happens?" she asked.

"When it first started, you would walk down the stairs into the living room asleep, mumbling as if you were talking to someone. Once Billy tried to wake you up and you screamed so loud and then sobbed for hours, but you wouldn't tell me or your mum what was up. Last night it got dangerous because you didn't come into the living room, you went out of the back door. We hadn't even heard you. It wasn't until you walked in the front door that we noticed that the back door was wide open. We have no idea how long you'd been gone or where you went. I haven't slept a wink all night worrying about you." He kissed her on the forehead and winked. She could see the concern in his eyes.

*

The back door slammed, and she jumped from her daydream, spilling tea all over herself. Her heart started to beat fast and for a fleeting moment she wondered... Could it be him? She had a constant daydream that he would come and find her. It was the only thing that gave her hope.

"Only me, dear, I have just been to the shop to pick up some bits. Thought I would pop in and have a cuppa with you." Mrs Dawkins smiled as she filled the kettle with water. "Why, you look like you've seen a ghost. Are you feeling OK? You look awfully pale."

"I'm fine, I was daydreaming, and you startled me, that's all."

"I'll make the tea." She went to the pantry to find Peggy standing there with her hands on her hips. "What does the old busybody want now?"

"She doesn't mean any harm. I think she is just lonely," Em said.

"Oh, I think she does, lassie, all that woman is interested in is gossip. Who do you think spread all over the village that you are a healer? I mean, you only made her a dandelion tincture for her skin. No bloody gratitude!" Peggy stood shaking her fists at Mrs Dawkins. It made Em chuckle.

"I know, I'll just have a quick cup of tea with her and then I'll get rid," Em whispered.

"Sorry, what was that, dear?" Mrs Dawkins shouted from the kitchen.

"Make yourself scarce," Em whispered to Peggy as she walked through to the kitchen. "Oh, nothing, I was talking to myself, I dropped something," Em mumbled.

"First sign of dementia, that. Have you seen a doctor recently?" Mrs Dawkins said abruptly.

"Not that it's any of your business, Mrs Dawkins, but no I haven't, I have been talking to myself for years and I've lasted this long, without too much trouble!" Em said as she sat at the kitchen table.

"Aww, talking of trouble, I was talking to Mrs Deacon in the shop and she told me that there is to be an emergency village meeting."

"Really? Why?"

"Well, you know that young woman, in the new house? Two kids, no husband. Well, apparently, she reads those awful witches' cards. She been doing readings for all the young ones!" Mrs Dawkins said in her thick west country accent, looking really pleased with herself.

"Do you mean Tarot cards?"

"I don't know what the cursed things are called! Anyway, the Reverend is fuming. The meeting is tomorrow over Zoom. Will you be joining?"

"No, I don't think so. It's none of my business, and I cannot see how it is harming anyone. After all, we are in the 21st Century, and not in the dark ages." Em just about managed to contain her anger and gave Mrs Dawkins her most innocent smile.

"We thought that's what you would say, being one of that kind."

Em nearly choked on the last of her tea! "One of what kind?" Her voice now raised, she was trying not to lose her temper.

"Not now. Calm down. It's the wrong time," Peggy whispered in Em's ear.

"Anyway, must go, Jeremy will be wondering where I have gone to get his Pedigree Chum. Thanks for the tea. I will see you soon," Mrs Dawkins said as she collected her shopping bags and hurried to the door.

"Not if I see you first," Em said under her breath. "See you soon," she said as she forced a smile.

She watched as Mrs Dawkins waddled past the window and up the road.

"NOSY OLD BAG!" she shouted. "Bloody cheek. Who do these people think they are!"

*

Once the snow had cleared, which seemed to take forever, Em thought a long walk would do her the world of good. She had been stuck indoors for the past fortnight; the fresh air might help her clear her mind. She had put that many layers on she looked four times bigger than her small frame!

Walking along the tree-lined road, she took in a good deep breath. The fresh, crisp air felt amazing as she filled her lungs with it. She said hi to all the trees that she passed, not caring if anyone saw her. Everyone thought that she was bat-shit crazy anyway!

She got to the five-bar gate and used the kissing gate next to it to reach the clearing. This was her favourite place. As she lived away from the sea, this was the place, her go-to. She knew the trees, the bracken and even some of the squirrels that would get a bit brave if she had nuts in her pocket. She loved this place!

As the cold began setting into her bones and the sun was getting lower in the sky, Em decided to start heading back. As she approached the kissing gate, she could hear raised voices in the distance. She moved a little closer to hear what was being said.

"You are not welcome here. It was decided at the village meeting that you should get your affairs in order and leave this village at the earliest convenience, young lady. We cannot tolerate your sort, undermining the integrity or faith in this village. Everyone agrees."

It was the voice of John Greggs, landowner; he thought he owned the village. *Pompous prick,* Em thought.

"I only read cards for a bit of fun, and to make some extra money. I am bringing up two children on my own, and the kids love it here. Please don't make us leave. I promise I won't read cards anymore," the young woman pleaded.

"Is it any wonder your husband left you, carrying on like that?" He spat the words out.

"I think that's enough, Mr Greggs. You have attacked this poor woman enough. Off you go and count your pennies. There's a good boy," Em said as she appeared next to the now sobbing young woman.

"You would pipe up, wouldn't you? Do you both belong to the same coven? Or is she your apprentice, Ms Wells?" Em wanted to wipe that bloody smirk from his face.

"Unlike you, Mr Greggs, I do not like to conduct my business in front of the entire village, nor will I react to your unfounded accusations. So, I will bid you good day, and escort this young lady home, just in case another of your posse decide to verbally abuse her." Em took the woman by the arm and walked in the opposite direction to the now gathering crowd.

"Thank you," the woman said between sobs.

"No need to thank me. They are all bullies. They need putting in their place. Honestly, it's not the 1700s. They all need to get a grip!" Em could feel the rage bubbling up again.

"Haven't I seen you at the school?" the young woman asked. "Are you the lady that lives on the edge of the village in the cottage all by itself?"

"Yep, that's me, and my little cottage, and yes, I work for the school. I'm usually there on Wednesdays. Well, for now anyway."

"Oh, really! Are you leaving?"

"I don't stay in one place for too long and going by the infuriating attitudes of the people around here, I think my time here is nearly done."

"That's a shame. You look like you belong here," she said as she started sobbing again.

"Why don't you come and have a coffee at the cottage?" Em said.

"Thank you, that would be lovely."

The warmth of the cottage and the smell of freshly baked bread made it feel very welcoming indeed!

"What a gorgeous home!"

"Thank you. Now firstly, what's your name? And secondly, would you like tea or coffee?" Em asked with a warm smile.

"My name is Claire," she said as she laughed.

"Pleased to meet you, Claire, I'm Em."

"Pleased to meet you, Em, and I would love a coffee. White with two sugars, please."

They sat by the fire and chatted for an hour or so. Em was looking at Claire; her face seemed very familiar. Claire asked Em why she didn't stay in any one place for too long.

"I think it's because I have always been a little different to most people, and I don't really like people very much. Let's say, I have trust issues," Em said, looking into the fire.

"I can relate to that! My husband had an affair with our next-door neighbour, and then moved in with her! The final straw was that they had a baby and yet, he won't give my children the time of day. That's why we moved here. Fresh start and all that."

"I'm sorry, that's shit. What a bastard!" Em looked at Claire and noticed tears welling in her eyes. "I wish there were something I could say that would make you feel a little better, but I know there's not. All I will say is that time is a great healer, and there are some good people in the world, you've just got to find them." Em thought of his beautiful face, his strong arms wrapped around her; she missed him so much! She felt that she was no closer to finding him.

"What about you, Em? Do you have a family?" Claire asked.

Em could feel the sting of tears in her eyes. "I had a family once. I lost them. Long story."

"I'm so sorry! Was it an accident?"

"No, they disappeared."

"Really! How awful. When did this happen?"

"Like I said, long story, trust issues, I would rather just leave it there. I have only known you for an hour and in that time I have told you more about me, than I have anyone in years."

"Sorry, I er, I didn't mean to pry," Claire said as she looked at her watch.

"You had better make a move and collect your little ones from school," Em said.

"Yes. I didn't realise it was that time. Listen, Em, I cannot thank you enough for today, you are too kind."

"No problem. Come on, get going, I have work to do." Em was tapping her watch.

"Yes, sorry. Well, thank you again. Hopefully, I'll see you soon," Claire said as she was walking out of the door.

"See you," said Em as she waved and closed the door. She put her back against the door and slid to the floor, sobbing. Would she ever find them?

She picked herself up, wiped her face off and looked in the freezer for something for dinner. She took a coffee up to her study, switched on her laptop. She had better get some work done! As the laptop was loading, the news pages came up. She took a mouthful of coffee and was organising herself when an article caught her eye.

FAMILY APPEAL FOR INFORMATION ON MISSING HUSBAND.

As she scrolled through the story it all seemed so familiar. Loving husband and father. Loyal, faithful and totally out of character.

She sat with her head in her hands in deep thought.

"This is not your problem, Em, you have enough to worry about without taking on others' problems," Peggy said.

"Maybe I can help them," Em replied. "I need to do something, Peggy. If I can't find my own family, then maybe, just maybe, I can help them."

"But you need to concentrate on finding Ronnie, your mum and your dad."

"It's useless! It's ridiculous that I have a gift that can help find people, people that I don't even know, but I cannot use it to find the people I love the most." Em could feel the despair building. "WHERE THE FUCK ARE THEY, PEGGY?" she screamed.

"You need to calm down, NOW," Peggy said as she looked directly at Em. "For weeks now you seem to have given up. You are never going to find them hiding away here, are you?"

"I am NOT hiding away! I followed the dreams, the crystal ball, the Tarot cards. They all led me here. To find what? A bunch of bigots and fuck all else!" Em shouted.

"Right, lassie, you need to tune back into your gift. Tune back into nature, concentrate on building your energy back up, and stop feeling sorry for yourself. Where is that strong woman that I know and love? Come on, get back on track!" Peggy said sternly.

All intentions of work had now diminished, Em knew she could not concentrate. She looked out of the window, wondering how it had got so dark so quickly. She looked at the clock; it was 6pm. Em closed her laptop and went down to the kitchen and started to prepare the food she took out earlier. She had zero appetite, but she knew that Peggy was right. She needed to build herself back up, both physically and mentally.

She put some logs on the fire, put on the TV, poured herself a glass of wine and sat down with her lasagne. She was eating when the phone rang. Em looked at the screen. *OH shit,* she thought as her sister's number flashed up. She really wasn't in the mood for her right now.

"Hello."

"Hello, stranger, how are you?" Jade said.

"I'm OK. How are you?" Em really couldn't care less. To say she had a very strained relationship with her sister was an understatement!

"Are you still in the West Country?" Jade asked.

"Well, for a little while, yeah. Why?"

"Lewis and I thought that we might pop down and see you. We could both do with a break, and we haven't been down to the West Country in years."

Shit! How the hell am I going to get out of this? Em thought to herself.

"Em, are you still there?"

"Er, yes, sorry. Er, when were you thinking of coming?"

"Well tomorrow, it is Friday, and we are both off until the following Thursday. Is that OK with you?"

"Sure, what time do you think you'll get here?"

"About 6 in the evening. Honestly, Em, you could sound a little enthusiastic!" Em frowned as she imagined her sister pouting at that very moment.

"I am! I mean, it will be lovely to see you both. Will you be having supper?" Em said, trying to sound a little more excited.

"Supper will be lovely. Just remember I am now vegetarian, and Lewis is gluten intolerant. If you are cooking meat, don't give him too much. I am trying to wean him off it."

"He is not five, Jade. He is a fifty-year-old man. I'm sure if he wanted to be vegetarian, he would be!" Em said in disbelief.

"Emily, meat is not good for you and I am just trying to do the best for him, not that it is any of your business! I'm going now, need to get packed. I will message you in the morning with our travel itinerary."

"OK, can't wait, see you tomorrow," Em said, trying her hardest not to sound sarcastic. "Bitch!" Em said as she hung up. This was all she needed; trying to get herself in a good place, and that stupid cow turning up. What a nightmare!

CHAPTER 2

*C*omplete *darkness engulfed her; she felt as though she was suffocating.* "*Peggy, PEGGY!" she screamed. She could just make out Peggy's silhouette in the darkness.* "*Is it here?" Em whispered.*

"*Aye, I can feel it, the negative energy," Peggy whispered back.*

A low growling sound was growing in the silence. Em felt pressure around her neck; she was struggling, fighting to breathe. "*FIGHT IT, EMILY!" Peggy shouted.*

"*I WANT WHAT'S MINE," it growled, that all too familiar unworldly voice. Its grip tightening around Em's neck. Em fought hard but it was impossible. She couldn't breathe.*

She woke up choking, covered in sweat. "Peggy, Peggy are you here?" she called out between coughing and sobbing – nothing. *Oh shit – where is she? Has it got her?* Em thought to herself.

She got out of bed and went down the stairs, she opened the fridge and took out a bottle of water. Shit, her throat hurt. She downed the water and looked at the clock: 4:20am. Why did it always happen then?

Em walked back upstairs and went to her study. There was no way she was going back to sleep after that! She switched on her laptop.

"You are not going to look at that family again, are you?"

"Peggy!" Em cried. "Thank the Goddess, you are safe!"

"Oh, it'll take more than a thing like that to stop me protecting you, Em." Peggy winked.

"What is it? What does it want? Do you have any idea?" Em asked.

"To be honest I have come across these things before, but I have no idea what it wants, Em."

9.30 a.m.

ON THE ROAD NOW. TRAFFIC IS GOOD. SHOULD REACH YOU AT 6.00 PM APPROX. WILL UPDATE AT 1.00PM. X

Great! Em had just finished her morning meditation, so her reaction wasn't half as bad as it could have been!

Em had a shower and then decided that she had better drive to the local supermarket and get some food in for her visitors.

Em was unpacking the shopping when the back door opened and in walked Mrs Dawkins. "Nice of you to knock," Em said as she turned to face her.

"Now don't be like that, dear. I haven't seen you in a while, I thought I had better check and make sure you are OK." Em felt a pang of guilt and smiled at her.

"I'm fine, thanks, would you like a cuppa?"

"Love one," she replied. "That's an awful lot of groceries for one person. Do you know something we don't?" Mrs Dawkins said as she chuckled.

Fishing again! Em thought. "No, my sister and her husband are coming to stay for a few days. You know, like a mini-break."

"Well, the company will do you good, no doubt," Mrs Dawkins said.

"Hmmm," was all that Em could reply.

"Ooh, there's something I have to tell you!" she said excitedly.

"Really?" Em replied with about as much enthusiasm as a snail.

"Yes – you know that young woman, you know the one that was told—"

"Yes, I know the one," Em interrupted.

"Well, she did a moonlight flit, left her furniture and everything!"

"Really? Maybe she has gone on holiday or to see her parents," Em said.

"No, you see Mrs Deacon told me that she sent Mr Greggs a letter."

"Why did she send him a letter?" Em asked.

"Why, I reckon is cause he's her landlord."

"Oh, I see."

"Well, he went to the house, see, and all her stuff was still there. What's even stranger is that he found a load of photos of you! All over the place, he said they were! Said he knew she was your apprentice!"

"What do you mean, photos of me? Photos doing what?" Em's head was reeling.

"Well, she didn't go into details, but by all accounts, they were everywhere."

"And where are these photos now?" Em asked impatiently.

"I don't know, dear. Mr Greggs probably has them. Anyway, must be getting on. I'll leave you to get ready for your family, dear," Mrs Dawkins said as she finished the last of her tea.

Em looked up as the back door closed. *SHIT*. How the hell was she going to get these photos, and what the hell was Claire doing with them? She couldn't ask Mr Greggs for them; the last time she saw him they didn't exactly part on the best terms.

"What about that teacher at the school? Suzie, isn't it?" Peggy said.

"What about her?" Em looked puzzled.

"You get on well with her, she loves what you do for the children. Maybe you could ask her if she knows anything. You know what this place is like for gossip, she probably knows everything."

"I'll message her now," Em said, as she picked up her phone. She didn't expect a reply until later as Suzie would be teaching and it was lunch time.

Em was making up the guest bed in the spare room when her phone pinged. She ran into the study and was disappointed to see it was a message from Jade.

1.00PM STILL ON TRACK, TRAFFIC GOOD. SEE YOU AT 6PM. JADE

"Oh, fuck off, Jade!" Em shouted, as she threw the phone on her desk. She went back to the spare room and finished off. She picked up her phone on the way downstairs and noticed one message and a missed call. She opened the message first.

WELL! THANK YOU FOR THE REPLY SIS. HAVE YOU FORGOTTEN YOUR MANNERS? LOOK FORWARD TO SEEING YOU. JADE.

The missed call was from Suzie. *Shit!* She couldn't call her now; she would be in lessons. The phone pinged again, and it was a message from Suzie:

Hi Em, tried to call in my break. Will give you a call at 4.30 when I finish. Suzie.

Em made herself some lunch and a coffee and took it up to her study. She was employed to do lesson plans and care plans for the children with learning difficulties at the local primary school. She worked from home every day, except Wednesday when she worked at the school. She had got so behind, she really needed to catch up.

Em closed her laptop and looked at her watch: 4:20. Suzie would be calling in ten minutes. There was a large crash from downstairs. Em ran down into the kitchen to find all of the cupboards open and her mum's casserole dish smashed in the middle of the floor. "What the hell?" Em said as she went to see if any of the doors or windows were open. Nothing. Em cleared away the broken pieces of her mum's dish and put the kettle on. Her phone rang; it was Suzie. "Hi Suzie, thanks for calling," Em said.

"Hi Em, how's things?"

"A little bit strange at the moment. Listen, there is something I need to ask you."

"Fire away, I'm all ears."

"It's about Claire."

"Claire?"

"Oh, sorry, Claire Hoskins, her son Josh is in your class."

"Oh, I see." Suzie's typically happy voice turned quite strained. "Look, Em, I needed to speak to you anyway, but not over the phone. There are some nasty rumours going around the village. Would you be able to pop round to mine this evening? I would come to you, but Rob is on night shift, so I have got the twins," Suzie said.

"Hmm, it's a bit awkward, my sister is coming from Kent tonight,

I can't really just leave her."

"What about tomorrow? I have to drop the twins off at the pool, but I could meet you after?"

"That would be better. What time?"

"Shall we say 12:30 at Victoria Park?"

"Brilliant! See you then."

"See you then, Em."

"I have found out some things from the ancestors," Peggy said, from behind her.

"For crying out loud, Peggy, we need to sort out some sort of warning for you, you scared the bloody hell out of me!" Em stood holding her heart, for fear that it would jump right out of her chest.

"Sorry, lassie, I didn't mean to scare you. You are very jumpy at the moment." Peggy looked concerned.

"I was upstairs, and I heard an almighty crash come from the kitchen. When I came down all the cupboards were open and Mum's dish was in pieces in the middle of the floor," Em said.

"Oh, dear. I think that we need to create some protection works, especially now I know what I do."

"Oh, the ancestors," Em said, looking puzzled.

"That thing, last night."

"Yes, what about it?"

"It's a manifestation."

"And?"

"It is an extremely negative spirit, and it's pretty powerful. It is from ancient times and it's on the hunt." Peggy sounded worried.

"Shit, what time is it?" Em said to herself. She looked at her watch – it was 4:50. There was no way she would have time to create protection works before Jade turned up.

"I won't have time to do any working before Jade gets here. Shit!"

"So, we wait until they go to bed. Set your alarm for 2:30am — that's when the moon will be at waning phase, the best time to do it." Peggy winked and then disappeared.

Em made herself a cup of coffee, lit the fire and sat in front of it. She just wanted to enjoy the peace while she could.

*

They were in the big open-air market at the seafront. Mum and Jade were looking at some saucepans and Em was looking through some clothes rails on a stall that sold ethnic boho clothes. Mum called over. "Em, coffee time, it's my round. What do you want?"

"I'll have a hazelnut latte please, Mum!" Em shouted back.

"OK love, I won't be long, I'll meet you both at the boating pool," Mum said as she disappeared amongst a swathe of shoppers.

"I don't know why you buy that tat," Jade said as she joined Em.

"Because I happen to like it, and it doesn't involve sweat shops or slave labour," Em scowled.

"Well, I think it's over-priced rubbish, and it's scruffy," Jade said, as she turned her nose up.

Em shook her head and took the items to a small Nepalese woman, who ran the stall.

"All I can say is, that it must be busy at the coffee shop. Where the hell is Mum?" Jade said as she looked at her watch. "Lewis is picking me up in ten minutes, at this rate I won't have time to drink my tea!" she added, as they waited at the boating pool.

"Shame," said Em, laughing.

"God, you are intolerable, Em!"

"Yes… yes I am," Em said.

Jade's phone pinged. "I'm off. Lewis is parked at the taxi rank and cannot wait. Tell Mum thanks for the tea… it was delicious."

"Sure will," Em replied as she looked at her watch. Mum had been gone forty-five minutes. She had better go and look for her.

She went to the coffee cabin; there were so many people! She pushed her way through the people and walked inside. No sign of her. She pushed through the queue of people, who started tutting, and shouting out that there was a queue. "I know that there is a queue, I am not buying anything, I just need to ask something," Em said as she turned to face the queue of people.

"Excuse me," she shouted to the young girl working at the coffee machine. Nothing. "EXCUSE ME!" Em shouted.

"What! Christ, can't you see I'm run off my feet!" the young girl shouted.

"I just need to ask a quick question," Em said over all the noise.

"Well, what is it?" the girl asked impatiently.

"Was there a woman in here about 50 minutes ago? She's about this high, mid-length grey hair?"

"Have you seen the amount of people in here? I have seen about a hundred people like that," the girl said as she rolled her eyes and turned her back on Em.

"Well, could I at least show you a photo?" Em said, scrolling through her phone.

"I haven't got time for this! Have you seen the queue?" the girl huffed.

"Well, thanks ever so much, you have been most helpful!" Em said. She scanned the cabin and then stormed out. "Rude bitch," Em said as she managed to get out of the crowds of people.

She took out her phone and called her mum's number – straight to voicemail. "Mum, can you just let me know where you are? Jade's gone home, and I have had enough of this place and just want to go home."

Em hung up and her phone rang. It was Ronnie. "Hey babe," he said in his gorgeous northern accent.

"Hey, have you finished work now, babe?" Em asked.

"I finished about half an hour ago, you gonna be long?" he said.

"Well, I want to come home, but I have lost Mum. She went to get the coffees an hour ago and I haven't seen her since." Em was starting to worry.

"I'm sure she has bumped into one of her friends, you know how your mum likes to talk. Look, I'll come down and meet you. I can help you look for her. OK?"

"OK, thanks babe, I'll wait by the boating pool, see you soon."

"See you soon, sweetheart, love you."

"Love you too." Em looked at the phone. Nothing.

She tried her mum's number again; this time it said, "The number you have dialled has not been recognised."

"What the hell?" Em tried the number again. Same thing. She looked around, but there were still so many people, it was like looking for a needle in a haystack. She made her way back to the boating pool and waited for Ronnie. Even if Mum had bumped into one of her friends, she would have let Em know where she was. This was really out of character.

It was a comforting sight, to see the love of her life wading through the crowds of people. She stood and waved to get his attention. He spotted her and made his way over to her.

"You are a sight for sore eyes," Em said as she threw her arms around Ronnie's neck.

"Alright babe," he said before he planted a big kiss on her lips.

"Where the bloody hell is she?" said a cockney voice behind Ronnie.

"Dad! What are you doing here?" she said as she looked at Ronnie with raised eyebrows.

"Well, it might have escaped your attention, but she is my wife!" Dad said. He was really agitated. Dad became anxious really quickly, which is why Em hadn't phoned him; she knew he would panic. Especially about Mum; he worshipped the ground she walked on.

"I know! I just didn't want to worry you; I knew you were watching football this afternoon," Em said.

"Where have you looked?" Ronnie asked.

"I have been to the coffee cabin, but they were as much use as a chocolate teapot! To be honest, there are so many people here, it's so hard to search out one person."

*

The doorbell rang, and Em looked at her watch. 6pm. *SHIT, it must be Jade and Lewis.* It rang again. Jade never was known for her patience! "Alright, alright, I'm coming!" Em shouted. She opened the door and Jade barged past her.

"It's bloody freezing out there, what took you so long? I thought you had gone out!" Jade said as she threw her coat off and onto the sofa.

"Where's Lewis?" Em asked.

"Oh, he had to take an important phone call, so he is still in the car. Come on, get the kettle on, I'm parched." Jade said as she marched into the kitchen.

Em saluted, and Peggy, who was standing beside Em, laughed. "Where do you keep your teabags?" Jade said as she rooted through the kitchen cupboards.

"Well, funny thing, this. They are in the tea caddy. Who would have thought that I would keep them there?"

Jade threw Em a filthy look and then opened the caddy. "Oh, what sort of tea is this?" Jade said, screwing her face up.

"It's clipper tea, absolutely no plastic and a lovely cuppa," Em said, smiling.

"Don't you have any flavoured tea? I only drink Twinings at home," Jade said.

"Well, you should have brought some with you. I am afraid that, in my house you get what I have or go without," Em said, feeling extremely pleased with herself.

The doorbell rang. "That will be Lewis. Go and give him a hand, will you?" Jade looked at Em.

"Why of course, ma'am. Anything else? A foot rub, hot bath…"

"Just go and get the door, he'll catch a death." Em huffed and went to the door.

CHAPTER 3

Once they were settled and had supper, they were sitting in the cosy lounge, in front of a roaring fire. Em was in her big cuddle chair, and Jade and Lewis sat upright on the edge of the sofa. Jade yawned and Em looked at her watch. 10:30. "Well, I'm shattered, so I am going to call it a night," Jade said as she stood up.

"Always were such a party animal, weren't you Jade?" Em said and smiled at Lewis, who was trying to hide a smirk.

"We have been travelling all day and I am usually in bed by 9:30. Come on, Lewis," she said and beckoned him with her head.

"I might have a coffee before I go to bed, I'm not really that tired," he said, looking almost scared of Jade's reaction.

"Suit yourself, but don't disturb me when you do come up. Oh, and only one coffee. It's not good for you!"

Em made the coffees and took them into the lounge. "So, how are you?" Lewis asked.

"Oh, you know me, just trying to get on with life," Em said, staring into the fire.

"We both know that's not true. I hear that you are still searching for them. It's been a year; don't you think it's time to give up now?"

Lewis said, so matter-of-factly.

"DO NOT TRUST HIM," Peggy whispered in Em's ear.

"I don't!" Em said out loud, without thinking.

"I know you don't want to, but I think you are wasting your time. You should be more like Jade; she has come to terms with the fact that she will probably never see them again," he said, glugging down his coffee. Well, at least he hadn't realised that she was talking to Peggy!

"I am NOT Jade. I know they are still alive, and I WILL find them!" Em was close to losing it. "Now, if you don't mind, I would like to turn out and go to bed!" She didn't even look at him.

Em threw herself on her bed and sobbed into her pillow. What a prick! Why was Jade so quick to just write them off! What the hell was wrong with her? Em yawned. She set the alarm on her phone and crawled under the covers.

She was in a large building, like a derelict stately home. There was little furniture. She could hear voices, in the distance. She followed the voices up the huge concrete staircase. She heard her name being called. "MUM, IS THAT YOU?" she called out. Now there were lots of voices, all calling her name. The hallway started to spin.

Em fell. Darkness. Then the sound of that awful growling. She felt IT getting closer. "WHAT DO YOU WANT?" Em screamed.

"YOU KNOW WHAT I WANT!"

She felt its grip around her throat. She screamed, "GET AWAY FROM ME. YOU WILL NOT HARM ME," and blew all the love that she had in her soul, for Ronnie, for Mum, for Dad and Peggy, at it, and it disappeared.

"Well done you!" Peggy said as she sat on the edge of the bed.

"Hmm, somehow I don't think that will work for much longer. I can feel the power building in that thing," Em said as she put her head in her hands. "What does it want? I really haven't got a clue, Peggy."

"I'm working on it. We need to get the protection works done for a start, and then maybe you should look at your crystal ball," Peggy said, looking troubled.

There was a *tap, tap* on the door. "Is everything alright in there?" It was Lewis.

"Yes, fine thanks," Em said.

"I heard you speaking to someone."

SHIT!

"OH, I was using my Dictaphone, couldn't sleep so I decided to do some work," she said, crossing her fingers.

"OK, so long as you are alright. Night."

"Night," she called out, nearly bursting into laughter.

"I don't trust that one. I think he knows something," Peggy said.

"Like what?" Em whispered.

"I'm not sure, but the truth will out. Just be careful what you say to either of them!"

*

The alarm was going off. Em reached out to her bedside table and looked at the time. 7:30. She hadn't finished the protection works until 4am, all she wanted to do was crawl back under the duvet, but she could hear voices downstairs. *Great!*

As she got to the bottom of the stairs, she heard them talking. "Your sister is not right in the head. I heard her talking to someone at around 2am and then heard her walking around at 3:30," he said.

"Oh no, she hasn't started sleepwalking again, has she? She used to do it all the time as a child. If she has, it means trouble for us," Jade said.

"What means trouble for you?" Em said cheerfully as she walked into the kitchen.

"Oh, er, the people that put an offer in our house, we think they are going to pull the plug," Jade said. Em nearly laughed, but managed to hold it in. "Anyway, Em, I have written our itinerary for the day. You don't have long, so a quick cuppa, then you need to get ready," Jade said, changing the subject.

"No, sorry, I can't today, I have work to do," Em said as she shoved a slice of heavily buttered toast in her mouth.

"Why are you working on a Saturday? And you shouldn't eat so much butter, it will clog your arteries."

"I have a meeting with one of the teachers. Neither of us had time during the week. Sorry, can't be helped. I am sure you both of you will have a great time without me anyway," Em said.

"I shall go and get showered then. Don't bother about food tonight, we are going to book a table somewhere," Jade shouted as she was walking up the stairs.

Em was sitting at her dressing table drying her hair, when the large photo of Ronnie fell off. *Shit*, she thought. She bent down to pick it up and luckily it hadn't broken. She looked at the photo and remembered the first time she saw his beautiful face. Em was 18 and working in a restaurant part-time, while she was at college. The restaurant was on the seafront in the fishing town where she was born and had grown up in. It was a Saturday night; it was always busy on a Saturday, but they were fully booked all evening as there was a massive motorbike show being held in the town. To say she was run off her feet would be an understatement.

At around 10pm, Carol, the manager, told Em to go for her break. After grabbing a few chips and a bottle of water Em went out the back for a cigarette. It was quiet out in the beer garden, just two couples at different tables.

"Sorry, but have you got a light?" a sexy northern voice said.

Em looked up and there he was – tall, handsome, with the most beautiful blue eyes she had ever seen. "Oh, er, yes, sure." Em felt herself going seven shades of red as she fumbled in her apron pocket for the lighter.

"Would you like one?" he asked, holding out the packet.

"I'd better not, I'm only supposed to be on a quick break," she said. She *so* wanted to stay.

"I'm sure it won't hurt; you have been rushed off your feet all night," he said as he shook the packet at her.

"Oh, bugger it. Go on then," she said as she helped herself.

"Don't suppose you would let me take you for a drink when you've finished?" he asked, looking at the floor.

"I probably won't finish until 1:30, there isn't anywhere open then," Em said. She felt like saying, 'Fuck it, let's just go now,' but she needed the job and didn't want to let Carol down.

"Em," Carol shouted from the door.

"Coming," Em called back.

"Come on, love, the other girls need to take a break too," Carol said.

SHIT!!!!!

"Duty calls," she said as she stubbed out her cigarette. He looked disappointed.

"Em," he called as she opened the door to go back in.

"Yeah?"

"My name's Ronnie."

"It was lovely to meet you, Ronnie," Em said as she rushed back in.

They finally finished at 1:40am. They were sat at a table while Carol was sorting out the tips. "Somebody was popular tonight,"

Nicky, one of the other waitresses said.

Carol looked straight at Em. "Yes, that young northern gentleman was quite smitten with our Em." Carol winked at Em, and Em could feel herself blushing.

"He didn't stop looking at her all night," Nicky added.

Em stood up and yawned. "I think that's my taxi," she said as she looked out of the window.

Carol gave Em her tip money. "See you tomorrow, love," she said.

"See you all tomorrow," Em called out as she got in the taxi.

*

Em woke up to the smell of kippers, and Dean Martin blaring out on the living room stereo. She looked at the clock – it was 10:30. *Shit!* She felt like she had only had an hour's sleep. She went down to the kitchen, where Mum was at the cooker. "You look knackered," Mum said. "What time did you get home?" she added.

"About 2," Em yawned.

"They work you too hard at that place, maybe you should look for something else. You will run yourself into the ground. What with college and working every weekend," her mum said as she swept Em's fringe out her eyes.

"I'm fine, Mum. I like working there, and I need the money," Em said as Dad walked into the kitchen to eat his kippers. Em didn't tell her mum that she had been awake most of the night thinking about the most beautiful man she had ever seen and would probably never see again.

She sat opposite her dad at the kitchen table eating a bowl of cereal. Dad looked up from the newspaper. "You have a sparkle in your eye, Em, got something to tell us?" he asked as he winked at her mum.

"What are you talking about? You silly sod! She looks bloody knackered." Her mum laughed.

"I don't have anything to tell you," Em said, not making eye contact with either of them, but going redder by the second.

"You sure?" Dad said, looking at her over his glasses. He knew! How did he do that! She could never keep a secret from him. He had this thing, like he could almost read her mind.

"Well, a guy came in the sea shack last night and he was really nice," Em said.

"I see, and has he asked to take you out?"

Here we go, Em thought. *Inquisition time!*

"Well, he asked if he could take me for a drink after work, but I finished too late. Not that it matters because he comes from up north somewhere, so I will never see him again," Em said solemnly.

"How do you know?" Dad said. "Maybe he lives down here."

"I doubt it, he was probably down here for that motorbike show."

"I have a feeling you will see him again, my darling," Dad said as his gaze turned back to the paper. She spent the entire day locked in a daydream. She could not stop thinking about him.

Em was full of energy, so she decided to walk to work the beach way. There were lots of people about even though it was a bit chilly. When the Sea Shack came in sight, Em could see someone sitting on the wall outside. Her heart started to beat fast as she realised it was Ronnie.

"Hello again," she said, as she strode up to him, full of confidence.

"Hi, I thought if I caught you before you started, you might have time for a chat," Ronnie said.

"How did you know I was working tonight?" Em asked, bubbling with excitement inside.

"I asked your boss last night," Ronnie said. It was his turn to blush now.

They sat and talked for 20 minutes before Em had to start. She found out that he was from Chester and was indeed there for the motorbike show. Sadly, he was going back tomorrow. Em stood up as her shift was about to start.

"I could come down next weekend," Ronnie said. "Maybe you could book a night off and I could take you out for dinner," he said. How could she resist? Em took her pad out of her apron pocket and wrote her home number on it. She handed it to Ronnie. "Make sure you call me and let me know that you are back safely," she said as she leant over and kissed his soft lips. Her legs turned to jelly.

*

Her phone pinged, bringing her back to earth with a bang. *See you at 12.30 Suzie*, the message read.

Em was waiting by her car in the car park at Victoria Park. She saw Suzie in the distance, gave her a wave and started to walk towards her. Suzie held out a coffee in a take-out cup. "I took the liberty of grabbing us a take-out. Got you a latte, is that OK?" Suzie said.

"Lovely," Em said, as they started to walk the pretty path around the perimeter of the park.

"So, about this Claire," Suzie said. "What did you want to ask me?"

"I take it you know that she was ordered out of the village."

"I knew she was moving; she wrote me a letter to say that the children would be moving to a different school. Who ordered her to leave the village?" Suzie asked.

"The bloody committee, that's who, bunch of bigots." Em was trying to be polite and not swear but they all made her so angry.

"Why? How did they make her leave? On what grounds?"

"Mr Big Pants Greggs was her landlord, and he is head of the committee. It's because they found out that she was reading Tarot cards and said that she was compromising the faith and integrity of the village. What a joke!" Em had started to shake with anger.

"So, what do you need to ask me?" Suzie said, blowing on her coffee.

"Mrs Dawkins came round for a cuppa yesterday and told me that this Claire had done a moonlight flit. When Greggs went to the house to check it, he found photos of me everywhere!"

Suzie nearly choked on her mouthful of coffee. "Really? Did you know her well?"

"I met her once. She was being balled out by Greggs in the middle of the village, so I took her back to the cottage to calm her down."

"How odd," Suzie said, rubbing her forehead, "but I don't see how I can help, Em, I didn't even know any of this had happened."

"Well, you know how Rob's dad is friends with Greggs, I wondered if you would be able to find anything out for me that way," Em said. "I'm sorry to have to ask, but I had words with Greggs when he was shouting at Claire and he more or less called me a witch. I don't think he will take too kindly to me asking for the photos," Em said.

"I'll see what I can do, but I can't promise anything. You know what that lot are like, cliquey bunch."

"Thanks, Suzie. I would appreciate anything at the moment. I have no-one else to ask."

"Hmm, I know, your name is mud all over the village at the moment. The reverend came to the school the other day and asked me what I thought about your values and moral integrity."

"What the fuck! Oh, sorry." Em put her hand over her mouth. "Well, that's made my mind up, I am leaving this place as soon as I can," Em said, horrified by what Suzie had just said.

"You can't leave, Em, you are such an asset to the school, and you make such a huge difference to the children's lives."

"Well, tell that to that bunch of arseholes that call themselves the committee then," Em said as tears filled her eyes.

"Stay calm, don't let this upset you and cloud your judgement. You are here for a reason, Em," Peggy said in her ear.

Em wiped the tears away and shook herself. "Come on, girl, get a grip," she told herself. "Right, well I had better get on, lots to do," Em said, forcing a smile.

"Em, look, I'll do my very best to find out what's going on, but please, please don't make any hasty decisions about moving on. Give me a couple of days at least," Suzie asked.

"OK, I'll think about it. See you soon," Em said as she turned and walked away from Suzie.

Em couldn't stand the thought of going back to the village just yet, and she wished that she had never moved there. All the dreams she had, led to the West Country, as too did the crystal ball and the Tarot. The cottage was in the ideal position for Em to try and find them, yet every avenue came to a dead end. She got in her car and lit a cigarette, wondering what do with herself. "Those things will kill you," Peggy said from the passenger seat.

"You sound like Dad," Em said and chuckled.

"Why don't you go to the sea for a bit? I know that you miss it. It might help clear your mind," Peggy said.

Em turned to say something but she'd gone. "Boscastle! That's where I'll go. Thanks, Peggy," Em said out loud.

*

As she was walking through the pretty fishing village she immediately began to feel better. She could smell the salty air from the sea, and it was pretty quiet because it was out of season. Em grabbed a take-out coffee from the tourist information café and headed to the rocks above the sea. She must have been sitting, just watching the waves for about 20 minutes, when a very friendly collie dog ran over to her and started to lick her face. "He likes you," said an older lady, who was now standing beside her with a lead in her hand.

"He's lovely. What's his name?" Em asked.

"Merlin," chuckled the woman. She had long grey hair, and a truly kind face.

"Hello Merlin," Em said as she was stroking this very playful dog.

"Do you have one? A dog, I mean," asked the woman.

"Unfortunately, no. I would love one, but I move around a lot, it wouldn't be fair," Em said solemnly as she remembered Butch, her beloved boxer.

"You search for something, you cannot find," the woman said, looking out to sea.

"Er, er, yes. How did you know?" Em was feeling a little uneasy now.

The woman turned to look Em straight in the eye. "There is great danger ahead for you, you are looking in the wrong place, you need to be strong, follow your instincts and believe in your gift."

Em turned to look at the waves crashing over the rocks. "How, how do you know?" Em was afraid to ask, but she needed to know. She turned and the woman had gone. Em stood and looked all around her. No woman, no Merlin. *What the hell just happened!* Em thought to herself.

CHAPTER 4

Em was in her kitchen, preparing her dinner when the front door opened. It was Jade and Lewis. "Don't mind us, we are just going to shower quickly and then we are off out," Jade shouted as they were walking towards the stairs.

"OK," Em shouted back "Thank the Goddess for that," she mumbled under her breath. "For a second I thought they had changed their minds about going out for dinner," Em said, breathing a sigh of relief. Em went into the lounge, lit the fire, poured herself a large glass of wine. She went to the turntable – well, it was Ronnie's pride and joy, he loved music – and she put on one of Ronnie's old Blues albums; it always made her feel close to him.

Em decided that rather than sit with her dinner on a tray, watching mindless crap on the TV, she would sit at the table and listen to music. She put her pie in the oven. She would wait until Tweedledee and Tweedledum went out before she ate.

She heard footsteps coming down the stairs. "What is that awful noise you are listening to?" Jade piped up.

"Ronnie's favourite album." Em looked her straight in the eyes.

"Sorry, Em, that was insensitive. Anyway, must go, we have a table booked for 7:30," Jade said, looking at the clock.

"Where are you eating?" Em asked.

"At the Manor," Jade said with a beaming smile.

"Oh, very la-di-da," Em said and smiled. "Have a great time!" she shouted as the door was closing.

"Don't wait up," Jade replied.

As Em sat and ate dinner, she was reminiscing about the times that she and Ronnie would lay the table and cook a posh meal, when Dad took Mum out for dinner. Neither of them really liked people so they preferred to 'fine dine' at home.

Em felt a chill behind her; it made her shiver. "Peggy, if that's you, NOT FUNNY," Em called out. She looked around, nothing there.

She got up to check if there was a window open that was causing a draught, but everywhere was shut up tight. The cold air seemed to be following her. She heard her name being whispered. "Emily, Emily…"

"PEGGY, IS THAT YOU?" Em shouted. "Where are you?" Every hair on her body was standing to attention.

Em walked back to the table and picked up her plate. As she turned to take it into the kitchen, there, right in front of her stood a vision of her mum. Em dropped the plate. "Mum, Mum what's happened?" Tears started to sting Em's face. The vision disappeared. Em picked up the plate and took it to the kitchen. She put the kettle on. *Time for a cup of tea,* she thought. Maybe she had had too much wine. She cleared the dishes, grabbed her mug of tea and went to the living room.

She was curled up on her big armchair, in front of a roaring fire, when the front door flew open. Em jumped. "What the—" She went outside to see if it was windy, but it was calm. She walked back into the cottage. It was impossible for that door to open on its own. What the hell was going on?

Where was Peggy? Em hadn't seen or heard her since the park. That was not like Peggy; she was always around. Em felt something in the cottage, it felt familiar. "Em, you must help them. They need your help." It was her mum's voice again. As she turned she saw her again, but then she faded to nothing. It was at that point, she knew. Her mum had died, she just knew it. She crumbled to the floor and sobbed.

Later, the front door opened. "What on earth is the matter?" Jade said as she walked over to pick Em up.

"SHE'S DEAD. SHE'S FUCKING DEAD!" Em screamed, and Jade slapped Em's face as hard as she could.

"And you are hysterical. For goodness' sake, CALM DOWN." Jade started to shake. "How do, how do you know? Have the police been?" she asked.

"No, she was here. She was standing right there. She spoke to me," Em said, choking the sobs back.

"Now you just listen here. Do not start with that mumbo-jumbo crap. Until I hear it from the police I refuse to believe it, especially when it's one of your weird fantasy visions. Honestly, Emily, aren't you a bit old to be seeking attention?" Jade stood shaking her head.

"Get out of my house now. BOTH OF YOU!" Em screamed.

"Em, calm down. Look, we can't leave tonight, we have both been drinking. We will both go upstairs and stay out of your way. We will leave first thing. I promise," Lewis said, his eyes so wide they looked like they were about to pop out of his head.

*

Em wiped her eyes and looked at her phone. It was gone 2; she had been sobbing for hours. Where was Peggy? She needed her more than ever. Em decided that the only solution was to go into trance to see if she could find her.

She was walking through the wood when she came to the clearing. She climbed the steps up the hill until she reached the mist. Her heart was pounding. Peggy was usually here with her. The mist parted and she walked through. There, on a bench was an older woman, the same woman that she saw at Boscastle, and yes, Merlin the collie was sitting at her feet. "Excuse me," Em said quietly.

"Peggy is not here. Something has happened. She is needed elsewhere." The woman spoke without even looking at Em.

"Is it my mum? Has she died?" Em pleaded for an answer.

The woman walked over to Em and said, "Child, that is not for me to answer. Peggy will be back with you very soon. In the meantime, if you need assistance, call me and I'll come." She was smiling, that kind smile.

"But, but I don't know your name." Em trembled.

"I am Carrie, your great-grandmother," she said. "Remember, just call my name."

Em woke to constant knocking at the front door. She looked at her phone. It was 5:30am. She crawled out of bed and ran down the stairs. She opened the door to find Lewis standing there. "Erm, I forgot the car keys," he said. Em stood to the side to let him in. As he came back through he looked at Em and said, "Maybe you should seek some professional help, you are clearly unwell."

"And maybe you should both just fuck off out of my life. I never want to see either of you again," Em said as she slammed the door behind him.

She walked into the kitchen and put the kettle on. It was still warm; the cheeky bastards had made themselves tea before they went!

Em looked around the cottage; it felt so empty. Now she realised how much she relied upon and missed Peggy.

Em's phone started to ring. She didn't know the number. She answered. "Ms Wells?" a voice with a thick Welsh accent said.

"Erm, yes," Em replied.

"This is DS Tarbuck, from the Conwy constabulary. I'm afraid to inform you that we have reason to believe we have found the body of your mother."

*

For about an hour Em just sat, shellshocked. She had to go to Wales to identify the body. Apparently Jade was too distraught, and Billy wasn't in the country. The detective told her it would be a good idea to come with someone she was close to. *Well, that's a bit hard when they are missing,* Em thought as he said it. There was only one person who Em would consider taking with her. Adam was her cousin. He was Mum's sister's son. In fact, he was more like a brother to Em. As teenagers they were close because Di, Adam's mum, met a new man and he and Adam didn't get on, so Em's mum and dad took him in.

Now, Adam was a highflyer; Em very rarely saw him. Adam lived in London, as he was a games developer. It made sense; he could afford to live there, and the lifestyle suited him. Em took a deep breath and called Adam. "Sorry, can't get to the phone right now, so I must be really busy. Leave your number and I'll get back to you when I'm not really busy."

Em was trying to compose herself and hold it together. "Hi, er, hi Adam, it's Em. I need to ask you a big favour, can you—"

"Em, I'm here. What's up? You sound terrible."

"Adam, I need your help."

So, after an hour's conversation, and Em sobbing through most of it, it was decided that Adam would catch the next available train from London. Em looked in the mirror. She looked awful. She tidied up and showered and then sat waiting for Adam to call, to give her a time to pick him up from the station. She looked in the freezer for dinner. For years Em and her mum would have one day a week, where they would prepare the meals for the week. It was a routine Em found hard to break. She took out two individual shepherd's pies and put them on the side. She made herself a coffee and took it out to the small garden. She felt stifled in the house, she needed some air.

Even though it was chilly, the sun was shining and Em could feel a little of its warmth on her face. She heard a *caw, caw* and looked round to see Arthur, her resident crow, picking at the nuts she had put out for all the garden birds. Em looked at Arthur. "Hi Arthur, how's the family?" she asked.

"Caw, caw," he said and flew up into the small willow tree. Em's phone was ringing inside. She jumped and ran just in case it was Adam.

"Hi Em, it's Suzie."

"Oh, hi Suzie. What's up?" Em asked.

"Are you OK, Em? You, you sound different," Suzie said.

"No, I have just had some really bad news which I can't talk about at the mo'," Em said, her voice beginning to quiver, her eyes filling with tears.

"Oh, I'm sorry to hear that, it's just, well it's just that I have some information about Claire. I'm sure it can wait until you are feeling better," Suzie said awkwardly.

"No, no, honestly Suzie, it's fine. What is it?" Em asked.

"Well, I had no joy with Rob's dad or Greggs, but I do have the address for the children's new school. You have to promise that you won't say that it came from me. They will sack me."

"Brilliant! Of course, my lips are sealed. Thank you so much, Suzie," Em said.

"OK, I have written it down and will post it through your post box on my way to the shops," Suzie said.

"Thank you again, Suzie, I can't tell you how much I appreciate it," Em said.

Then Em's mobile rang. "Suzie, I have to go, my mobile is ringing," she said as she hung up and grabbed her mobile. It was Adam.

She had two hours before she had to be at the station, so she went and stripped the guest bedroom, and made up a fresh bed for Adam. As she was carrying the bedding downstairs she felt a chill behind her. As she turned, she missed her step and tumbled down the stairs.

Everything was swirling, like a whirlpool. She was falling faster and faster, and then darkness. Within the darkness she could hear breathing; it was getting closer. She could feel an icy breath on her face, but couldn't see anything. "What do you want from me? JUST FUCKING TELL ME!" she screamed.

"TIME IS RUNNING OUT. TICK TOCK, TICK TOCK," it growled in her face.

"Em, Em! Shit, what the hell happened?" Adam was kneeling beside her, gently shaking her.

"What?" Em said. Pain shot through her head. As she rubbed it, she said, "Shit, my head hurts, I fell down the stairs."

"Well let's get you somewhere more comfortable," Adam said as he bent to pick Em up.

"I can manage," she said.

Adam made coffee and took it into the lounge, where Em was curled up on her cuddle chair. "How did you get here?" Em asked Adam as he passed her a coffee.

"I waited ten minutes for you, then called your mobile, and your home phone. When there was no answer, I decided to grab a cab," he said. "More importantly, how did you get those cuts all over your face and arms?" he asked.

"What do you mean?" Em asked, feeling her face. "Ouch!" Em

looked at her arms; they were covered in what looked like deep gouges and were bleeding. "I have no idea."

"I think we need to clean those up," Adam said as he got up. "Do you have a first-aid kit?"

"Nope. I think there may be some antiseptic wipes in the bathroom cabinet," Em said as she stood up to look in the mirror. "Shit! How the hell did this happen?" Em said.

Adam cleaned her wounds, put the shepherd's pies in the oven and lit the fire, then took his stuff up to the spare room.

After they had eaten Em looked at Adam. "I'm sorry," she said.

"What for?"

"Dragging you down here, for having to sort me out. It wasn't exactly the welcome I was hoping to give you," she said.

"Hey, that's what families are about, isn't it?" he said.

*

They were on the road at 5:30am. It was a long drive to Wales. Adam wanted to go by train, but Em couldn't face strangers all day. They took turns driving and finally reached the police station at Bangor. As they walked towards the main doors Adam grabbed Em's hand. "I can do this, if it's going to be too hard for you," he said.

"Thanks, but I need to see for myself," Em said. She was shaking from head to toe.

The officer in charge took them to a room. He couldn't give them any information except that the body was found near the bottom lake on Mount Snowdon. He gave them the address of the mortuary and said he would meet them there in an hour.

They went to a café in the centre of Bangor and grabbed a couple of coffees. Adam had a sandwich but Em couldn't face food.

The mortuary was around the back of a hospital. DS Tarbuck was waiting at the door for them. As he led them in he said quietly, "Now

I would prepare yourself, there are quite a few injuries to the face."

Em felt her mouth fill with water, and she had to choke back the vomit. A man in medical scrubs was standing outside a door and shook DS Tarbuck's hand. They walked into the room, and Em could see a table with a body covered up. The smell hit the back of her throat and the room spun. Adam grabbed hold of her as she stumbled. "Em, I can do this," he whispered. Em shook her head.

As they stood by the table, the man in scrubs looked at Em. "Are you ready?" Em nodded. He pulled the sheet back, just enough to reveal the face. Em took one look, vomited on the floor and then collapsed.

They sat in the car, not saying a word. Em felt numb. "I will do the drive back," Adam said. Em just nodded.

They pulled away from the hospital car park and a voice came from the back of the car. "I'm so sorry, lassie."

"Oh, Peggy!" Em was so relieved to see her.

"What about her?" Adam asked, looking puzzled. Em had forgotten that Adam knew nothing about her gift.

"Oh, it just made me think about when Peggy, you know," Em said.

"Yeah, me too. It makes you realise how much you miss them, don't it?" he said.

"I am sorry you had to see that, Em. I know you can't speak now, but we need to get a move on and find Ronnie and your dad. We MUST make it a priority," Peggy said. Em nodded.

*

They spent the journey talking about Adam's latest girlfriend Abbie, and Ronnie, who Adam missed terribly. Adam had become really good friends with Ronnie when he and Em first met. They both shared so many of the same interests. They talked about the old days, the times they had as children. Throughout the journey they had laughed and cried. As they reached the town before the village, where Em's cottage was, they decided to grab fish and chips.

"Right, you warm the oven and put the kettle on, and I'll light the fire," Adam said as they got out of the car.

"Sounds like a plan," Em said as she hugged the fish and chips packet for warmth. She put the food in the oven and filled the kettle. "Table or lap?" she shouted through to Adam.

"Don't mind, either," he shouted back.

Em laid the table. "Sod the tea, I'm having wine. Do you fancy a beer?" she asked.

"Yeah, why not?" he said.

After they had eaten they sat at the table reminiscing over old times. They then started talking about Em's search and how far she had got. She knew that she had to tell Adam about her gift, about Peggy, but she was worried how he would react.

"Adam, I need to tell you something, but I need you to have an open mind," Em said.

"OK, what is it?"

"It's a long story, so it might take a while."

"Go on then."

"Well, do you remember that as a child I used to sleepwalk?" He nodded. "I stopped sleepwalking and then started to jump in my sleep. It got so bad that Mum and Dad moved me into their bedroom, they were so scared I would die. I used to float in mid-air! Anyway, they took me to a friend of theirs who was a 'white witch'. Her name was Sally. She sat and spoke to me for a long time, asking me questions, and then went off and spoke to Mum and Dad. She sent us home and gave them things, that, she said would help. They told me that she had picked up that I could communicate with spirits, that there were many, and that they were constantly trying to speak to me, even through me sometimes. Most of them were good, but there were some bad ones too. Sally gave them some herbs to burn around me every night, and they had to put a circle of salt around me, because it was through sleep that they would contact me."

The colour had drained from Adam's face.

"Shit, Em, why didn't anyone tell me?" he said.

"I think they were worried that people would think that we were either all bat-shit crazy, or that I was some sort of demonic child. Things settled down, the sleepwalking and the jumping stopped until I hit puberty and it got pretty bad again. I took myself to Sally and asked for her help. She agreed as she said that I had a very powerful gift, but I needed to learn how to use it properly. I trained with Sally for three years, and I have been able to control it. A week after Peggy died, I woke up and she was sat at the end of my bed. She told me that she was my spirit guide and that she would look out for me in the other world. I can pass through, you see. So, when I shouted, 'Oh, Peggy!' in the car, it was because Peggy was in the car. I know that this is a lot to take in, and you probably do think I'm tapped in the head, but I am telling you the truth, Adam. I am only telling you because I trust you," Em said, looking at the floor as she was too scared to see Adam's reaction.

"It is a lot to take in, but know this, Em, I believe every word of it and I will do whatever I can to help you," Adam said as he stood up. "I'm gonna hit the sack now, I'm knackered, and I need to call Abs," Adam said as he rubbed the top of Em's head.

"Ouch!" she squealed.

"Shit, sorry, I forgot," he laughed. "Anyway, night, hope you sleep well, and remember I am only across the hallway if you need me."

"Night Adam, and thanks for everything," Em said.

"Any time."

Em was sitting in bed. She was wide awake. Where was Peggy? She really wanted to speak to her! Em's mobile rang. She looked at the number and put the phone back on the bedside table. "Nope," she said out loud. She could not face speaking to her sister. Not now, not ever! Then her phone pinged. Message from Jade:

I know that we did not part on good terms, I just want to know how you got on today. She was my mum too. Jade

"UNFUCKINGBELIEVABLE!" Em threw the phone across the bedroom.

"You are going to break that phone!"

"Thank the Goddess you are here!" Em said as Peggy perched herself on the end of Em's bed. "Do you have any idea what happened to Mum?" Em asked.

"I have been with your mum, she needed me. All I know, Em, is that all three of them were taken by the same people, but they were separated. You have something that someone is desperate to get their hands on, to the point that they kidnapped all the people you love," Peggy said.

"I haven't got a clue what it is though, Peggy, or where Ronnie or my dad are. Do you think they are in Wales too?" Em asked. Shit, she felt so helpless. "How the hell am I going to find that out?" Em had her head in her hands.

"What about Suzie, has she found anything out?"

"Oh, I need to check the post box," Em said as she jumped out of bed and ran down the stairs.

CHAPTER 5

PEGGY....

*P*eggy was the sister of Robert (Em's dad) Wells. When Peggy was six and Robert three, their father died of consumption. Their mother was not a wealthy woman; she lived in a small, rented cottage in rural Scotland. The landowner told their mother that if she gave Robert to him that she and Peggy could live in the cottage for free, and that they could both work in the Manor house.

Reluctantly Robert was given away and was taken to London. Peggy wasn't to see him for 15 years, but she thought about him and missed him every single day. When Peggy was 12 her mother died, and the landowner sent Peggy to live with her elderly grandmother, Carrie. Peggy had never met her. Peggy's parents had moved to the Scottish Highlands when she was a baby. Her grandmother lived in the middle of nowhere, on the Scottish borders. Carrie was a very stern woman, who hardly spoke to Peggy for the first two years of her living there. Life was extremely hard for Peggy. Carrie became very poorly, and bedridden, so Peggy became her nursemaid.

In the two years before she died, Carrie warmed to Peggy. Carrie was not a stern woman at all, she was just unable to trust people, because of the way she had *been treated, because of her gift. She moved around all the time because she was labelled a witch. Peggy then realised that Carrie was actually a really kind, lovely woman, who had led an incredibly hard life.*

Carrie told Peggy of the gift, that she too had the gift, and that one of Robert's daughters would have it also. She made Peggy promise to find Robert in London. That his family would need her in the future.

Whilst caring for Carrie, Peggy became very friendly with a young worker from a nearby farm, called William. After Carrie died, Peggy and William got married and lived in the tiny cottage that Carrie left Peggy.

A few years later, Peggy, knowing that it was coming up to Roberts 18th birthday, with William travelled to London to find him. It took six long months to track him down, and the reunion was emotional. Robert's life in London was as hard as Peggy's in Scotland. They instantly became remarkably close and Peggy was devastated when she had to go back to Scotland.

They stayed in touch and Peggy and William would travel to London to visit Robert. Peggy wanted Robert to move to Scotland, but he had met the love of his life Maggie and they had decided to move to Kent.

Peggy and William couldn't have children, so when they went to stay with Robert and his family, they would spoil the children rotten. Peggy adored them!

Peggy and William lived a contented life in Scotland. They were incredibly happy. William had a good job as farm manager, and Peggy was well loved and respected in the village. The locals were always popping into the cottage for palm readings, ointments or card readings.

When she was 60, William came home from work one day to find Peggy unconscious on the kitchen floor. She had suffered a massive stroke, and she died the next day. Everyone who knew her was completely devastated.

Em opened the post box and amongst all the junk mail, she found a handwritten envelope, which she recognised as Suzie's handwriting. She sat in bed and opened it; the address was in a place called

Penrith. Em Googled it. It was in the Lake District. *What is she doing up there?* Em thought to herself. Well, she would worry about that tomorrow. Her eyes were heavy; she needed to sleep.

She was in some sort of tunnel. It was dark, wet and dimly lit by small lights in the walls. The walls were black and the smell in the air was tar-like. There was water dripping down the walls. It was so quiet. There was a silhouette in the distance, but the light was so bad she couldn't make it out. As she got closer the silhouette started to walk away. She quickened her pace to follow. She had no idea who or what this was, but she guessed it to be the outline of a woman.

The woman was moving faster and faster until Em was jogging to keep up. Finally, the woman turned a corner, and Em followed. She was in a big opening, like a cave. Em looked around for the woman, but she was nowhere. Then, she heard chanting; it became louder. Em turned to look behind her and there she was, the woman she had been following. She was kneeling in front of what looked like an altar. The woman had the longest, wild red hair and really scary green eyes. She looked at Em, picked something up and held it above her head. She began laughing and screeching. She picked up a knife from the altar and poked the thing with it. Em felt a massive, sharp pain in her leg. The pain was so bad Em dropped to the floor.

"Em… Em… EMILY!" she heard. She turned and looked towards a boulder and saw her mum. Em tried to stand but the pain was too much, so she began to drag herself over to her mum. The woman stopped laughing and looked over. She went to put the knife in again, but Em's mum roared in her face and the woman disappeared.

"Em, EM! For Christ's sake, wake up." Adam was shaking her.

"What? WHAT?" Em shouted as she woke with a jump.

"Jesus Christ, you have just scared the living shit out of me!" Adam was shaking violently.

"What's happened?" Em said as she tried to get out of bed. Em yelped. "What the hell has happened to my leg?" she said as she pulled back the quilt to reveal a blood-stained sheet and a deep gash on the side of her knee.

"Something woke me up, it was shaking me. I opened my eyes and could have sworn I saw Peggy leaning over me. Then I heard screaming and laughing coming from your room. I came in and you were asleep but thrashing about and laughing, well, it was more like screeching," Adam said, still shaking.

"Oh, Adam! What the hell is happening?" Em said as she put her head in her hands and sobbed.

Em was becoming hysterical when Peggy appeared and stood beside her. "Emily, for goodness' sake, calm down!" Peggy said in her sternest voice.

"Where in the Goddess's name were you? I was all alone! You are supposed to be my spirit guide and protect me!" Em shouted.

"I am your spirit guide, this is true, but that woman, is no spirit. She is very much alive, my darling. You were most certainly not alone. Correct me if I am wrong but didn't your mum save your arse, and get rid of her?" Peggy said, with her hands on her hips. Em nodded. "Now, young man, wee Adam, you need to get Em to the hospital as that wound is going to need stitches and antibiotics," Peggy added, looking straight at Adam. Strangely enough, he was looking right back at her.

"Can… can you see her?" Em asked Adam. He nodded his head yes. He had turned grey in colour.

"Yes, he can see and hear me," Peggy said as she smiled. "He has always had the gift, but until now chose to ignore it."

"But how? I don't understand. I thought that the gift came from Dad's side of the family. Adam is Mum's side," Em said.

"Ah, but Adam's father was also Carrie's grandson. Anyway, enough of this chit-chat. You need medical assistance, young lady," Peggy said, and then she disappeared.

*

After three hours of being in A&E, being prodded and poked, stitched up and sent home with a goody bag of tablets, Em was shattered. Adam got her comfy on her chair, with a big footstool in front of it, and told her to sleep, while he popped out to get some shopping so that he could cook dinner for her. Em was too scared to go to sleep, in case that bloody woman came back. She decided to research Claire on her phone instead.

She woke up to the smell of something delicious cooking; it was then she realised that she was starving! "Do you feel better for that sleep?" Adam asked her when he brought her in a giant mug of coffee.

"To be honest, I was too scared to sleep, but those pills must be bloody strong, I don't even remember dozing off," she said as she smiled at him.

"Well, you look a million times better for it," he said. "Em… there's something I need to ask you."

"What's that then?" she replied.

"Well, Abs is a bit lonely, with me down here. You know we have spent the last three months together every day, and—"

"Yes, of course she can come down. You silly sod, you didn't have to ask," Em said.

Adam looked relieved. "I didn't like to, what with your mum and that."

"It's fine. When is she coming?" Em asked and then took a big slurp of coffee.

"Er… her train gets here in an hour," he said as he blushed with embarrassment. He just couldn't say no to Abbie. She was the sweetest, most beautiful thing he had ever met.

"Right, well I'll go and check dinner and then you can tell me the plan of action," he said, with the biggest beaming smile.

How lovely, Em thought. When someone makes you *that* happy, you should never be apart. She missed Ronnie so much that her entire body hurt. Suddenly, like a bolt of thunder, she felt the energy inside her build, until she thought she was going to burst. "Adam, we have got to find them," she called out.

In the hour before Adam had to go and collect Abbie, Em told him all about Claire, the photos and the fact that Claire was now in the Lake District.

"Well, there's only one thing for it, then. You need to get yourself better, and then it's off to the Lake District for us."

"But what about your work?" Em said.

"I am self-employed, and I haven't had any time off for about three years. I want to help, Em. You're my only family."

"Thank you, Adam, you truly are a good soul. Ronnie always used to say it," she said, as the tears welled up.

*

Adam went to collect Abbie. Em managed to get off the chair to look in the mirror. She looked a mess. If Ronnie saw her now, he would run a mile! Em showered, blow-dried her hair and put a little make-up on. She felt a million times better. "That was a poppet," Peggy said. Em jumped.

"I'm sorry? What was a poppet?"

"That thing she held in the air. It's made of wax. Usually, it will have something of yours put into it. Like hair. How would that woman have your hair?" Peggy looked concerned.

"I have absolutely no idea."

"To be able to do what she did, she must have used very powerful magic indeed," Peggy said, "and the reason that your mum was there, and I was not, is because, your darling mum will not be peaceful until this monster is stopped, and your dad and Ronnie are found. You will be seeing much more of her, Em."

"Well thank the Goddess for that!" Em thought out loud.

It was a really nice evening, getting to know Abbie. Em could see why Adam was so smitten. She was slim, had the thickest, shiniest brown hair, and a gorgeous face. She was also extremely sweet. Em thought it was funny how Adam squirmed as he told Abbie about his gift and the family. It reminded Em of when she had to tell Ronnie the same thing! He was so cool about it and was always checking in on Em to make sure she was OK. She only had to go into a daze, and he would ask her if she was OK. The times he would wake her up during the night because she was moving about or sleep-talking. His arms enveloping her, telling her he would always look after her.

Em was shattered, and as soon as her head hit the pillow she drifted off to sleep. The next morning, she woke up, pleasantly surprised that she had had no visions or night terrors. She climbed out of bed. Shit, her leg was sore, so she reached for her painkillers. While she was waiting for them to kick in, she sat on her bed with her laptop. She researched Claire's name. She scrolled down until she found a newspaper article, dated three months ago. It was about a woman who had gone missing, with her two children, from Kent. It said the husband had reported that it was out of character and that there had been no marital problems. The description the husband gave of his wife and the two children matched Claire's family, but the surname was wrong. Hmm… Em pressed print on the article, then went downstairs for much needed coffee.

Adam and Abs were sitting at the small kitchen table; the smell of freshly brewed coffee filled the cottage.

"Morning," Em said cheerfully.

"Morning. I take it that you had a peaceful sleep," said Adam, smiling.

"Oh yes," Em replied, pouring her coffee and handing Adam the article that she had printed off. As Adam was reading it Em said, "The description and everything is the same, but the surname is different."

"Was there a photo of her? I mean it would make sense, wouldn't it?"

"I didn't see one. Hang on, I'll grab my laptop," Em said as she hobbled back to the stairs.

They scrolled through the article and right at the end was indeed a photo, and yes, it was most definitely Claire. "Well, one of them is lying," Em said.

"My bets are on her. Why would the husband put it in national newspapers if he had left her for the neighbour, and didn't want anything to do with the kids?" Adam said.

"I have to go and get my dressing changed at the doctors this morning. I'll ask if it is OK to travel, and if it is I think that the trip to the Lake District should be sooner rather than later," Em said.

"What time?" Adam asked.

"10:45," Em said, chewing on her toast.

"OK, well Abs will drive you. I will go and hire a bigger car. I am not travelling all that way in your micro car. Wales was bad enough!" he said and laughed. "I still can't straighten my legs properly!"

*

As they were coming out of the doctor's surgery, they bumped into Mrs Greggs. "Ms Wells, isn't it?" she asked with a smile.

"Yes, the one and only," Em said as Abs elbowed her in the side.

"Look, I know you haven't much time for my husband, and

goodness knows I don't blame you, but I understand there were some photos of you at that strange girl's house," she said.

"That's right, have you seen them?" Em asked.

"My dear, I have hidden them. I do believe that you should have them, they belong to you," she said in a very West Country accent.

"Brilliant! I think you are a wonderful human being!" Em said excitedly.

"Well now, just so we don't cause any suspicion I will leave them in an envelope for you at the school office. Will that do?" she asked, looking around to see if anyone was watching.

"That will be perfect. When do you think you will drop them off?"

"I'll go home and grab them as soon as I have finished here, then I'll take them into the school. I'll pretend they are raffle tickets, OK?"

"That's wonderful! I can't thank you enough, Mrs Greggs," Em beamed.

"No need for thanks, dear, and the name's Dawn." Em shook her hand and Abs helped her hobble to the car.

"Would you like me to style your hair for you?" Abs asked.

"Are you a hairdresser then?"

"Hair stylist, darling," Abs said in her poshest telephone voice and they both burst out laughing.

*

"Wow," Adam said when he walked in. "What a transformation." He walked over and gave Abbie the biggest kiss. "All down to you, I suppose." He winked at Em.

"Well, yes, apart from the beautiful face. That, I cannot take the praise for," Abs said as she blushed.

"Ahh… You are the sweetest!" Em said as she gave Abs the biggest hug.

Em's house phone started to ring. It was DS Tarbuck. While Em was talking to Tarbuck on the phone Abs brought Adam up to speed about the photos and told him that the doctor had given Em the all-clear to travel.

DS Tarbuck had called to tell Em that they had arrested a man from Kent, in connection with her mum's murder, but they hadn't charged him yet. When Em quizzed him about the man's connection, he wouldn't give her any information, other than that he was being questioned. He told her that they were doing everything possible to catch whoever did it, and that as soon as they charged someone, he would give her more information.

Em relayed the conversation back to Adam and Abs. "Well, I suppose it's down to us then," Adam said. "I am going to pick up the rental car at 2. Do you want me and Abs to pop in the school and pick up that envelope for you?"

"Nah, I had better go, Penny the receptionist is a bit of a funny bugger. Besides, the walk will do me good." Em smiled.

"Will you be able to walk all that way?" Abs asked.

"It's only up the road and I'll take a walking stick," Em said as she laughed.

*

The walk to the school was hard work and even though it was chilly, the sun was shining, and the air was good. Em did her usual, talking to the trees and the birds as she walked.

Penny gave her the envelope and Em gave her two weeks' lesson plans. She told her she was going away for a break. "Em," she heard coming from the corridor. She turned and saw Suzie coming up the corridor towards her.

"What are you doing here?" Suzie asked.

"Oh, I have just dropped two weeks' lesson plans off as I'm going away, for a break," Em replied.

"Any news on Claire?" Suzie asked.

"Not really, I have been a bit preoccupied," Em said.

"Is there anything I can do?" She touched Em's shoulder.

"Thank you, but no. I think the time away will do me good," Em said as she walked towards the door.

"See you when you get back," Suzie said. Em nodded and waved.

*

"Make sure you pack plenty of warm clothing, the weather forecast says we have another cold snap coming," Em said as she hobbled up the stairs to pack.

Em was checking her list (she loved lists) to make sure she had packed everything and realised her bobble hat wasn't there. After turning everything upside down there was still no sign of it anywhere.

"When did you wear it last?" Abs asked. Em thought back. The last time she could remember wearing it was after the snow. It was the day she took Claire back to the cottage!

"The hair!" Peggy shouted.

"What?"

"The poppet!"

"Shit, yes."

CHAPTER 6

"The photos!" Peggy shouted.

"Shit, where did I put them? I got so carried away with planning the trip that I completely forgot about them!" Em started rifling through her bag. She was pulling everything out in a panic. "Phew, they are here," she said with a sigh of relief. She took them out of the envelope and put them face up on the coffee table. They were not what Em expected. There were photos of Em as a child sitting in her small rose garden. Photos of her at Christmas; there were even photos of her and Adam as teenagers. There were two of Em with her mum and dad and two of her and Ronnie.

"So, she either broke into your house in Kent or knows someone who had access to those photos," Peggy said.

"There were never any break-ins, not that I can remember. No, Mum and I got the photos out a few weeks before she went missing, so they were not stolen," Em said, "and Dad went through the albums when Mum went missing, to give the police photos of her," she added.

"Who gave them to her then?" Adam was deep in thought. "Right, we are not leaving until Friday, that gives me two days to do some poking around," he said as he scratched his stubble. "I just need to go and make some phone calls. Abs, see if you can find this Claire on Facebook or Instagram, will you?" he shouted from the bottom of the stairs.

"What do you want me to do?" Em shouted.

"Rack your brains, think back, did anyone in the house mention someone called Claire?" he shouted.

Em went up to her bedroom. She thought if she meditated that might help her remember.

*

She was in her garden, helping Dad dead-head the roses. Dad looked drained; you could tell it was taking its toll on him. Mum had been missing for 3 weeks and it was driving him mad. Ronnie had been driving him around every day, just looking. The times he had seen someone from behind and jumped out of the car, only to be bitterly disappointed, that it wasn't her. Dad suffered from severe anxiety, and Mum always knew how to calm him down. Now he was going to pieces and Em didn't have a clue how to help him. She felt so helpless. Every night she and Ronnie would lie in bed and hear him sobbing. If it wasn't bad enough that her mum had vanished into thin air, the fact that she had to watch her dad's heart break a bit more every day was devastating!

She had called Billy every day since Mum had disappeared, begging him to come and see Dad. She thought it might help. He made excuses for four weeks until finally he gave in and came home for the weekend. Little did Em know how much of a nightmare that would turn out to be! She had arranged for Jade and Lewis to come for dinner on the Saturday night.

Jade, Lewis, Billy and Charlotte (Billy's awful little wife) took Dad to the pub, while Em and Ronnie prepared the food.

Between them they prepared a lovely meal. Ronnie made

homemade tomato, basil and roasted pepper soup for starters with homemade bread. They were doing steak, with spicy wedges and salad for main, and Em had made her dad's favourite pudding, baked apples, for dessert. They were both up to speed with the food when they all walked in. You could have cut the atmosphere with a knife.

"Hey, did you have a good time?" Em asked as she kissed Dad's cheek.

"Ask them," he said miserably as he walked into the kitchen to see Ronnie.

"What's happened?" Nobody said anything, but it was obvious there had been a row. "Anyone want a drink before dinner?" Em asked. They all gave her their drinks orders. *Bloody cheek!* Em thought to herself.

Dad was chatting to Ronnie as she took the tray of drinks into the living room. "Dinner will be in ten minutes," Em said to Dad as he sat down in his armchair with a bottle of beer. He winked at her and she went to the kitchen to see if Ronnie had found anything out.

"He didn't really say anything, except that Billy and Jade have always had their own secret club and that neither of them could give a toss that your mum is missing," Ronnie said as he raised his eyebrows in a Groucho Marx kind of way. Em laughed. She loved him so much.

"They always were sitting away from everyone else, even as kids. Mum always used to say they were plotting!" Em said as she grabbed the basket of rolls and followed Ronnie and the soup into the dining room.

Everyone was sitting eating and not one word was said. *AWKWARD!* Em thought to herself as she looked at Ronnie and could sense that he was thinking the same thing.

"This soup is absolutely delicious, Ronnie," Em said.

"Yeah, it's lovely Ron," Dad said. It was the first time he had looked up from his food since everyone began eating. He forced a smile at Em and then scowled at Jade.

"Do not keep throwing me filthy looks!" Jade shouted at Dad. Lewis nudged her with his elbow and Charlotte was trying not to snigger.

"Hey, don't speak to Dad like that." Em stood up.

"Well, we can't all be as perfect as you, can we? Dear sweet Emily."

"No, you can't, and you might want to take a leaf out of her book!" Dad roared and pointed to Jade and Billy.

Jade stood up. "I do not have to take this crap. Come on, Lewis, we are going," she said with her hands on her hips.

"Don't bother, I need some air. I'm going for a walk," Dad said as he got up and grabbed his coat.

Em jumped up and ran after him. As he opened the door Em said, "Wait, Dad, where are you going?" Her eyes filled with tears.

"Em, darling, I just need a bit of thinking space. I'm only going to walk around for a bit, I'll be ten minutes," he said, rubbing Em's head.

"Well, take Butch with you then."

Dad laughed. "Em, I used to box years ago; I don't need our silly dog to protect me!"

"Please, Dad, it will make me feel better and he'll be company for you," Em said as she put the lead on Butch. Dad took the lead and kissed Em on the forehead. Em went back to the dining room door and heard raised voices.

"Well get the fuck out then!" she heard Ronnie shout.

"Who the fuck do you think you are, telling us to get out of our family home?" Billy shouted back.

Em ran in just as Ronnie and Billy were squaring up to one another. "STOP!" Em screamed. Jade barged past Em with Lewis following closely behind. They left.

"I think it would be best if you and Charlotte booked into a hotel. I asked you to come because I thought that it might help Dad, but it seems to have done more harm than good," Em said, now sobbing.

"We are staying here. God, you are so self-righteous. It is my family home too." Billy smirked.

"You might want to act like you are part of this family then. Four weeks! Four weeks our mum has been missing and where were you? Oh, I forgot, Billy big bollocks. He's got that many businesses he doesn't know what do with them," Em retaliated.

"You know what? We will book into a hotel. It's quite clear we are not welcome here, darling," Charlotte said as she took hold of Billy's arm and smirked.

I would just love to wipe that smirk off her face, Em thought to herself.

When they had gone Em looked at Ronnie. "What on earth are we going to do with all that steak?"

Ronnie laughed. "I don't know, Em," he said as he held her tightly.

An hour passed; they had cleared everything away. "Where the hell is he?" Em looked at her watch. "He said ten minutes." *Am I paranoid because of Mum?* she thought to herself.

"I'm sure he's fine, babe, probably just walked further than he meant to," Ronnie said and smiled.

"You said that about Mum."

"Harsh, but true. Come on then, let's go and find them," Ronnie said as he got up from the comfy sofa.

*

All night they were out looking. No sign of them. Em had become hysterical so Ronnie took her home on the promise that he would phone the police and report them missing.

They both woke up on the sofa to banging on the door. Ronnie looked out of the window. "It's the police," he said.

It was like déjà vu, Em thought. Four weeks ago, they were doing all of this for her mum. What the hell was going on? Another knock on the door. It was the family liaison officers. With them, they had a dog lead and collar that had been found on the search. Em knew it belonged to Butch before she even looked at the name tag. Em fell to the floor. They had found the collar and lead on a small piece of common land not far from the house.

In her conscious mind Em was thinking, *Claire, Claire,* then…

The senior family liaison officer said, "OK, well I have to get these back to the station to be recorded as evidence, so I will leave you in the hands of my colleague, Officer Claire Savides."

That's it! Em sat up. She knew that Claire's face was familiar. How did she not recognise her?

She ran down the stairs, shouting, "I've got it!"

"You have remembered something?" Abs looked up from her phone.

"Yes, she was the assistant family liaison officer when Mum and Dad went missing. Her surname wasn't Hoskins though, it was—"

"SAVIDES," Abs and Adam said at the same time.

*

Over a cup of coffee and a slice of chocolate fudge cake, Adam told Em what he had managed to find out. A friend of his worked at the newspaper that ran the story about Claire's disappearance and with a little persuasion he gave Adam the phone number of the husband, Marcus Savides. Adam was meeting him the next day. Abs had found Claire on Facebook and Instagram under the name Claire Hoskins, but she hadn't been active for two weeks. So, the plan was, Adam was to drive to Kent to meet with Claire's husband, while Em and Abs stayed at the cottage to get everything ready for the trip.

Em sat in bed and all the memories were swirling around in her head. Mum, Dad, Ronnie and Butch. Why had they all been taken? What was it that they wanted? Em was sobbing; she was so heartbroken. She felt a cold draught all around her. "Not again," she cried out and put the pillow over her face. She was so afraid that it would be Dad or Ronnie.

"Em, it's me," Peggy said in her ear.

"Thank goodness." Em was still sobbing; she could hardly breathe. As she took the pillow away she noticed that Peggy was not alone. She immediately put the pillow over her face again. "Em, Carrie is with me," Peggy whispered. Very slowly Em moved the pillow, to see Carrie standing at the side of her bed with Merlin.

"Oh, my dear child, how my heart breaks for you," she said softly. This made Em even more emotional and she was at the point of hysteria.

"Emily," Peggy said sternly. She always knew how to ground her.

"You must listen, Emily," Carrie said. "This, what is happening now, goes back to many years ago, when I was about your age. We come from a long line of... shall we say, gifted folk. Our bloodline pre-dates the first witch trials," Carrie said. Em rubbed her eyes. "You see, when I was your age, I lived in a cottage in the middle of nowhere. I had no choice. There were other families, from other bloodlines, not good ones, that wanted something from me. These families practiced very dark magic. There is something in the arcane that can aid them to create incredibly evil manifestations, and to be able to control the minds of others so that they can wreak havoc across the lands," Carrie said mournfully.

"Did… Did you give it to them?" Em asked.

"I most certainly did not! When I was a child I was just like you. I would sleepwalk and jump in my sleep. One night I had left the house; when I came back I was covered in mud. My mother asked me where I had been, and I told her that I did not know. She tried to beat the truth out of me but, I genuinely did not know, and to this day I still do not know."

"I don't understand," Em said. "What has this got to do with me?"

"I believe that you have the same gift as I, and because it always happened when we slept, neither of us remembered what happened during that time. Does that make sense to you?" Carrie asked. Em nodded.

"Then we have to find a way of helping you to remember, don't we?" Peggy said.

"Tell me, Emily, do you have a connection to a specific Goddess?" Carrie enquired.

"Er, yes… Cerridwen," Em answered.

"Excellent! You must go to her place in Wales. Make contact with her and ask for her assistance. Do you know where this place is?"

"Yes I do, but we are going to the Lake District."

"Time is not on your side; you need to find the people you love before they suffer the same fate as your mum. I am sorry if that sounds brutal, but it is the truth." Carrie started to fade and then she was gone.

Em put her head in her hands. "SHIT!" she shouted.

"Get some sleep. You need your energy levels need to be working on all cylinders," Peggy said as she rubbed the top of Em's head.

"Ouch!" Em yelped. "Why does everyone keep doing that? My head is still bloody sore."

"Sorry, lassie, I forgot." Peggy laughed. Em laughed.

Darkness again. She could hear waves crashing; she must be near the sea. She was walking through a cave. She could smell the salty air. She could see nothing. LAUGHING, CACKLING, getting louder and louder. She heard a dog barking. She moved forward, slowly getting closer. The opening again, the same altar, the same woman and a dog. She hid behind a boulder. Please, Mum, I hope you are here, *she thought to herself.*

Growling. She turned to see a dog next to her, foaming at the mouth, bearing its teeth. Butch?? No, it can't be.

The woman turned to face her; she had what looked like blood dripping from her mouth. "ATTACK!" she shouted. The dog leapt at her and sunk its teeth into her shoulder, locking its jaw. The pain was unbearable.

Without thinking, she sunk her teeth into the dog. It yelped and jumped back. "Butch, Butch, it's me." *The dog had his tail between his legs; he started to walk over to her.* "Good boy," *she whispered.*

"HERE!" the woman shouted, and the dog ran back to her.

"HE'S MY FUCKING DOG!" Em shouted.

"Not anymore." The woman started to laugh and then picked up the poppet. The woman picked up the knife, but before she could do anything Em's mum was on her back.

"LEAVE!" Mum screamed at her.

Em woke up, covered in sweat.

"What the hell is going on?" Abs shouted as she ran in the room. "OH my god, Em, what has happened to your shoulder? You are bleeding!"

CHAPTER 7

Em was shaking. She knew she had to pull herself together and be strong. Abs went downstairs and made them all hot chocolate. It was 3am! Em told Adam and Abs what had happened earlier with Peggy and Carrie and about the vision.

"Firstly, Em, you need to clean your shoulder up, then you need to get some sleep. We can still travel to the Lake District; we will just have to drive to Wales in between," Adam said.

While Em jumped in the shower, Abs changed her sheets. Back in bed with clean pyjamas, painkillers and her hot chocolate, Em started to feel very sleepy.

She was in a place that felt incredibly familiar. She walked along a pavement; she could smell the sea, and fish and chips cooking. At the end of the pavement was an old man beckoning to her. She walked to him. He said nothing but pointed to a narrow path in the undergrowth. She looked at him, and he nodded, still pointing. She started to walk on the path. It was leading towards the sea. She was going downhill and it was steep. The path levelled out and then split into two. Now what? She took the path that veered to the right, and as she looked ahead, the old man was there. He nodded. She carried on until she came to a huge mound of rocks, which led to a small shingle beach. She clambered over the rocks. She was standing on the beach, the tide was coming in. She didn't have long. She heard a dog bark to her left, she turned to look. It was Butch. She ran over to where he was. When she got there he disappeared, but down beside a boulder was a scarf. She picked it up. It was Ronnie's scarf!

Tears were streaming down her face. She had to write this down, making sure that she had every detail. After she had done that she looked at the clock on her phone. It was 6:30am. She went downstairs and made herself a cup of coffee. *Right,* she thought. *Mum, Dad and Ronnie all went missing in Kent. Mum's body was found in Wales.* The dream she had about Ronnie was definitely not in Kent. She racked her brains; she had definitely been there before. Where was it?

By the time Adam and Abs surfaced, Em had cleaned the cottage and laid a table for breakfast. She had even cooked pancakes. They both looked pleasantly surprised by this renewed energy that Em had. "Adam, would you be able to check in on the house while you are in Kent?" Em asked. "I haven't done it this month."

"Of course," he said, eating a mouthful of pancake. "These pancakes are delicious," he added.

"Mmm." Abs nodded her head in agreement.

Em was clearing away the breakfast things, and Abs was helping Adam get ready for his trip to Kent, when the back door opened. "Oh my! What on earth has happened to you?" Mrs Dawkins said, with her hand over her mouth. Em had forgotten about all the cuts and bruises.

"Oh, I had a little accident, that's all, Mrs Dawkins. Nothing to worry about," Em said.

"The last time I saw someone in that state was when I took my niece to Tintagel and she slipped over some rocks." Mrs Dawkins was looking at the cuts on Em's arms.

"THAT'S IT!" Em squealed.

"I beg your pardon! What's it?" Mrs Dawkins looked quite shaken.

"Oh, sorry Mrs Dawkins. I was racking my brains earlier about a beach I went to years ago, and you have just reminded me, that's all." Em laughed. Peggy laughed too! Em quickly scribbled the word 'Tintagel' on her notepad.

"Hey Em, could you make Adam some sarnies for the journey?" Abs called from the upstairs landing.

"Yeah, sure. Will ham and salad do?" Em called back.

"Perfect."

Mrs Dawkins was twisting her neck to see who it was that was talking. "I'm sorry, dear. I thought that your family would have gone by now."

"Oh, no, that is my cousin's girlfriend, we are all going to the Lake District tomorrow for a break," Em said, as she took things out of the fridge.

"How lovely for you. Well, I shan't intrude any longer, make sure you look after yourself," she said as she hurried out of the door.

"If only she knew!" Peggy said.

"Right, what shall we do once we are all packed?" Abs asked.

"Well, I thought about a nice drive to the coast. The sea will help to bring my energy levels up," Em replied.

"Ooh, sounds good. We need to wrap up, though, it was cold outside when I was seeing Adam off."

*

They pulled onto the main car park. The pavement in the dream was just around the corner, she was sure of it. Yep! She was right. Abbie had no idea why they were there as Em decided not to say anything about the dream. "I think the beach is this way," Em said, pointing in the direction of where the old man was standing in the dream.

"Do we *actually* have to go down to the beach? Can't we stay up here? I can smell the sea. Just take a big whiff," Abs said, as she sniffed in really hard.

"No, I need to touch the water. Anyway it's not as cold here, we'll be fine."

"It's just that, I am afraid of heights and that looks like a big drop down there." Abs looked worried.

"OK, why don't you wait at the top and I will nip down, touch the sea and come back up?"

"But Adam said that I wasn't to leave your side," Abs said, biting her nails.

"Abs, I'll be fine. Peggy is with me. She will take good care of me."

Em walked the same path that was in the dream; every now and then she would look up and wave at Abs. She got to the boulders and very carefully got down onto the beach. She looked up but couldn't see Abs from where she was. She walked down to the sea and put her hands in. She felt the energy pulsate through her. She heard a dog bark. She turned but there was no dog. She saw the boulder. She walked over to it and heard a dog bark again. It sounded high up. There on the cliff top was Abs with an old woman and a dog. She was waving. *Shit!* Em thought. There was no scarf. She hurried over the boulders and ran up the path. She was so out of breath when she got to the top she thought that she was going to collapse! She could just about make out the three of them in the distance, so she hurried. As she got nearer, the old woman, who looked familiar, gave her a wave and then turned and walked off with the dog.

"Who was that?" Em said, so out of breath she could hardly manage to get the words out.

"She was extremely sweet. I didn't catch her name, but she knew you. She told me to give you this." Abs handed her the scarf. Ronnie's scarf.

"What is it?" Abs asked.

"I have no idea," Em lied.

"And why does it smell of cow poo?" Abs added. Em smelt it. She was right. Why did it smell of manure?

Adam called when they got back to the cottage to say that the meeting went well and that he had found a few things out. He was just making his way to the house and then he would be on his way back.

Em and Abs prepared dinner and made a packed lunch for the long drive to the Lakes the next day. They had rented a cottage in Pooley Bridge near Ullswater. It wasn't far from Penrith, where Claire had moved to.

Adam didn't get back to the cottage until 9:30pm. Abs jumped at him as he walked through the door.

"You must be knackered. Go and get comfy and I'll bring the food in," Em said, feeling like a bit of a third wheel!

They all sat and ate in the living room. Em cleared the plates and took in a tray of coffees and some cakes. "Well?" she said as she put the tray on the coffee table.

"Well, Mr Savides, or Marcus as he told me to call him, was very informative. I had to pretend that I was a student who was doing a final piece on missing persons, and that if he gave me information I might be able to find things that have been overlooked by the police," Adam began.

"Very clever," Em smiled.

"So, he told me that he thought that Claire was having an affair, and that she had become friends with a strange woman called Katarina. Marcus didn't go much on her; said she was one of those."

"One of what?" Abs asked.

"In his words, one of those nutters that think they can see into the future. Apparently, she was helping Claire with the Tarot," he said.

They all laughed. "So, does he think that Claire has ran off with the guy she was having the affair with?" Em asked.

"That's when he started to get a bit cagey. He definitely knows who it is, but he wouldn't say. He looked quite scared."

"And that's it?" Abs asked.

"With him it is. I went to check on the house and guess who was there?"

"Billy," Em replied.

"How did you know?"

"Wild guess," Em said.

"He was rummaging through your mum and dad's wardrobe. When I asked him what he was doing, he told me to get out and that it was none of my fucking business!"

"Nice. Sounds like Billy," Em said.

"What did you say?" Abs asked.

"I told him that I was checking the house for Em and not to be so rude!"

"And?"

"He just went on a rant about you, Em, and then stormed out of the house," Adam finished.

"So apart from that, was everything OK?"

"It all appeared to be fine," he said.

*

Em double checked her case to make sure she hadn't forgotten anything and then set her alarm for 5am. She did some meditation before she jumped into bed. She was just about to switch the light off when, "So, what do we make of the scarf?" Peggy said.

"Well, I think it means that Ronnie is close by," Em said hopefully.

"I think you are on the right tracks, Em." Peggy winked.

"So, do you think I should stay here and look for him, instead of going to the Lakes?" Em asked.

"I think you should go to the Lakes, go to Wales, make contact with Cerridwen. These people are drawing you in, so I think that Ronnie and your dad are safe for a wee while."

"OK. Thank you, Peggy. Night-night," Em said as she switched the light off.

"Sleep well, lassie," Peggy whispered.

*

On the road at 5:30am. It was still dark and bloody freezing. Adam was doing the first stint of driving, so Em cuddled up on the back seat with a blanket. She was thinking how she and Ronnie had always said they would go to the Lakes one day, and now she had to go without him. She thought back to the day that Ronnie had moved into Mum and Dad's. They were going to rent their own place, but Mum and Dad wanted them to stay there. Ronnie got on so well with both of them that everyone decided it was a good idea. Well, everyone except Jade and Billy. Jade moaned that she was never given that option and Billy said that he thought that they were both scroungers, who wanted to sponge off Mum and Dad.

After they had put Ronnie's things away, Dad drove them all to the Swan Inn, a quaint country pub that served lovely meals. It was lovely, and Em couldn't have been happier.

Life ticked away nicely, for a while anyway. Word had got round the town where they lived about Em. There was always someone knocking on the door or ringing up, wanting either healing, Tarot or something lost to be found. One woman actually came and asked Em, if she could find out where she had put a tin of beans that she couldn't find! It all took its toll on Em and she became drained and then quite poorly. As a family they decided to move somewhere a little more isolated, to give Em time to recover.

That was Em's only problem with having a gift. Especially healing. So much of your own energy is used, that over time you become drained.

They moved to a lovely house, which stood all by itself. It had a sweeping driveway, and its own small wood at the bottom of the garden. It had four double bedrooms, a lounge, dining room and a snug. Ronnie and Dad converted an old outbuilding into a workshop/ritual room for Em, where she could make her elixirs, and ointments. She loved it in there. They kept themselves to themselves and it was peaceful.

Ronnie carried on working as a marine engineer. He was really good at his job, and very well respected. He built boats. The move meant that he had to travel for work, but for the sake of Em's health, he did not mind. He loved the very bones of her. People always commented on how they 'were meant to be'.

She thought about THAT fateful day. The day when he never came home. It was a day like every other. They had breakfast together, then Ronnie went to the cabin to oversee Dad's business. Dad had built up a good building firm over the years, and Ronnie would check in every day to make sure everything was good. Pete, who was Dad's right-hand man, had been brilliant since Dad had gone. He took over and kept everything running smoothly.

So, the plan was that Ronnie would pick Em up in an hour and do the usual, go looking for them. Except this time Ronnie never came back. Devastated was not the word. Em went to pieces; nothing and no-one could console her, well, no-one except Peggy. It was from this moment that she became so reliant on Peggy. The visions were becoming more and more frequent, and they all involved the West Country. The crystal ball and the Tarot were all suggesting a journey west.

So, after two months Em took the plunge and rented a cottage there. Then the visions stopped. She was getting nothing, until now.

"Em. EM!" Abs was shaking her.

"What, what's happened?" Em said.

"Nothing. We have stopped for a break; you know, to grab a coffee and go to the loo," Abs said, grinning.

"Where are we?" Em asked, rubbing her eyes.

"We are just outside Chester," Adam replied.

*

They grabbed coffee and food to go and were back on the road. This time Adam was in the back, so that he could have a nap. Abs was driving and Em was co-pilot. Em was wide awake and taking in the scenery. "Em, you need to keep looking at the map," Abs said, laughing.

"I know I do but isn't it beautiful!" Em was wide eyed, wishing Ronnie were with her. They had the best road trips! The closer they got to the Lake District, the higher the hills and mountains got. It was breath-taking! They stopped at Kendal, parked up and stretched their legs. It was really busy. They found a coffee shop, grabbed a takeout and had a walk around. It was lovely. "Ronnie would love it here," Em said as she watched all the people in their hiking gear, heading up to the Fells.

They decided to go as they didn't want to be driving in the dark, so they headed off for the final part of the journey. Em was back on the back seat, as her leg was really sore. As the light faded, Em drifted off to sleep.

She was walking through a field full of sheep. All around were rolling fields. She could see a building in the distance, with a small light in one window. Growling, getting louder. She began running. She turned and looked behind her. She could see nothing, but knew it was getting closer. Darkness. It was there in front of her. This monstrous thing, that had haunted her for such a long time. "Peggy, where are you?" she called.

"You are all alone. No-one to save you now," it growled.

"YOU DO NOT SCARE ME; I AM STRONGER THAN YOU," Em roared back at it. "Now get out of my way!" she shouted. It jumped at her, bearing blood-stained fangs. She hit the ground. It was above her. Its huge claws around her neck. She was struggling to breathe. Then it disappeared. She got to her feet, choking for breath. She could no longer feel its presence. She looked around; she was alone. She walked slowly towards the building. She could hear sobbing. "I'm coming," she called out as she began to run.

"Em, we are here," Adam said, as the boot slammed shut behind her.

They unpacked all their things. The cottage was very quaint. Well, Abs called it old fashioned, Em preferred quaint. They were sat in the living area, in front of the fire, drinking hot chocolate. "Right, is it tomorrow that we need to go to Wales?" Adam asked.

"No, the day after. I thought that tomorrow we could have a look and see if we can find Claire," Em said.

"Yep, sounds like a plan," Adam and Abs agreed.

"Maybe we should get the map out tonight and plan the journey to Wales, just in case something crops up," Abs said.

CHAPTER 8

The sun was streaming through the light material of the curtains. Em looked at her phone to see what time it was – 5:30am. She had slept like a log, with no visions or night terrors. She slipped on her dressing gown and slippers and crept down the stairs. She didn't want to disturb the others; they needed the rest after the mammoth drive.

It was cold, but when the sun streamed through the windows it felt warm. Em made herself a coffee, opened the door and took it outside. The scenery was absolutely stunning. "Wow," Em said out loud as she took a deep breath in. There was a small metal bistro table and two chairs, so Em sat herself in the line of the sun.

There were so many different species of birds, it was incredible. A robin landed on the table next to Em's coffee cup. "Hello Mr Robin," Em said as she smiled. The robin cocked his head to the side. Em stood up, to go to the kitchen to grab a biscuit, but the robin flew off. She came back outside armed with two digestive biscuits. She broke one up into crumbs on the table, and within seconds the robin reappeared and landed next to the crumbs. When it had eaten enough, it looked at Em and then flew off.

She didn't know if it was the change in air or scenery, but Em felt like she was full of energy and optimism. Probably both. Then the dark cloud appeared. Something was troubling her. It was the fact that since she had left the West Country, she had not seen or heard Peggy. It bothered her because she relied heavily on Peggy's presence, especially in the other realm, and the last time Peggy went quiet, her mum had died. This was not a good sign; Em's optimism was slowly disappearing.

Em walked back to the kitchen, to refill her coffee, and was a little shocked to see Adam drinking coffee. "I thought that you would have wanted a lie-in," she said as she refilled.

"Nah, the sun woke me up. To be honest I didn't really sleep well, so I was glad to get up," he said.

"Oh, is everything OK?" Em asked.

"Yeah, everything is cool, Em. Probably being in strange place. I just kept waking up, that's all," he said, yawning. "Anyway, do you have the address handy for this Claire? I was going to put it in Google Maps."

"It's in my bag, hang on, I'll grab it," she said. "I think we should go as early as possible," she added, whilst emptying the entire contents of her bag all over the kitchen table. Adam shook his head in disbelief, at the amount of crap she had in her bag.

"Why, what's up?" He looked worried.

"Nothing's up, it's just that I haven't seen or heard from Peggy, since we left, and it's worrying me. I would rather get this over and done with, and then maybe, just maybe we might have some sort of lead to go on." She tried to smile.

*

They drove past the cottage that Claire was renting, and then Adam parked in the pub car park around the corner. "Right! Let's do this," Adam said, taking off his seatbelt.

"Actually, I think it's best if I go on my own. She might get spooked if all three of us are standing there," Em said.

"NO WAY, EM!" Adam shouted. "I am not letting you go there on your own. She had photos of you. She could be an absolute nutter," he said, shaking his head.

"Alright Winston, calm down!" Em said, laughing.

"Look, there is a small café right opposite the cottage. Why don't we sit in the window seats over there? Em has her phone if she needs us. We give her, say, 20 minutes, and if she hasn't come out, we go in," Abs said, looking pleased with herself.

"Hmm. I have a bad feeling about this," Adam said, rubbing the stubble on his chin.

So, Adam and Abs went to the café and Em made her way to the cottage. There was no car outside, which wasn't a good sign, but it was only 8:10am. *Where would she have gone at this time of the morning?* Em thought to herself. She rang the doorbell. She had butterflies in her tummy. She felt strangely nervous. Em turned to look over at the café and could just about make out Adam sitting in the window seat. She shrugged her shoulders.

"Ring it again," she heard Peggy say. Em looked all around her, but there was no Peggy.

Em rang the bell again and she heard, "Hang on, I'm just coming." It was definitely Claire's voice.

The door opened, and sure enough it was Claire. "Oh my god. What are you doing here?" She looked truly stunned.

"I need to talk to you, Claire," Em said.

"Well, I suppose you had better come in." She sounded quite put out. She led Em into a tiny living room. There was hardly any furniture. Just a small sofa and a small television on a table. Em looked around. It was so sparse.

"So, what do you want?" Claire said, standing with her hands on her hips.

"Well firstly, I'd like to know why the bloody hell you had lots of photos of me," Em said. She was seething. She stopped this girl from getting a public tongue lashing, and this is how she repays her, bloody cheek!

"Don't know what you are talking about," she said defiantly.

"Don't give me that crap, I have got the bloody photos!" Em shouted. She was shaking with anger.

"Well, if you have got them, I can't have them. Can I?" She laughed. "Anyway, if that's all you came for, I'd like you to leave," she added.

"I'm not going anywhere until I get an honest answer." Em now had her hands on her hips.

"Look, either you get out now, or I will call the police," Claire said nervously.

"Oh, you mean your colleagues," Em said and smirked.

"What... What are you talking about?" Claire was now shaking.

"You thought that I didn't recognise you, Officer Savides." Claire slumped on the sofa. "My cousin has also spoken to your husband. I'm sure he would be over the moon to know of your whereabouts," Em said smugly.

"Oh Christ, please don't tell him," Claire pleaded.

"I won't tell him, if you tell me why you took those photos," Em said, trying to hold it together.

"I took them for someone else," Claire said, looking at the floor.

"Who?"

"I... I can't tell you. She will kill me."

"I guess you can look forward to seeing your husband again very soon," Em said.

The door opened and a small voice said, "Is it Uncle Billy?" It was Josh, Claire's son. "Oh, hello Miss Wells, what are you doing here?" he asked.

"Hello Josh, I am on holiday here and thought I would pop in to see how you all are," she said, lying.

"Joshie, you need to get up the stairs and brush your teeth. Miss Wells was just leaving," Claire said. Em raised her eyebrows. Josh ran back up the stairs.

"Look, there was this woman. I met her at a psychic fair. She said that I had a gift, and she could teach me how to read Tarot. I went to her for a reading. She saw in my cards that I was on the case of your missing parents. She offered to show me how to help you. First she told me to get the photos, she said that she needed them to heal your pain, then when you left she told me to follow you and update her on how things were going. She even paid for the house and the move! Listen, I thought that she was genuine. It wasn't until she told me to take one of your hats, which I did, but she told me that I had to make a poppet of you. I said no and she got really nasty, which is why I did a flit so quickly and ended up here. Please don't tell anyone where I am," she pleaded.

"I need a name and address," Em said.

"Her name is Katarina. I don't have her address on me," Claire said.

"You don't remember a house that you used to visit? Fuck off, Claire, you must think I'm stupid!" Em shouted.

"If you have any sense you will stay away from her. She is dangerous, Em. You will get hurt." Claire was rocking back and forth on the sofa.

"SHE HAS MY BOYFRIEND AND MY DAD, YOU STUPID

COW!" Em bellowed at her. The doorbell rang. Claire looked at Em. "That will be my cousin," Em said. The doorbell rang again. Em walked to the door; she could see through the glass, that it was Adam. "I will be back for the address in two days. If you don't give it to me I will tell your husband where you are. Do you understand?" Em said. Claire nodded and Em left.

*

Back in the car Em told the others what had been said.

"Do you believe her?" Abs asked.

"Jury's out on that one," Em replied.

"She's lying," Peggy said. Em looked to her right... and there she was. Phew!

"I know you are right, but she did look genuinely frightened," Em said as she turned to face Peggy.

Abs turned from the front seat and then looked at Adam and shook her head. "I just can't get used to her talking to thin air," Abs said to Adam. He laughed.

They had a day of driving around the lakes. Not too far though, tomorrow was going to be another mammoth drive. They had to book into a bed and breakfast as Em had to try and make contact with Cerridwen after the sunset.

They stopped at a pub on the way back to the cottage, to have dinner. It was lovely. Exposed beams and exposed stonework. The meal was lovely and after two large glasses of wine, Em and Abs were quite tipsy. They got back to the cottage at around 8. When they walked through the door they could all smell a strange smell. It smelt like something was rotting.

They put all the lights on, Adam checked all the windows, while Em and Abs searched for what was causing the awful smell. The smell was stronger as they came to the bottom of the small staircase.

Em went up first, with Abs following slowly behind her. "You check your room and I'll check mine," Em said to Abs. The smell hit her as soon as she entered the room. It was so pungent. Em turned the light on and looked around the room. Nothing appeared to have been moved. The smell was coming from the bed. Em looked under it, but there was nothing. She pulled the duvet back and there it was… A dead crow. It had been slashed with a knife. Its intestines were spilling out. Em's mouth filled with water. She ran out of the room and towards the bathroom, for fear that she would vomit. Abs went into Em's room and screamed.

Adam took the crow outside and buried it in the garden, while Abs held the torch so that he could see what he was doing.

Em changed the bedding. Luckily, she found fresh bedding sets in the linen cupboard. Em made the tea while Adam and Abs showered.

They were sitting in the lounge. "Who the hell would do a thing like that?" Adam said.

"Well, I don't think it's the old lady that owns the place, she seems too nice, and besides, what reason would she have?" Em said.

"Was there any sign of a break-in?" Abs asked Adam.

"Nothing, no sign at all, so we are either looking for a master hacker or someone with a key," Adam sighed.

"Or they used magic," Em added.

"You know, right now nothing would surprise me," Adam said, rubbing his eyes and yawning.

"I don't think that you should sleep in that room on your own tonight. Why don't you share with Abs and I'll sleep in your room?" Adam said.

"Look, I'll be fine. I have been on my own for a year now. I can take care of myself. Anyway, I'm sure Peggy is here somewhere." Em yawned. "I'm going to hit the sack now. Big day tomorrow," she said as she hobbled towards the stairs. Her leg was really painful.

She showered, checked to make sure she had everything ready for Wales and then crawled under the covers. She could still smell that awful smell, and every time she closed her eyes, she saw that poor crow. She heard Adam and Abs go to their room, and finally she drifted off.

She was in an old building. The walls were stone, and the floor was concrete. She heard voices coming from behind a closed door, then cackling. It was HER. She heard a man's voice too. A voice she recognised. She slowly and quietly opened the door. It was enough to see what was going on. The woman was sat in the middle of a black pentagram, which had been painted on the floor. In front of her, tied to a chair was what looked like a man, with a hessian bag over his head. She was holding something in her hand. She lifted it up. It was a poppet. She struck the poppet with the knife and the man screamed and bent over in pain. "STOP!" Em screamed. The woman turned to face her.

"I have been expecting you." She smirked.

"What do you want from me? How can I give it to you if I don't know what it is?" Em was shaking with fear. "Please, just tell me," she pleaded.

The woman leapt forward and knocked Em to the ground. Em was trying to fight her off, but she was so strong. The woman ran her hand over the dressing on Em's leg, and instantly maggots were coming from inside the dressing, crawling over Em's leg. Em was screaming and fighting with as much energy that she could muster.

"EM, EM FOR CHRIST'S SAKE, WAKE UP!" Adam was shaking her violently. She sat bolt upright and threw the quilt off of her and looked at her leg. She screamed as she saw that the maggots were still there, and there were more now.

"FUCKING HELL!" Adam shouted. He grabbed Em and carried

her into the bathroom. He sat her on the side of the bath, and turned the taps on. He began to remove the dressing. Em was sobbing and close to hysteria.

"EMILY, YOU MUST CALM DOWN!" said a stern voice. Em looked up, it was Carrie.

"Where – where is Peggy?" Em sobbed.

"She is needed elsewhere. I am here to help you, but you need to preserve your energy," Carrie said.

Adam had managed to get the dressing off and wash the wound. "There is a new dressing pack in my case," Em sniffled.

"ABS, ABS!" he called out. "That woman could sleep through an earthquake, I swear," he said as he dried his hands and went to wake her.

"How on earth am I going to stop that woman?" Em asked, as she washed the last of the maggots down the drain.

"You do not give yourself credit, child, you are so much stronger than she," Carrie replied.

"EM, SHE'S GONE!" Adam shouted from the bedroom. Em swung her legs out of the bath and hobbled as quickly as she could to Adam. "I have checked everywhere. She is definitely not in the house!" Adam was panicking.

Em walked around the small cottage, checking all the cupboards and wardrobes, but there was no sign. Adam had joined her in the kitchen. "Maybe she went outside," Em said.

"In the middle of the bloody night? Em, get real, they've got her." He collapsed on the kitchen floor.

Em grabbed the torch and went to the back door. She reached up to take the key off of the hook, but before she could put the key in the door, it opened. There she stood covered in mud with huge scratches down either side of her face. "Thank the Goddess!" Em was so relieved. She threw her arms around her. Abs stood as stiff as a board, saying nothing.

"Where the hell have you been? I thought that they had taken you. What has happened?" Adam was now close to hysteria. "ABS, ABS TALK TO ME!" he shouted, shaking her.

"ADAM, STOP! FOR GOODNESS' SAKE. DON'T YOU THINK SHE HAS BEEN THROUGH ENOUGH?" Em shouted as she moved him away from Abs. Abs started to scream, uncontrollably. Em had no choice. She slapped her hard around the face. Abs' screams then turned to sobs as she sank to the floor. Adam sat beside her and held her in his arms.

Em searched the cupboards for a first-aid kit, and finally found one in the bathroom cabinet. She cleaned Abs' wounds and ran her a bath. Adam sat in the bathroom to keep Abs company and Em re-dressed her leg. *Shit!* In all the commotion she forgotten about Carrie's visit, and the fact that Peggy was needed elsewhere. "Oh no!" she cried out loud.

"It's OK, Em, nobody close has died, there are just other things that I need to do," Peggy said.

"Thank the Goddess." Em sighed a huge sigh of relief.

Em had barely slept. She tossed and turned all night. She couldn't stop thinking about the hooded man. Was it Ronnie? Was it Dad? He didn't sound like either, but his voice was familiar.

The following morning, they all sat around the small kitchen table, all pretty shellshocked. "Listen, I've been thinking. I am going to get the train to Wales, to give you two some time away from this madness," Em said.

"I don't think so," Abs replied, shaking her head.

"We do this together. Now go and get sorted, we need to be on the road," Adam piped up.

*

Abs was asleep in the back of the posh 4x4 that Adam had hired. Em turned to look at her and then turned to Adam. "Has she said what happened?" she whispered.

"Nope, just said that one minute she was tucked up in bed with me, and the next she was outside, and it was pitch black. She said that she couldn't see anything but heard growling," he whispered back.

"Poor thing." Em shook her head and looked out of the window.

They stopped at Chester for a coffee break, and to stretch their legs. Em bought them all a sausage roll, and Belgian bun. They sat at a table outside. The temperature was pretty mild, and the sun was shining. Abs was just picking at her food. "You look miles away, Abs, you OK?" Em asked between mouthfuls.

"I'm fine, just a bit tired," Abs answered, not looking up from her food.

"Tired! How could you possibly be tired? You have slept the entire journey so far," Adam said as he nudged her. "Let me see your face."

"Why, what's the matter?"

"The scratches, they have almost disappeared! They were like deep cuts last night." He looked at Em.

"I did some healing on them when I cleaned them," she said, blushing.

"That was really kind of you," Abs said as she touched Em's hand.

Em jerked back. "OUCH! You just gave me a massive electric shock!" Em said, rubbing her hand.

"Shit, it's blistered!" Adam said as he inspected Em's hand. "Touch my hand." He looked at Abs. She touched Adam's hand and it happened again. "SHIT!" he shouted.

"What's wrong with me?" Abs looked panicky.

"I think it is where you slept in the car, with your head against the window. You probably have a lot of static." Em tried to reassure her. "Hey Adam, my leg feels OK today. Shall I do a stint of driving? I'd like to." Em smiled.

"That would be grand, Em, I'm knackered." Adam yawned.

So, the final stint of the journey was Adam asleep on the back seat, Em driving and Abs as co-pilot. Nobody had said a word since they left Chester, which felt like an eternity. They were an hour and a half into the journey, and for all that time Abs just stared out of the window.

Em pulled over in a lay-by and got her phone out of her bag. She connected it to the car stereo and put on her favourite road trip music. She and Ronnie always listened to it on a road trip. Em was in her element driving, and listening to music, Abs remained silent and Adam slept the whole time.

It was 4pm when they finally reached the apartment that sat just next to the shore of Bala Lake. It was stunning. They were going to stay in a B&B, but Em found the apartments on the internet and they had availability. It was expensive for one night, but Em thought to herself at the time, *I might not be alive tomorrow, so bugger it!*

They unpacked the car and had a good look around the apartment. There were big patio doors that led onto a balcony overlooking the lake. It was beautiful. Adam and Abs went to the bedroom to unpack, Em made coffees and took hers out onto the balcony. There were lots of people about, which was not surprising. The weather was lovely, and the scenery was stunning, Em thought to herself.

Em's phone pinged.

Oh no!

It was a message from Jade:

HAVE YOU HEARD FROM WILL? CHARLOTTE CALLED ME LAST NIGHT. HE HAS BEEN MISSING FOR THREE DAYS. JADE.

Em replied:
Will??? Do you mean Billy? If you do, then no I have not heard from him for months. Em.

It pinged again.

From Jade:
WELL, YOU COULD AT LEAST SHOW A LITTLE CONCERN. HE IS YOUR BROTHER! JADE.

Em contemplated a reply, but really could not be bothered to get into another slanging match with her sister, so she took the phone inside, and went back outside to finish her coffee. The sun was slowly disappearing; Em thought that she had better get herself ready.

Adam and Abs went into the town and grabbed some takeaway pizzas for dinner, so Em put all the things that she needed into her basket. She was just getting out of the shower when they came in with the food.

They all sat in silence, eating the pizza. Abs occasionally scowled at Adam, and he just put his head down. "I take it that you two have had words." Em looked at them both. Neither of them replied. Em took her empty plate to the kitchen area, made herself a coffee and took it out onto the balcony. After a few minutes, the door opened, and Adam walked out. He looked at Em and sighed. "What's going on with you two?" Em asked.

"I haven't got a clue. She hasn't spoken to me properly since last night, and she keeps scowling at me. When we went to grab the pizzas, I went to put my arm around her, and she shrugged me off."

"To be honest, she didn't speak once during the entire journey," Em said.

"Maybe they have enchanted her," Peggy said. Em smiled, her biggest smile.

"About bloody time!" Em said as she laughed and winked at Peggy.

"I think that you should stay here with Abbie tonight, Adam," Peggy said.

"No way. There is no way that I will let Em do this on her own!" he said angrily.

"Em will be safe, Adam, I promise that I will not leave her side. If they have enchanted Abbie, which I suspect they have, it would be dangerous for her to be there. She could lead them straight to Em."

"Abs wouldn't do anything to hurt Em, she loves her." His eyes were full of tears.

"Look, sweetheart, let Em do this, then as soon as we are back we will work to release Abbie from the enchantment."

"What time are we doing this thing?" Abs said as she appeared through the doors. Em looked at Adam. He shrugged his shoulders.

"I am doing it alone, Abs," Em replied.

"Oh." She turned and went back inside the apartment.

"You must watch her when I leave here, Adam. She must not follow me." Adam sighed and put his head in his hands.

Em went to her room, double checked that she had everything she needed. It was quiet in the apartment. She looked out from her room; there was no sign of Adam or Abs. Em guessed they were in the bedroom. Em grabbed the basket, put on her new woolly hat and zipped up her coat. Quietly she crept out of the apartment and closed the door. Earlier in the day she had made a mental map in her head of where she needed to be, from the balcony. She turned on the torch and began her journey. "Peggy, are you here?" she whispered.

"Aye, lassie."

Em found the perfect spot, just on the shoreline. She took her small cauldron out of the basket and placed it to face north. She laid out her altar cloth and on it she placed a moonstone, a sunstone and the six herbs of Cerridwen. *Right, vervain, acorns, rowan, oak, myrrh and pine.* She rhymed them off just to make sure. She lit charcoal in the cauldron, added the herbs and in the light of the moon, she began her ritual.

It was so quiet. Em was quietly chanting. The wind speed picked up and suddenly Em heard footsteps coming from behind her. Every part of her was shaking with fear. The cauldron lit up and the brightest light began to shine from it. There were things flying from the cauldron; they were dandelion seeds. Em stood and the seeds were flying all around her. She was awestruck!

The footsteps stopped. Very slowly Em turned, and there in front of her stood the Goddess Cerridwen. Em dropped to her knees. "My lady. I am humbled that you heard my call." Em was bursting with emotion. She had never, in her entire existence, felt like this.

"Please stand, child." Cerridwen beckoned her to rise. "I know why you called upon me. I cannot share all of the answers that you ask of me, however, there are some that I can."

"Thank you, my lady," Em said as she bowed.

When Cerridwen had shared the knowledge that Em needed, she said, "I must go now. Do what you will, but always do it with the purest of heart." She touched Em's face and the energy pulsated through her. There was the brightest of light, and then darkness. Em was blown away! She had never experienced anything like it. She felt amazing! Em scrambled around looking for her torch. She gathered all her things up and headed back to the apartment.

There was no sign of life in the apartment when she got back. She put her basket in her room, made herself a hot chocolate and took it out onto the balcony. Wow! She had never felt so good. "That was absolutely beautiful," Peggy said.

"I do not have the words to describe how I feel right now," Em beamed.

"So, you understand that when she put her hands either side of your head, she gave you what you need to know."

"I understand perfectly, Peggy." Em yawned. She went inside. Still no sign of life. She went to her room, crawled into bed, her head nestled into the soft pillow and she slept.

*

Em woke to the sound of pots banging in the kitchen. She got up to investigate. Adam was the culprit. "Blimey! All this noise, it's only 6:30." Em yawned.

"I wanted to cook breakfast, thought I would use it as a peace offering, but I can't find a frying pan."

Em opened another cupboard and handed Adam a frying pan. "Where's Abs?" she asked. Adam beckoned to the bedroom. "No better between you then?"

"Nope. We spent the whole night lying in bed, her with her back to me."

"Is she asleep?"

"Yeah, well she was when I got up."

"I'll be back in a bit," Em said as she peeked through their bedroom door, and then went to hers. Seconds later she appeared with her basket and crept into their bedroom.

Adam was frying bacon; the smell was wandering throughout the apartment. Em was famished. After a few minutes Em reappeared, smiling. Abs was behind her. Abs ran over to Adam, threw her arms around his neck, and through her sobs told him how sorry she was.

Adam looked at Em in bewilderment. "I have reversed the enchantment. We have our Abs back!" she grinned. She went out onto the balcony, to give them time to kiss and make up.

*

The journey back was much more comfortable than the journey there. They were all very happy and chatty. All three of them took turns to drive, co-pilot and chill. It was Em's turn in the back and she was enjoying the scenery. They passed a sign for Kendal. *Not far now,* Em thought.

She heard a voice. "Look out of the window to your left." She looked.

"STOP THE CAR!" she bellowed.

Adam slammed the brakes on. "What's wrong?"

Abs turned to face Em. Em pointed to a field with a building three quarters of the way up. "What? What is it, Em? You are freaking me out." Abs was shaking.

"That building. There is someone in it. It has something to do with them. I have seen it before." Em hadn't taken her eyes off the building.

The three of them started to walk through a field full of sheep. Abs was holding on to Adam for dear life, and Em was in front, striding with determination. They hadn't even discussed a plan of action, Em had just marched across the field, with Adam and Abs following behind.

Em got to the building first. She walked around the perimeter and looked through the tiny window. There was so much dirt on the window that it made it difficult to see, but she could just about make out a figure lying on the floor with a hessian hood over its head. "We have to get in there now!" Em called to the others. Without waiting, she went to the door and with her hardest kick, booted it in. The smell inside nearly knocked her over; it was a million times worse than the dead crow! She put her scarf over her face and moved towards the body. It was clearly a man; he was lying face down. Em touched the body with her foot.

Nothing. Very slowly, she removed the hood. It was Joel, her brother's best friend. Adam ran in. "SHIT. Is he... Is he... you know?"

"Most definitely," Em replied. Adam bent down to look at something in Joel's hand. He took it from him. It was an envelope. Em took it from Adam and opened it. Abs had arrived now, and she stood with her hand over her mouth. Inside the envelope was a photo. Em took it out. It was a photo of Claire and her two children, bruised and battered, tied up in what looked like a barn. There was also a note. Em read it out loud.

TICK TOCK TICK TOCK.

CHAPTER 9

Back at the cottage, they all slumped into the chairs, exhausted. They had all been grilled by the police and were finally allowed to go. "So, first thing in the morning, we go to Claire's, and then head on home." Adam yawned.

"She probably isn't going to be there, judging by that photo," Em replied wearily.

"Ah, but maybe that's what this Katarina wants you to think." Adam scratched his stubble, deep in thought. "In fact, I might drive over there now," he added as he jumped up.

"You have got to be kidding me, I'm bloody shattered," Abs said, shaking her head. "No way, Adam!"

"Look, I can go on my own, it'll only take ten minutes to drive there, I'll be back before you know it."

"If you are going, then I am coming with," Em said.

"Right!" Abs huffed as she stood up. "I'll get my bloody coat on."

*

They pulled up outside of Claire's cottage. "OK, look, no lights, it's obvious they are not in there, well, not unless they enjoy sitting in the pitch black," Abs said, shivering.

"I think we should nip around the back and have a look through the windows," Adam said.

"No way! If the neighbours see us and call the police, how the hell are we going to talk our way out of that one?" Abs replied.

"What about, say, we park somewhere close, and walk around the back, one at a time," Em said.

"I think you should turn the car around and go back. This is a trap."

"Who said that?" Em looked around. It wasn't Peggy or Carrie's voice.

"Said what?" Adam and Abs both said in unison.

"Adam, turn the car around quickly. This is a trap; we need to get out of here." They both just gawped at Em. "NOW!" she yelled.

Adam spun the car around and slammed his foot down. The car was silent the entire journey back.

They all sat around the table blowing on their hot cups of tea. "Didn't you recognise the voice?" Abs asked.

"No, not at all." Em took a sip of her tea. "I think we should leave here as early as possible tomorrow. I need to get back to the West Country and look for Ronnie. Hopefully, the police will follow up on Claire," Em said.

At 5:30 they were on the road. Em couldn't sleep so she got up, packed everything, tidied everything and made breakfast to go. Adam and Abs were doing the driving, so Em was in the back.

The wind was howling, she was close to the sea, she could hear the waves. It was hard to see through the driving rain. There was a building, a white building. It was calling her. She fought against the wind and rain, trying to run. There was a car parked outside the building. It was red. Yes, it was a red 4x4.

"Em, come on, I'm parched," Abs said.

"Where are we?" Em rubbed her eyes.

"We are at yours," Abs said and laughed.

"Have I been asleep the whole time?"

"We thought we would leave you to sleep, so Adam and I took it in turns for toilet breaks and coffees. Come on, Adam has unloaded the car and lit the fire."

*

After she had unpacked and sorted through her dirty washing Em went downstairs. She checked the answerphone. One message from Jade, DELETE, and one message from DS Tarbuck. It was just a call to let her know that the man that was being questioned had been released with no charge. Also, that her mum's body was ready for release.

Em called the local undertakers and asked if they could collect her mum, and she would then come in to arrange the funeral.

Adam and Abs came through the back door with bags full of groceries. "Adam is going to make us one of his specialities tonight," Abs said.

"Oooh lovely," Em replied as she was putting on her scarf and coat.

"Where are you going?" Adam asked.

"I just have to pop into the school about work, and then to the doctors to get my stitches out."

"Hang on and I'll drive you," Abs said with a mouthful of jam doughnut.

"No need, I'm fine to drive, in fact I'm looking forward to getting in my car again. I shouldn't be too long!" she shouted as she shut the door behind her.

She was driving slowly towards Tintagel; that white building had to be somewhere around there. She parked in the main car park and strolled along the pavement, alongside the many tourists. She took the path and walked down to the sea. There were so many people!

Back from the beach she found a small kiosk selling pasties. She grabbed one and a coffee to go. She drove a short while and found somewhere on the clifftops to pull over. She walked along to a bench and sat and ate her pasty. She was looking around the coastline, but the only white building she could see was a church. *Bugger!* she thought to herself. She thought that maybe, just maybe, she might be onto something. She found a bin and threw her coffee cup and empty pasty bag in.

"Beyond the church is a farm." She turned, nobody there. It was the same voice.

"Who are you?" she called out. Nothing. She walked back to the car.

She drove towards the church. "Turn left," the voice said. She was then driving on a lane away from the church. "Turn left again." Now she was on a farm track. She pulled into a lay-by. It was probably safer to walk, she thought to herself. The track was going uphill, it was quite steep. Em was out of breath as she got to the brow. There, straight ahead of her was the white house. She heard a vehicle coming up the track, so she jumped over a small hedge and hid behind it. It was the red 4x4. A man and a woman got out, but they had their backs to her. The man then turned and walked back to the car. *BASTARD!* Em swore when she caught a glimpse of the man's face.

She waited until both of them had gone into the house, then she walked towards it, but stayed in the field. She had better cover there. The field swept behind the house. Barns. There were two of them. She climbed through a hole in the fence and skirted around the side of the first one. As she got closer she could tell by the smell and the noise that cows were in there. She went behind the first barn and through all the mud and muck to the back of the second barn. As she turned the corner, someone came out of the barn. She ducked down and back crawled to behind the barn. She wanted to look again, so very slowly she crawled forward and poked her head around. It was HER!

When Em thought it was safe she crawled around to the barn door. *SHIT.* It had a massive padlock. "Touch the lock," the voice said. Em looked all around to make sure it was clear and with both hands grabbed the padlock. It opened and dropped to the ground. Em picked it up and put it in her pocket.

She opened the barn door just enough to squeeze through, and pulled it closed behind her. The only light in there came from cracks in the wood. Em fumbled in her pocket for her phone and put the torch on. She got up and slowly pointed the light around the barn. She heard a low groan coming from the corner. She was trembling so bad that she dropped the phone. She picked the phone up and very slowly she walked towards the sound. It groaned again. She stopped. She carried on until she was close enough to see clearly. *OH, MY GOODNESS! WHAT THE FUCK HAVE THEY DONE TO YOU!!!!* There he was, tied up and gagged. Beaten black and blue. Half starved to death. HER FUCKING RONNIE!

She ran over to him. She was sobbing at the very sight of him. She managed to get the gag out of his mouth. "Thank fuck," he whispered. His eyes went wide and before he could say anything she felt a hand over her mouth, and she was being dragged backwards. She was kicking her legs behind her, trying her hardest to fight back. She was pushed face down to the ground and her hands were tied tightly. She was kicked in the side so hard she thought her insides were going to explode. She was turned over, so she was on her back and could clearly see her assailant. What her assailant did not know, was that they were just about to be smacked over the head with some sort of heavy metal contraption.

He was just about to say something when *WHAM!* Adam hit him over the back of his head, and he dropped to the floor. Adam untied Em. "Is he out?" she asked.

"Out cold." They both ran to Ronnie, who was being untied by Abs. "Fuck," was all that Adam could say, when he looked at Ronnie.

"We need to get him to the car, quickly. Where's yours parked?" Em looked at them both.

"Behind yours," Adam said.

"Shit! Can you carry him? He is too weak to walk. I think they have drugged him." Em was beginning to panic. She knew that they needed to be gone NOW!

Abs crawled out of the barn door first. She gave Adam the all-clear and he dragged Ronnie. Em followed. They all got away from the first barn safely. Abs led the way behind the second barn. Adam managed to get Ronnie to stand. He threw Ronnie's arm around his shoulder and together they hobbled around to the second barn.

Em heard a growl, coming from behind her. She turned but there was nothing. She heard a yelp and as she turned, she saw Charlotte clawing at Adam's face. Adam let go of Ronnie, who was now on the ground, his face pouring with blood, Adam's too. Em took a run at her; she took the padlock out of her pocket and smacked Charlotte around the head as hard as she could. She hit the ground. Em called Abs, then she grabbed hold of Ronnie and pulled him to his feet. Adam took Ronnie again and they moved as fast as they could, through the field to the cars.

Back at the cottage, Em could not stop sobbing. She was trying to clean Ronnie's cuts, but seeing what those bastards had done to him broke her heart. *I am going to kill every fucking one of them,* she thought to herself.

"Purest of heart," the voice said.

"I know," Em said out loud.

*

Ronnie had lost consciousness while Em was cleaning him up, so Adam and Abs helped her get him into her bed. "I think he needs to sleep those horrible drugs off," Adam whispered.

Downstairs drinking coffee at the kitchen table, Abs had cleaned Adam's face, but the scratches were really deep. Em got her special ointment and rubbed it into the cuts. "How did you know where to find me?" she asked.

"Well, we knew that your doctor's appointment isn't until tomorrow, it's over there on the memo board, so we followed you," Abs said.

"Just as bloody well that we did! Why didn't you tell us what you were doing? Don't you trust us?" Adam said. He looked truly hurt.

"Of course I trust you! You have both been through so much, and it's all because of me. I just thought that I would give you both a break. I'm sorry," Em said, tears streaming down her face.

She went out to the small back garden to peg out the washing. "He needs to talk about it," Peggy said. "The only way he will truly heal, is if he speaks about it."

"I know, I was just giving him time to rest. Believe me, Peggy, I wanted to sit and watch him, but Abs said to let him rest." Peggy nodded, and Em took the empty basket back in.

"I heard movement upstairs; I think Ronnie is awake," Adam said as he was taking things out of the fridge. Em ran up the stairs. She opened the bedroom door and saw that the bed was empty.

"Ronnie. Babe?" Em called out. To her relief, he walked out from the en-suite. He had showered and cut his massively long beard. It revealed even more bruising. Em's eyes filled with tears.

"Come here, you," Ronnie said as he held his arms open. Em ran into him and held him as tight as she possibly could. "Argh! Mind the ribs, babe," he said.

"Sorry," she said and laughed, tears streaming down her face.

"It's this beautiful face that has kept me going. I have missed you so much, every second of every day." He took Em's face in his hands and wiped her tears away. "Em, there are not enough words to thank you, for finding me and saving my life. You are the bravest, most beautiful person and I love you with all my heart." Tears now spilling down from his eyes. There was a knock on the door.

"Come in!" Em shouted.

Adam came through the door. "Er, sorry, I didn't mean to intrude. Abs and I wondered if you wanted us to go out for a bit. Give you two some privacy." He looked awkward.

"Don't be daft," Ronnie smiled at him. "Em is going to take me for a walk, show me the area," he added. "So Adam, my friend, when we get back, I expect a roaring fire, a delicious meal and beers chilling in the fridge." He winked at Adam.

"Of course, mate, goes without saying," and he threw his arms around Ronnie. "Good to have you back, my friend," he said. Em laughed as she saw Ronnie's face screw up in pain as Adam held him so tightly.

As they walked slowly hand in hand towards Em's go-to place, Ronnie began his recollection.

"Before I begin to tell you, Em, I need to ask you a question," he said.

"Anything, my love." She beamed at him.

"Where the hell are we?" Em burst out laughing. She had completely forgotten that he would have no idea where he was.

"We are on the border of Devon and Cornwall, my love."

"Why here?"

"After they took you, the visions started again, the Tarot and the crystal ball all led me here. So after two months I rented this place, in the hope that I would find you all." Sadness crept all over her face. They sat beneath the ancient oak tree and Ronnie began.

"I went to the cabin to check in with Pete. I was just about to leave when Pete took a phone call. This man came into the cabin and asked if I could move my car as he had to make a delivery. I moved the car, and then he came over and asked if I could give him a hand as Pete was on the phone. I walked over to the back of the open van. The next thing I knew, I was smacked over the back of the head. I was knocked out cold.

"I woke up and the van was moving. I was tied up and gagged. It seemed to take forever to get to wherever it was, and then I was blindfolded, dragged out of the van and taken into a house. I was thrown onto a hard floor and the door then closed and locked. The blindfold came off and I can't tell you how relieved I was to see your mum standing over me. Then your dad came over and he helped her untie me."

Em was sobbing.

"Anyway, for three months, we stayed in this one room. Disgusting food was brought to us, but there was a sink in the room, so at least we had plenty of water."

"How did you all go to the loo?" Em asked.

"In a bucket!"

"Aww, I bet Mum loved that."

"Well, your dad would take a blanket off one of the mattresses, and hold it up, and he told me to sing loudly!" He chuckled.

"Did you ever see the people that kept you there?"

"Nope, they all wore balaclavas. One day a woman in a balaclava came in. I could see red hair underneath it. She tied us up, gagged us, blindfolded us and loaded us into a van. Again, we drove for hours. Then we were taken to a different room, not much better but it did have a toilet. We were in there for another five months."

"How did you know?"

"Your dad and I would scratch the days on the walls."

"Very clever. What did you all do all day?"

"Talked about you, mostly, hatched our escape plan, oh, and played cards. Your mum always won, of course." He chuckled again.

Thank the Goddess they were all together, Em thought to herself.

"Your dad and I came up with a plan. This room had wooden beds. You know, the ones with slats. We took one slat from each of the beds and managed to hold them together with the screws. God knows how, but you know how clever your dad is with these things." Em nodded.

"Well, we waited until the last food of the day was being brought in. I hid behind the door. Two came in; I smacked one of them over the head with the wood and your dad smacked the other one the tray of food, while your mum was kicking the living daylights out of him. We managed to get out. We ran to the front door, but the bloody thing was locked. Then we saw her. This woman with long red hair and the scariest green eyes I have ever seen."

Em nodded again. "I have seen her too. She is in my dreams, and she can physically hurt me."

"Bitch! She set the door on fire. Then about four of the hooded fuckers came in, dragged us back to the room and beat us all to a pulp." Em's mouth filled with water; she wanted to throw up. "The next morning, we were separated. They took your mum first. Your dad went absolutely batshit, so they injected him with something. He was out cold when they took him. I was the last to go, I didn't get the injection though, they just smacked me over the head and knocked me out. I woke up in that barn where you found me."

"'I'm so sorry," Em said as she sobbed.

"Hey, none of this is your fault, babe, don't ever think that it is." He held her face in his hands. "It was in that barn that I discovered how much your brother and the poisoned dwarf were involved."

"Didn't they cover their faces?"

"No. Billy took great pleasure in letting me know who was in charge. It wasn't them at first, they have only been there for the last two weeks. Funny though, one of the men's voices was very familiar."

"Joel?" Em looked at him.

"YES! How did you know that?"

"We found him dead two days ago," Em said.

"Shit. Where?"

"The Lake District."

"What the hell were you doing there?"

Em told him all about Claire, how it led them to the Lakes and the visions that she kept having.

"Maybe that's where your mum is, then? We should go up there and look."

Shit, he didn't know.

"Babe, Mum's body was found near the bottom lake, on Mount Snowdon." Em put her hand on his and they both wept.

CHAPTER 10

They headed back to the cottage as it was beginning to get dark. As they walked arm in arm, the two of them were completely shellshocked. They opened the front door of the cottage; the smell was wonderful. "Well, you two have surpassed yourselves," Em gasped as she looked around. The fire was roaring, the food was cooking, the table was laid beautifully and there was lots of wine and beer.

"It's the very least we could do," Abs beamed as she ran over and hugged Em.

They had a wonderful evening, talking about old times and times yet to come. All the things that they were going to do together, and all the places where they were going to go.

It was around nine when the phone rang. Em answered it. When she had finished she went back to the table; the colour had drained from her face. Ronnie stood up. "What's wrong?" he said, looking at Em.

"That was DS Tarbuck, the police sergeant that is dealing with Mum's case." She gulped.

"And…" They were all waiting.

"He had a call earlier from the police in the Lake District. The man that was held and questioned in Mum's case, was the one we found in that building. Joel."

"What, so Joel killed your mum?" Ronnie said.

"He said that there wasn't enough evidence to charge him. How could he? She was good to him." Em sat on the floor. "BASTARD!"

*

They all went up to bed. Em was so happy to be lying in the arms of 'her Ronnie'. It seemed she had waited an eternity for this moment. "Em, I love you." He looked deep into her eyes.

"Ronnie, I love you too. So much." And they drifted off to sleep in each other's arms.

She was in a tunnel. She could see the light at the end. It was dimly lit. Gas lights. Lots of noise. It sounded like horses' hooves. She reached the end. It felt like she had gone back in time. She walked through the cobbled streets until an old pedlar lady grabbed her arm. "This way, miss," she hissed and led her up a side alley. It was dark, everywhere smelt like smoke and sewage. The pedlar pulled her into a building. She walked her through a curtain to a back room, and there sitting at a table covered in dark red velvet, was Carrie. In front of her was a crystal ball. She looked very young.

"Sit," she said. She tossed at coin at the pedlar and shooed her away. "I need to tell you of what she seeks."

Em nodded.

"An age ago, our ancestor Abagail Walcott wrote a grimoire. It was based on writings by a man called Abraham of Worms. He practiced kabbalistic magic."

Growling, getting closer. The table lifted and the evil twisted thing that haunted her, appeared from beneath it, sending the table and Carrie flying. It leapt at Em. She felt power building up inside her. She opened her mouth and blew. Gold dust was covering the beast. It disappeared.

"Babe, babe are you OK?" Ronnie was leaning over her.

"Quick, I need to write this down," Em said as she felt around for a pen. Ronnie put the light on. He handed Em her pad and pen from the dressing table. As she sat furiously scribbling, Ronnie sat beside her reading it. "Who the hell is Abraham of Worms?" He laughed.

"No idea, but I need to research him," Em said and laughed too.

"So, it's 6am, shall I go and make some coffee and we can sit in bed and decide how the hell we are going to find your dad?" Ronnie said.

Back in bed, Em was trying to decipher her dream. It just wasn't bringing her any closer to finding her dad. Ronnie put the coffees on the bedside tables and jumped onto the bed. "So where do we think he is then?" he asked.

"Well, you were in Cornwall, Mum was in Wales, Claire was in the Lake District. I haven't a clue, Ronnie. It's not like there is any sort of pattern. Shit, he could be anywhere," she said.

"I think if you find Claire, you may get some answers to the whereabouts of your dad," Peggy said.

"But what about the notes? TICK TOCK. It screams to me that time is running out," Em said, looking at Peggy, who was standing beside her bed.

"Now that you have Ronnie back, the only thing that they have, that you love, is your dad. He is their bargaining tool. I think he is safe for a wee while." Peggy smiled.

"I hope you're right, Peggy." Em smiled back. "Oh, sorry I got a bit lost then." Ronnie chuckled. Em laughed. It used to be a regular occurrence, Em talking to thin air, before he was taken.

There was a knock on the bedroom door. "Come in," Ronnie called out.

"Would you both like a coffee?" Abs asked.

"Ooh! Yes please, Abs, we'll be down in a couple of minutes," Em said.

They walked down the stairs to the smell of croissants baking. Adam had laid the breakfast table, and Abs had picked some flowers out of the garden and put them in a vase.

Ronnie walked over to Adam at the cooker. "Smells good, mate."

"Well, we need to build you up. You are all skin and bones." Adam laughed.

They all sat around the table trying to figure out what to do next. "I don't know why, but I cannot get Pendle out of my head, I even dreamt about it last night and I've never been to the place," Adam said.

"What, THE Pendle? Witches Pendle?" Ronnie asked through a mouthful of croissant. Em laughed and brushed the crumbs off of his beard. "Ouch!" he yelped.

"Don't be a baby, really, after all that you have been through!" Em laughed, Abs laughed too.

"Yes, the very same, in my dream there was a derelict tower," Adam said.

"Would you know it if you saw it again?" Abs asked.

"Dunno, probably." Adam nodded.

"What time are your appointments today, babe?" Ronnie asked.

"Erm, doctors at 10:30 and undertakers at 1:30. Why?"

"Adam, when does the hire car have to go back?" Ronnie looked at Adam.

"I have it for two months, I leased it. Why?"

"Well I reckon, if I go with Em to her appointments, either you or Abs could look on the internet for accommodation in or near Pendle for a couple of days. What do you all think?" He looked around.

Adam and Abs were both nodding in agreement.

"Are you sure that you are up to it, babe? You have been through so much." Em touched Ronnie's bruised face.

"Sweetheart, I have been locked away, feeling so bloody useless for a year, I think that it will do me good."

"If you are sure," Em said as she put her arms around his neck and gently kissed his lips.

*

Stitches out. Funeral booked. Em and Ronnie walked back into the cottage to a hive of activity. Adam was in the living room on his phone; Abs was sitting at the dining table on hers. *Who the hell is that in the kitchen then?* Em thought to herself.

Then she heard her. *SHIT!* Em looked at Adam with wide eyes; he shook his head. "To what do we owe the pleasure?" Em said as she walked into the kitchen.

"Ronnie! When did you get back?" Jade walked over to Ronnie, who was behind Em and hugged him.

"WHEN DID HE GET BACK? I MEAN HE HASN'T JUST GOT BACK FROM HIS HOLIDAYS. HE HAS BEEN LOCKED AWAY FOR THE PAST FUCKING YEAR!" Em screamed at Jade.

"Do not tell her any details, Em, she is not to be trusted," Peggy whispered in Em's ear.

"DO NOT SHOUT AT ME! Who the hell do you think you are?" Jade screamed in Em's face. Jade lifted her hand as if to strike Em.

"Go on, I dare you. I have been wanting to give you a good hiding for years." Em was trembling with rage.

"ENOUGH!" Ronnie shouted as he stood between the both of them.

Abs grabbed Em's arm and led her out to the garden. "Right, you sit here and talk to Arthur, and I will go and make us both a cup of coffee and fill you in. OK?" Abs said as she sat Em on a chair. Em nodded; she was too angry to speak without bursting into tears. She most certainly didn't want Jade to think she was weak.

"Hey Arthur," she said to the crow sitting on a branch of the small willow tree. She wiped her tears before they fell. "How's the family?"

"CAW CAW," he replied. Abs came out with a tray of coffee and some iced buns. She offered Em a bun. Em shook her head.

"Well, what does the stupid cow want?"

"Apparently, her and Lewis came down to make sure that you were OK, as 'Will' and Charlotte haven't been in touch and she was worried about you. She also wants to know the funeral plans."

"Does she now? And why does she keep calling Billy, Will?"

"Look, Em, I know that it is none of my business, but the way I see it is, that if you act like you are not bothered by her, she will soon go away and try to get a rise out of someone else." Abs smiled.

Ronnie came out. "Gone," he said, rubbing his hands together.

"Really? What did you do, physically throw them out?" Em laughed.

"No, just sold them this sob story that you and I were going abroad for some 'alone' time, and Adam and Abs were going back to London."

"And they bought that?" Em raised her eyebrows.

"Well, they're not here, are they?" he said, looking mighty pleased with himself. "Anyway, missus, you need to get packed. We hit the road at fifteen hundred hours." He laughed.

"Aye-aye, sir." Em saluted him. As she got up to go inside he grabbed hold of her. Abs grabbed the tray and disappeared. He gazed deeply into her eyes. It gave her a fluttery tummy. She kissed him on the nose, slapped his bum and ran off laughing.

Adam was driving and Ronnie was up front with him. Em and Abs were in the back eating chocolate, while Abs was showing her the photos and details of the hotel on her phone. "Babe, it's got a heated indoor pool and a spa," Em said excitedly.

"Great! Did you pack our costumes?" he replied.

"Erm… no." Em blushed. They all burst into fits of laughing.

*

As they parked at Chester services Adam turned to them all and said, "They are going to think that we have shares in this place!" The girls laughed; Ronnie looked confused.

"It's because every journey we have been on lately, we always stop on these services," Em said as she kissed Ronnie's cheek.

Back on the road, Abs was driving, Adam was navigating and Em was cuddled up to Ronnie on the back seat. They both fell asleep.

All of a sudden Em went flying across the seat. Ronnie, who was still asleep was thrashing about, shouting and swearing. "Ronnie, wake up. You were dreaming," Em said as she gently shook him.

Ronnie rubbed his eyes and looked at Em. "Em, why are you bleeding?" Em felt something wet and warm running from her temple. She ran her finger over it and looked.

"It's nothing, sweetheart. I went flying when you were thrashing about. My head hit the window. They both looked at the window; there was a big crack in it.

"Oh my god! I am so sorry," Ronnie said as he put his head in his hands.

Em moved his hands and looked into his eyes. "Ronnie, I'm fine, it's just a graze. See? The blood has stopped." She showed him her finger as she rubbed it over the cut.

It was dark when they parked in the hotel car park in Clitheroe.

They were shown to their rooms. "Wow, this is a bit posh," Em said as she walked over to the super-king-size bed.

"Well, it's not quite as nice as the accommodation that I have been used to of late." Ronnie laughed. Em laughed too and threw a pillow at him as she went to check out the en-suite.

"Cool, it's got his and hers sinks, and a massive walk-in shower," she called out.

Ronnie came in to join her. "Wow! What's behind that door?" he asked as he opened it. He walked through. "Ooops, sorry, I didn't realise we had adjoining rooms," he said, laughing. Em followed him into the room. Adam and Abs were lying on their bed and both of them were blushing.

"Blimey, you two don't waste time, do you!" Em said. Abs hid her head under her pillow.

They all decided to call it a night and meet up for breakfast in the morning. Em and Ronnie both showered and crashed out as soon as their heads hit the lush pillows.

She was walking. There was a castle in the background. She felt as if she were not alone. It was dusk. Nobody else was about. All she could hear were the birds; no cars, no people. She kept looking behind her. Nothing. She came to a track and started to walk along it. It led to a house. There were no lights on inside the house. She heard rustling in the long grass running alongside the track. Then, a child screaming. It was coming from the house. The screaming was getting louder and louder. She began to run towards it. Then the lights in the house were turning on and off. It looked as though there was lightning inside. She ran faster and got to the door. She grabbed the handle and was thrown backwards. She was there, standing over her. "You will give me what I want." Em tried to get to her feet. The woman put her hand out, and what seemed like an electrical charge came from her fingers and pushed Em back. Em looked at her. Every time she used the charge, she aged, and now before her, the red hair had turned to grey and so had the piercing green eyes. Em summoned the energy inside her and blew as hard as she could. The woman flew backwards.

"Em, you are sleepwalking," Abs said.

"DON'T WAKE HER!" Ronnie shouted as he walked into the room. He took Em's hands and led her back to their room. "Sorry," he turned and said before he closed the door. He led Em to the bed, laid her down and covered her up. She sat bolt upright and burst into tears. Ronnie sat beside her. He said nothing, just held her in his arms. He had been through this so many times before. She stopped sobbing, rubbed her eyes and looked at Ronnie. "I have seen the place where I think they are keeping Claire and her children."

"OK, do you think we are in the right place?" he asked. Em nodded.

"There was a castle in the background."

"Right, sweetheart, I think we should both try to get some sleep for a few hours and go looking for her tomorrow," Ronnie said as he tucked Em back into bed.

*

In the dining room the next morning, Adam stood up and waved as Em and Ronnie walked in.

"Sorry about last night," Em said to both of them as she sat down.

"No problem," Adam said. "We are both getting quite used to getting up in the night with you, Em. Are you getting us ready for parenting?" he added as he laughed. Abs elbowed him in the ribs, and Ronnie and Em laughed.

Over a delicious breakfast – of course the boys both took advantage of the giant traditional cooked breakfast and the girls had croissants and coffee – they talked about Em's vision, and what the plan was for the day.

Adam went out to the foyer, to a stand full of leaflets of things to do and see in the area. He took a handful back to the table and handed a leaflet to Em. There was a photo of a castle on the front. "Was it that one?" Adam asked.

"Hmm, it looked similar, but I can't be certain, it wasn't very clear in the vision."

"That's Clitheroe Castle, it's not far from here. Shall we go there first?" Adam asked.

*

They parked the car and grabbed coffees to go. They could see the castle in the distance and began to walk towards it. "Does any of this feel familiar, sweetheart?" Ronnie asked.

"No, not really." Em looked disappointed.

As they got to the castle entrance Abs said, "Well, as we are here shall we at least have a look in the museum? They all nodded.

Adam, Abs and Ronnie were walking around looking at all the art exhibits, but Em was picking up on something. "Psst," she heard. She looked around her. "Psst." Again! She looked around. There was a dimly lit corner, with an old man leant up against the wall. He beckoned Em with his hand. "Come," he said. Em walked over to him. "You are looking from the wrong perspective; you need to be up high," he said quietly.

Em looked around to see if anyone was looking her way, as she turned she asked, "Where do I need to be looking?" The old man had gone. "SHIT!" Em said out loud.

Ronnie turned. "What's the matter, sweetheart?" he asked.

"There was an old man in that corner. He told me I was looking from the wrong perspective, that I needed to be up high. I turned around to make sure no-one was looking, asked him where I needed to look, and he was gone." She sounded agitated.

"I'll go and grab the others. Wait there." He smiled.

"I think we need to think about how many approaches there are to this place, and what surrounds them," Ronnie said. He always was so analytical!

Adam took out the map he had of the centre of Clitheroe. "Well, to one side there is a supermarket, and the other side is a station," He said as he looked over the top of his glasses. He looked like Em's dad and it made her giggle. "What's so funny?" he asked, looking puzzled.

"You looked like Dad when you peered over the top of your glasses, it made me happy," Em said as she smiled.

CHAPTER 11

They decided to carry on walking in the direction they came and then turn and walk back towards the castle. "I'm starving, can we get lunch soon?" Abs moaned.

They walked for about a mile, then turned and walked back towards the centre. It still didn't seem familiar to Em. They found a small bistro and went in for food. "Let's go back to the car. I don't think it was this castle," Em said as they came out of the bistro.

Adam had his map out again. "OK, how about we drive out to this place?" He pointed to a place called Whalley Nab. "It's a wooded hill, thought we might get a better view from up there. What do you think?"

"Anything is worth a try," Ronnie said, and they all nodded.

*

They were all out of breath when they reached the top. Em was bent double trying to get her breath back. As she stood, she looked around her. Although the view was breath-taking there was something else. There, in the distance. "There, it's over there." She pointed.

They all turned. Adam again looked at the map. "That's Whalley Abbey," he said. Once they all had their breaths back and had drunk water they started the descent. It was a lot easier than the ascent!

They walked towards the abbey ruins and sure enough, to the left of them was a track. "Should we go and get the car to drive here? I mean, in case we need a quick getaway?" Abs said.

"She has a point," Ronnie nodded.

"Why don't you two go and get the car, while Ronnie and I have a slow walk down the track and we'll meet you there?" Em said.

"Will you be OK?" Adam looked uncomfortable.

"We'll be fine, mate, just don't take forever," Ronnie replied as he and Em began walking down the track.

"Act with great caution, Emily, I fear there is great danger ahead," Carrie said, then disappeared as fast as she appeared.

"Maybe we should wait for them," Em said nervously.

"Sweetheart, I will let nothing come between us ever again," Ronnie said and pulled her in for a hug.

The house came into view. "Look," Em said, pointing.

"What?"

"Billy's 4x4 is parked outside," Em said.

"Fucker!" Ronnie said as his face screwed up with rage.

"I think we should hide over there in that long grass until we get backup." Em looked at Ronnie. He nodded in agreement.

They sat in the long grass near to a garage. Well, it was either a garage or a small barn. OK, we'll settle for small outbuilding. Em could hear crying. "Can you hear that?"

"What?"

"Can you hear crying?"

Ronnie listened. "It's coming from that outbuilding." He pointed and started to crawl through the long grass towards it.

"Ronnie! I thought that we were waiting," Em called after him. Ronnie carried on. Em followed. There was no way she was letting him out of her sight now. There was a small window on the side and Ronnie was looking through. "There's a little boy in there, tied up." He was pointing.

"Is it locked?" Em whispered. Ronnie got back on his hands and knees and crawled around to the door.

"It's padlocked," he whispered to Em.

Em crawled past him. He grabbed her arm to stop her. "I think I can get it off," she said. She carried on. She reached up, drew on her energy and held the padlock. It opened and before it could hit the ground, Em caught it. She put it in her pocket and nodded to Ronnie. He went in front and slowly opened the door. They both slid in and closed the door behind them.

Em's heart nearly stopped, when she realised that this small, frightened, badly beaten little boy was Josh! She crawled over to him. "Josh, it's me, Miss Wells. We have come to help you. You have to be a good boy and listen to what I tell you to do. OK, sweetheart?" Em said as she brushed her hand over his face. He nodded. He was trembling and sobbing.

"Josh, Ronnie is going to untie you now. If any of the bad people come in, I want you to pretend that you are still tied up, OK?" He nodded.

Ronnie untied his hands and feet and saw how deep the rope had cut into his skin. He was boiling with rage. They heard footsteps coming toward them. They both hid and the door opened. "Where the hell is that idiot wife of mine? She forgot to put the bloody lock on again," Billy mumbled to himself. He walked over to the small boy and backhanded him so hard across his face, Josh yelped out in pain. "I bet you distracted her, didn't you?" He looked at the child with such disgust. He raised his hand again and Em jumped on his back and dug her nails as hard as she could into his eyes. He was screaming. Ronnie joined in by punching him so hard in the stomach that he flew back and knocked Em flying. Ronnie could not stop. He just kept punching and kicking. The bastard deserved it.

"Sweetheart, he's out cold." Em grabbed Ronnie's arm. "We need to get him out of here," she said as she moved her head in the direction of Josh. Ronnie put the boot in one last time, just to make sure, while Em picked the boy up and rushed towards the door. Ronnie slowly opened the door – it was clear. He took Josh from Em and she went out first. Ronnie and Josh were close behind. They got him as far away and hidden as possible. "Now all we have to is wait for the cavalry. Where the hell are those two?" Ronnie looked at his watch. "Em, it's been an hour." He looked concerned.

"Josh, do you know where Mummy and Lois are?" Em whispered to Josh, who was still trembling.

"I think they are in the house." He pointed to the house.

"So why were you in the other building, sweetheart?" Em asked gently.

"Because the nasty lady said she was sick of me crying all the time," he said, sniffling. Em looked at Ronnie, her eyes were full of tears.

"Was it the lady with the red hair?" Em asked. Josh shook his head he looked puzzled.

"No, she has the same colour as you." He pointed to Em's hair.

"Charlotte," Ronnie and Em said in unison.

"Look, I think I can see Adam driving up the lane," Ronnie said. "I'll go and check."

"OK, be careful." Em blew him a kiss.

Ronnie crawled through the long grass and saw Adam's 4x4 pull into a layby. "Thank fuck," he said as he saw Adam and Abs get out. "What took you?" he said impatiently.

"Sorry, mate, the bloody car had ran out of fuel. We forgot to fill it up after the journey here," Adam said as he walked towards Ronnie.

"Er, where is Em?" Abs asked, with her hands on her hips.

"She is over there in the long grass with little Josh." Adam and Abs looked at one another and then at Ronnie. "Long story, we need to get them out of here and then I'll fill you in," Ronnie said as he began to crawl though the grass, with Abs and Adam following. Ronnie got to the spot where he had left them, but there was no sign of them. "OH NO!" Ronnie shouted.

"Listen," Abs said. There was crying coming from the grass to the right of them. Ronnie crawled over and found little Josh. Alone and sobbing.

"Josh, where is Miss Wells?" Ronnie whispered.

"The bad lady came." He pointed to the outbuilding.

"SHIT!" Ronnie shouted. "Adam, you and Abs get Josh to the car. If we are not with you in 15 minutes then Adam, you will have to come looking." Before Adam could answer, Ronnie had gone. He got to the outbuilding door. It was padlocked. "But Em put it in her pocket," he said to himself. He went around to the window. He could see someone tied to a chair but couldn't make out if it was Em. There was also someone on the floor face down. It looked like Billy. Ronnie was starting to panic. He went back to the door and tried to break the padlock. It was impossible.

Then he heard shouting, coming from the house. He turned to look. Em was at the door. "Hurry!" she shouted to him.

Ronnie ran as fast as he could. "Thank fuck you are alright," he said breathlessly.

"We need to get them out quick, Ronnie. Claire has lost a lot of blood and Lois is a nervous wreck," Em said as she led Ronnie through. Claire was lying on the floor, semi-conscious in a pool of blood and Lois was beside her rocking backward and forwards. "Can you carry Claire?"

"Sure," Ronnie said as he gently lifted her up. They went as quickly as they could, to find the car. Em took Lois by the hand and led the way. When she could see the car she started to wave her arms. They drove the car towards them.

"What the…" Adam said, as he ran over to them.

"We need to get her to a hospital," Ronnie said as he and Adam put Claire on the back seat.

"Right, if you and Em drive Claire to the hospital, Abs and I will walk the kids back to the abbey and call a cab. We'll take them back to the hotel," Adam said.

Driving to the hospital, Ronnie looked at Em. "So, what the hell happened?"

"I was talking to Josh, and Peggy shouted to watch my back. I turned around and Charlotte was just about to swing a metal bar around my head. I jumped up, grabbed the bar and whacked her with it. I told Josh to stay where he was and that you would be back, and then dragged her to the outbuilding. I tied her to the chair. Dickhead started to come round, so I smacked him again, and locked them both in. I went to the house and found Claire and Lois."

"Wow, you are so brave." Ronnie shook his head and smiled.

"Em, if you take her to the hospital, they will contact the police," Peggy said.

"But she needs medical assistance, Peggy," Em replied, looking around the car. Funny, she could hear her, but not see her.

"Try healing her. It would make your lives a lot easier."

"Where? I can't do it in the car."

"Do what?" Ronnie asked.

"Peggy thinks that I should try and heal Claire. The hospital will contact the police."

"There was an entrance to a wood back there. I could swing the car the around," Ronnie said.

They parked up at an entrance to the small wood. "Claire, do you think that you will be able to walk a little?" Em asked.

"I'll try," she replied weakly. Ronnie walked on ahead with the blanket that Em had used for the journey and laid it out on the grass. He took off his coat and made it into a makeshift pillow. Em put Claire's arm around her and walked her to the blanket. Em helped her to lie down. She looked at Ronnie in bewilderment. "She is so weak!" she whispered.

Then in front of her stood, not only Peggy but Carrie too. "You have the strength and healing power to help her. First you must empower your own energy," Carrie said. Em walked to an ancient beech tree and sat at the base quietly meditating, asking the earth to empower her energy.

"You are ready," Peggy said quietly in her ear. Em knelt beside Claire. She needed to see where the blood was coming from. She lifted Claire's jumper a little and could see a deep gash in her side. Em worked on Claire for about 30 minutes, and by the time she had finished Claire was not conscious. She looked at Peggy and Carrie for reassurance. "She is sleeping, lassie, you did very well," Peggy said, then they both vanished.

"Let's get her back to the car, it's beginning to get dark," Ronnie said. They took either side of Claire and carried her back to the car. "You look absolutely whacked out," Ronnie said as he rubbed Em's arm.

"I'll be alright, I could murder a coffee though."

Back at the hotel Ronnie went into the foyer first. He came out and told Em that the coast was clear. Luckily, Claire was awake and had enough strength to walk unaided into the lift. They took Claire into their room and Ronnie went through to Adam's room to let them know they were back. Both the kids were fast asleep in the bed. Abs was asleep at the bottom of the bed. Adam was sitting on the floor. He looked up when Ronnie walked through. "Thank the Goddess," he said as he walked over and hugged Ronnie. "I take it they kept her in," he said.

"What, Claire?" Adam nodded. "No, we didn't go to the hospital. Peggy warned us that they would contact the police."

"Shit, she is in a really bad way though. What are we going to do?" Adam asked.

"Em has done some healing work on her."

"And... has it worked?"

"Come and see for yourself," Ronnie said as he beckoned Adam back to their room.

Claire was sitting up on the bed drinking a cup of coffee. "Wow, you look a million times better," Adam said and smiled.

"Em is a very gifted lady," Claire replied.

"Lois and Josh are fast asleep," Adam told Claire.

"Good, they both need it after what they have been through," Claire said as tears streamed down her face.

"Well, I had better go back and keep watch. I'll bring them both through when they wake up," Adam said.

"Thank you," Claire sobbed.

Ronnie went through to Adam's room, to give Em a chance to find out what was going on. Em sat on the bed next to Claire. "You need to tell me everything you know, Claire. These people have killed my mum and they still have my dad."

Claire took in a deep breath. "OK, you already know about Katarina, yes?" Em nodded. "Well, I was having an affair with Joel. I met him one evening in the pub. He was with Billy. They came over to ask me if there was any news on your parents' disappearance. Long story short, Joel gave me his number and asked for mine. He messaged me a few times and then we met up. I met Katarina through Joel and Billy. They took me to her house. You know the rest where she is concerned."

"Yes, I know she wanted you to follow me, did Joel go with you to Devon?" Em asked.

"No, he said that he had a job in Wales he had to go to, but Billy came to visit a few times."

"Why?"

"So he could report back to Katarina, those two are as thick as thieves. I think they are in some sort of sadistic relationship," Claire said angrily. Em's eyes opened wide.

"What about Charlotte? I have had to whack that bitch a couple of times in the last few days," Em said and smirked.

"She thinks that they are doing it for money. Billy told her that they stand to gain a small fortune from it and the stupid woman believed him!" Claire laughed and then sadness filled her face. "I called Joel after Katarina had threatened me. He rented the cottage in the Lake District and promised me that we would be safe there." Claire was sobbing. "I can't believe I trusted him. The bastard!"

"So what happened after I came to see you?" Em asked.

"He came home, and I told him what had happened. He said that he had to go out and sort a few things. He told me not to answer the door, that he would be as quick as he could, and then we would move on. I haven't seen him since." She sniffed.

Shit! Em thought. *She doesn't know that he is dead.* "So then what?"

Em asked.

"I got the kids settled in bed and tried to call Joel. It went to voicemail. I got into bed and fell asleep. The next thing I know, there is a man in a balaclava in my room telling me to get dressed. I could hear someone in the kids' room shouting the same at them. They took us out and bundled us in a van. They drove us to where you found us."

"So who was there?" Em asked.

"Lots of people in balaclavas at first. Then the next day I had the royal visit from Katarina. She took Lois and I to this ancient hill and told us to dig."

"Dig for what?" Em asked.

"She said that she had been told that both Lois and I had the same gift as you, and that we should know what we were looking for. Em I didn't have a clue, but we dug anyway. When we didn't find anything she got her henchmen to beat me in front of Lois. She kept asking me over and over again where it was. When I couldn't tell her, she stabbed a poppet of me in the side. I passed out," Claire said as she looked at her mud-filled nails. "Would I be able to have a shower, Em?"

"Of course," Em said and showed her where everything was. "Claire, there is something I need to tell you."

"What is it, hun?"

"A few days ago, we found Joel dead in an abandoned building, in the Lake District. The police believe that he could have been the one who murdered my mum," Em said.

"NOOOOOO!" Claire screamed and shut the bathroom door.

CHAPTER 12

Ronnie ran into the room when he heard Claire scream. Em told him everything that Claire had told her. "Do you believe her?" Ronnie asked.

"I don't know. I feel bad for her and what she's been through, but my instinct is telling me not to trust her," Em replied.

"Em, don't trust her then, I sure as hell don't," Ronnie said as he leant forward and kissed her forehead.

"I told Adam and Abs everything. Neither of them trust her either. Adam called her husband, and he is driving up to collect her and the children," Ronnie said quietly.

"Shit, she went mad before when I said that I would tell her husband where she was," Em said.

"Well, Abs said that she had a long talk with the kids and they both said that they miss their dad so much and that they didn't even get to say goodbye to him. So he can't be all that bad. You only have her version of facts to go by," Ronnie said defensively.

"True, but if we tell her she might do a runner," Em whispered.

"Ah, already thought of that. We told the kids not to say anything, it was going to be a surprise for Mummy. Adam has booked us all a table in the restaurant for 6pm. Marcus is due to get here at 7 and meet Adam in the foyer." Ronnie winked an exaggerated wink at Em, and she laughed.

Claire came out of the bathroom in an untied robe. "Oh," she giggled, "I didn't realise you were in here, Ronnie," she added as she *very* slowly tied it up. Em shot her a look and Ronnie laughed.

"Ronnie and I are going to pop in to check on the children. Claire, get yourself ready as we have a table in the restaurant booked in half an hour. I expect you are starving," Em said.

"Oooh, I'm ravenous," Claire replied as she licked her lips and looked at Ronnie. Em pushed Ronnie into the bathroom.

"I do believe that she is flirting with you," Em said through gritted teeth. Ronnie laughed. "I WILL knock her out!" Em said.

In the restaurant Claire made sure she had a seat next to Ronnie, even though both of her poor children wanted to sit either side of her. Em was opposite Ronnie next to Adam. They had finished their starters and were waiting for the main course. Em looked across the table; Claire looked straight at Em and put her hand on Ronnie's arm. Em kicked him under the table. Ronnie pulled his arm away. Em nodded. "If you would excuse me, I must pop to the loo," Claire said and beckoned Ronnie with her head.

She left the table. "RIGHT!" Em said as she stood up.

"Don't do anything rash," Ronnie said and looked at the children.

"I won't," Em replied cheerfully.

Em walked into the ladies'. She looked under the cubicles and found the one that Claire was in. She waited. The door opened and Claire walked out. "Everything OK?" she said to Em whilst faffing about with her hair.

"As a matter of fact, Claire, everything is fine and dandy," Em said and smiled.

"Good," she replied as she reapplied her lipstick, well, Em's lipstick, that she borrowed and never gave back. Em held her hand out, and Claire reluctantly handed her the lipstick.

"I am just going to warn you. If you so much as look in Ronnie's direction again, I will pull your face off. Do you understand me?" Em said, trembling with rage. Claire walked out without saying a word. Em hurried behind her and sat down at the table. She checked her watch – 6:35. The mains were brought to the table. The children were eating like they had never eaten before. The plates were cleared, and Adam stood up. "Just going to nip to the loo," he said.

Claire was asking Ronnie about which was his favourite motorbike. *Bitch!* Em thought. Em looked up and saw Adam and a tall man walking towards the table. She smiled a discreet smile. "Daddy!" Josh shouted as he jumped from his chair and ran to the man with Adam. The look on Claire's face was a picture!

"How lovely!" Em said as she looked straight at Claire.

*

Em and Ronnie were sitting up in bed, recalling the day's events. "I haven't seen the green-eyed monster for such a long time." He laughed.

"I have only just got you back. There is no way I am going to let a tart like that muscle in on my man." Em laughed and nudged Ronnie.

"You should know by now, my darling, there has only ever been one woman for me." He winked.

Ronnie fell asleep straight away, but Em was struggling to settle. It was all running through her mind. How could her brother have his own mum killed, and dad kidnapped and beaten? What sort of monster was he? She thought back to her childhood. She was never close to either Billy or Jade. They used to bully her when her parents 't about and call her 'the chosen one'. Come to think of it, they weren't close to Mum or Dad. They were both really rude to both of them. Em thought back to one day in particular.

They had loaded the family camper van and left early in the morning. Both Billy and Jade moaned because they had to get up early, but Em was super excited. She loved weekends away. They drove for a few hours and stopped for something to eat. Mum made bacon sandwiches. Soon they were back on the road again. They got to the zoo at midday. Em was so happy. She spoke to every animal, in every enclosure, while Billy and Jade moaned the entire time.

Her dad knew that giraffes were Em's favourite, so he saved that for last. Em was in awe. One giraffe was about 20 feet away. Em was staring at it. In her head she was calling to it. The giraffe was looking back at her. "Come on, come and say hello," Em said.

"I told you she was a nutcase!" Billy shouted.

"Be quiet," Mum said and grabbed his arm.

"Come over here," Em said and beckoned the giraffe. It looked up and then began walking towards her. Em looked at her dad with wide eyes. The giraffe walked over to where Em was standing. It bowed its head, and Em bowed hers back.

Pleased to meet you, Em heard it say in her head.

"I'm very pleased to meet you," Em said out loud. Then all the other giraffes started to walk in Em's direction, and as they got close to her, they all bowed their heads. She bowed back. Jade was shaking her head.

"This is embarrassing!" she moaned.

The zookeeper walked over. "You must be a very special young lady," he said. "They are usually very shy," he added.

*

Later at the campsite, once the tent was pitched, Dad told them all to go and play so that Mum could cook the dinner. Behind the playpark was a wood. "Let's go and play hide and seek in there," Billy said.

"Yeah!" Jade agreed.

"Dad said we shouldn't leave the park," Em said.

"Aw, is the little chosen one scared?" Billy taunted.

"No," Em said.

"Come on then!" Jade shouted as she and Billy ran towards the woods. Em followed them.

"Right, Em, you are on it. You have to count to 100 then come and find us!" Billy shouted as he and Jade ran into the woods.

Em counted to 100 then began looking; she was going further and further into the woods. After about ten minutes she called out, "Come out. You win, I can't find you." Nothing. "Please come out, I'm scared," she cried out.

"Boo!" Billy pushed her from behind.

"That's not funny!" Em said as she began to cry.

"Shut up, cry baby," Jade said.

"Em, bet you can't climb up this tree," Jade said and looked at Billy. Em started to climb the tree. She reached the first branch, pulled herself up and sat on it.

"See, I could do it," she said, very pleased with herself.

Billy and Jade started laughing at her. "Now, get down," Billy said.

"Can you help me? I'm stuck." Em looked terrified. Billy and Jade ran off and left her. As much as she tried she could not get down. She sat back on the branch. It was getting dark. She would never find her way out of the woods in the dark.

Mum and Dad will be worried. "Oh, tree. Please help me," Em said out loud. The wind started to blow. It came out of nowhere. It was blowing really hard. All of a sudden there was a massive gust. It blew out of the tree and she landed on a big pile of leaves. She thanked the earth and ran as fast as her small legs would take her.

When she got back to the tent Mum shouted, "Em, what have we told you about running away from your brother and sister? Your dad has been frantic." Mum shook her head.

"But... they left me," Em cried. Mum clearly wasn't listening.

"Go and wash your hands, I'm just about to dish up," Mum huffed. "Billy, go and find Dad and tell him she's back." Em buried herself into her sleeping bag and cried.

"Em, what's the matter, sweetheart?" Dad said as he lifted the sleeping bag away from her face. Em told her dad exactly what had happened. He took her hand, led her to the camping table and sat her down. He looked at Billy and Jade. "I'll be having words with you two after dinner," he said as he scowled.

Em drifted off and had the best night's sleep ever. No visions, no lucid dreams.

*

The next morning, the four of them met up in the dining room for breakfast. They were discussing what to do on their last day there. "There's a fab golf course on site." Ronnie winked at Adam.

"I am not spending my last day here playing bloody golf!" Abs said. Em laughed.

"No, why don't you girls make use of the spa? It will do you both good," Adam said. The girls looked at one another.

"I suppose it might be quite nice to be pampered," Em said in deep thought.

"That's settled then. Shall I go and book?" Ronnie stood up and walked out to the foyer.

"I have never had a spa day," Em said. She felt a little nervous.

"Really? I have had loads, you will feel like a new woman

afterwards," Abs beamed.

Em spotted Ronnie walking back towards them. She still couldn't believe she had him back. Every time she looked at him, she had to pinch herself.

"Well I say, it's very posh in here!" Peggy said in a posh Scottish accent. She was stood next to Ronnie. Em and Adam both burst out laughing; she looked so comical, stood there with her hands on her hips. Ronnie and Abs looked at one another.

"What's the joke?" Ronnie asked.

"Peggy is stood right beside you with her hands on her hips, telling us how posh it is in here," Adam said, still laughing.

"So, you can see her too?" Ronnie looked puzzled.

"Yes, Adam has the gift too. Turns out that Adam's dad was Carrie's grandson, so Adam inherited the gift," Em said as she stood up kissed Ronnie's cheek and took the paperwork from his hand.

*

Abs was having a massage. Em opted out; she didn't like people touching her, so she had a facial instead. Em was lying on the bed with a mud mask on and cucumbers over her eyes. "Well, when you have finished bathing in luxury, maybe you could all get yourselves up to Pendle Hill!" Peggy said. Em took the cucumbers off.

"Is it important that we do?" Em asked.

"Lassie, I would not say it if it wasnee important," Peggy replied.

"Sorry, what did you say, Em?" Abs asked.

"Oh, sorry Abs, I was talking to Peggy," Em said. The therapist who was massaging Abs looked around the room, and then at Abs and Em in bewilderment. They both burst out laughing.

"Sorry, it's a private joke," Abs said to the therapist.

"Abs, we are going to have to cut this short. We need to grab the boys. There is somewhere that we need to be," Em said as she climbed off of the bed.

"You need the mud mask removed," the therapist said.

"I'll do it myself. Abs, come on!" Em said. The girls were laughing at the looks that other guests were giving Em with her mud mask on, as they walked through the hotel.

"Put something warm and comfortable on, it's a bit of a climb," Em called to Abs as they were going into their rooms. Em called Ronnie's new mobile.

"Hello beautiful, what can I do for you?" was the answer.

"Oh, sorry, I think I have got the wrong number," Em said and laughed.

"Very funny. What's up?"

"You two need to finish your game, we have to go to Pendle Hill. I have just had a visit from Peggy," Em told him.

"OK sweetheart, we'll be with you in ten," he said as he ended the call. Em washed the mask off her face. Blimey, it was like glue! She put on her walking gear and put Ronnie's out on the bed.

*

What a climb! They were all exhausted when they reached the top! The views were spectacular; it made the climb worth it. The others were all getting their breath back. Em heard someone call out. She walked in the voice's direction. It was coming from the stone storm shelter. A young girl poked her head out from inside. "Come quickly!" she said to Em. Em hurried into the shelter. The girl who was not much older than nine or ten, was very dirty and wearing rags. "Kent, you must go back there. Seek out Sally," the child said before she disappeared. Em walked out of the shelter and back towards the others who were walking towards her.

"Are you alright, sweetheart?" Ronnie put his arms around her. She told them all what had happened.

"Well, I think that we should go back to the hotel, have a slap-up meal and enjoy our last evening here. We can sort everything out once we get back to Devon tomorrow," Ronnie said as he rubbed his tummy.

They all had a lovely evening. Gorgeous food, wonderful company and maybe one too many drinks. Em felt quite sad the next morning as they checked out of the hotel. It was a quiet drive back. Everyone was reflecting on the recent past events. Ronnie was driving and Em was in the passenger seat next to him. "I suppose we should go back to London," Adam said from the back seat. Tears pricked Em's eyes at the thought. It had been so good, spending time with him and Abs. Abs was probably the only friend that Em had ever had in her life. In the short time she had known her, she had become more of a sister to Em than Jade had ever been.

"When do you think you will go back?" Em said, choking back the tears, as she stared out of the window.

"Tomorrow, I suppose. When are you two going back to Kent?" he asked.

"Em is going to give notice on the cottage tomorrow. So in a couple of days," Ronnie said as he put his hand on Em's leg. He could see she was upset. He looked in the mirror and saw that Abs had her head buried in Adam's shoulder; she was clearly as upset as Em.

"Hey, you guys both know that you are more than welcome to come and stay anytime, in fact it will be easier when we are back in Kent. We'll be closer," Ronnie said. Em put her hand on Ronnie's. *He is such a good soul,* she thought to herself.

*

After an emotional goodbye, Adam and Abs were on their way back to London. They promised that they would visit as soon as Em and Ronnie were settled back in Kent. Ronnie and Em spent the next couple of days sorting everything out, packing everything up and arranging removals. Em phoned Suzie to tell her; she couldn't bear to do it face to face. Suzie was disappointed that Em was leaving but understood and wished her well.

The day of the funeral. It was just Em and Ronnie. That's how Em wanted it. They had made arrangements for Mum's ashes to be couriered to Kent.

The morning of the move came. Em felt sadness creeping in. This was the place that helped her find Ronnie, and in a strange way she had become quite attached to the place. The small removals van had put the last of the things in and gone. Now in the cottage, it was just her and Ronnie. "We are going to find Dad. Aren't we?" Em was choking back the tears.

"Of course we are," he said as he wrapped his arms around her. "Come on, missus, we have a long drive." He kissed her on the head. She sadly closed the door for the last time and put the keys in the envelope for the letting agents.

As she walked to the car, someone touched her shoulder. Em turned and was surprised to see Mrs Dawkins standing there. "Mrs Dawkins!" Em said. She looked upset. "Is everything OK?" Em asked.

"Well, quite frankly, no it's not, my dear. You were going to leave here without so much as a by your leave. I thought that we had become friends," she said, clearly shaken up. Em put her arms around her a pulled her in for a big hug.

"I'm so sorry! So much as happened it didn't even cross my mind. Look, I'll write my address and telephone number down for you. We can still keep in touch," Em said as she scribbled it on a scrap piece of paper she had found in the glove compartment. She handed it to Mrs Dawkins. "Take care of yourself, Mrs D., and thank you for always checking in on me," Em said as she got into the car and pulled away. She wiped the tears from her face.

"Good riddance to bad rubbish," she heard from the back seat.

"Oh, Peggy!" she laughed.

*

It felt strange going back in the house. No Mum banging around in the kitchen, no Dad singing, no Butch knocking you flying every time you walked through the door!

Em picked up the mountain of post from the mat and put it on the table. The removals men had gone, so Ronnie and Em started to unpack. Em was in the lounge, sorting it out. There wasn't a lot to do. Em had only taken the cuddle chair and kitchen bits with her as the cottage was mostly furnished. She heard the front door close. Jade walked into the lounge, followed by Lewis. "Heard you were back. The vultures have landed," Jade said as she looked at Lewis and laughed.

"WHAT! Piss off, Jade, who invited you in anyway?" Em snarled.

"I do not need an invite into my own family home, Chosen One. Anyway, that's why I am here. I need to talk to you about selling," she said indignantly.

"Selling what?" Em looked at her in dismay.

"This bloody house. We may as well benefit from it," she said.

Em walked over and punched her straight on the nose! Jade grabbed Em's hair, trying to pull her to the floor. Em stuck her finger straight into Jade's eye. Lewis stood watching. Ronnie ran into the room, pushed Lewis flying and got between them. "What the bloody hell?" Ronnie said, looking at Em.

"She wants to sell the house!" Em yelled.

"Whoa, what house?" Ronnie asked.

"THIS FUCKING HOUSE!" Em screamed.

"Well, that's not going to happen, Jade. We have paperwork to prove that Em and I are joint owners in the property. We paid half.

Your mum's share automatically goes to your dad," Ronnie told her.

"What!" Jade looked shellshocked. "When did all this happen, may I ask?"

"Well that's exactly it. You were never around to ask or tell. Both you and Billy thought that we were scrounging off Mum and Dad. Well you were wrong!" Em said.

"And don't even think about doing anything to Dad. His share goes to me. So if it's the money you want so badly, you will have to kill me instead." Em looked at Jade with such despise.

"What makes you think that I had anything to do with Mum's death?" Jade stood with her hands on her hips.

"I never even mentioned Mum's death," Em said, shocked.

"Lewis, we are leaving, NOW!" Jade shouted and almost ran out of the door. Lewis following her like a little duckling.

"Did I just hear that correctly? She may as well have signed a confession to playing a part in your mum's murder!" Ronnie said.

CHAPTER 13

Ronnie was in the kitchen preparing the evening meal, and Em was trying to find Sally. Every time she thought she was getting somewhere it turned out to be a dead end. Em was racking her brain. *What was her husband's name… Kevin! That was it, Kevin and Sally Young.* She looked his name up on the internet. "Got it!" she shouted out to the kitchen.

"Have you found her?" Ronnie shouted back.

"I think so, I'm just going to call this number," she called back.

Em walked into the kitchen a few minutes later. "Was it her?" Ronnie asked.

"Yep, we have an appointment on Thursday, 12pm," Em said, feeling very pleased with herself. "Dinner smells gorgeous," she added and dipped her finger in the wok. Ronnie smacked her bum. She turned just as the phone rang. "Saved by the bell." She laughed as she went to grab the phone. It was Abs.

"Hey," Em said cheerfully. Abs was in a terrible state. After 20 minutes of Em trying to calm her down, Ronnie came through to the lounge.

"OK, text me what time your train is due in," Em said as she ended the call.

"What's going on?" Ronnie asked.

"We have a problem." Em looked troubled.

Em spent the next 20 minutes telling Ronnie about the conversation she had just had with Abs.

"So is Adam coming with her?" Ronnie seemed truly concerned.

"I don't think so, he didn't come home last night, and when she called him, he told her to give him some space, that he needed to think." Em sighed. "It just seems so out of character. He adores Abs," she added.

"I think I'll give him a call. He might talk to me," Ronnie said.

"OK sweetheart." Em kissed him as she left the room. She was getting the guest room ready when her phone pinged.

Train will be in at 6 Abs X.

"It's her! Nothing but trouble, that one." Peggy was in front of Em.

"What, Abs?" Em asked.

"No, Abs is a lovely girl. I'm talking about that harlot, whose life you saved!" Peggy was angry.

"Oh, you mean Claire. What has she got to do with it?" Em was intrigued.

"You should have taken the wee girl and left her there!" Peggy said. Em laughed.

"Peggy, why do you think that she's involved?" Em asked.

"I don't think, lassie, I know."

"And…?"

"She has been messaging Adam. She got his number from her husband's phone. I told him she was devious, but he would not listen to me. She has him under some sort of enchantment." Peggy looked sad. Ronnie came into the room.

"Well?" Em asked.

"He said he has some personal issues he has to deal with. To be honest, Em, he sounded as if he didn't really want to speak to me," Ronnie said. Em told Ronnie about her conversation with Peggy.

"Have you got an address for Marcus?" he asked.

"No, but I could probably find it. Adam did." Em got her laptop and started to search Marcus Savides.

"Got it!" she said. "It's a twenty-minute drive from here."

"Why don't I go while you pick Abs up from the station?" he said.

"No way! What if it's a trap? Safety in numbers, Ronnie. I think we should go together. Besides, it's you that she set her sights on, so she is probably using Adam to get to you," Em said.

"OK, fair point, how long have we got?" he asked.

"Two hours."

"Let's get going then."

*

They pulled up just along from the house. Close enough to see it. It was a nice semi-detached house with a drive and garage. They could see Josh playing basketball on the drive. There was a knock on the window Em's side. Em turned to look. It was Lois. *SHIT!* Em opened the window. "Hi Lois! How are you?" Em asked.

"OK, I guess, what are you doing here?" she asked.

"Oh, we popped by to make sure that you all got back safely," Ronnie leant over Em to say. "Is your mum at home?" he asked. She shook her head. "Oh, that's a shame, do you know when she will be back?" She shook her head. Em nudged Ronnie as she saw Marcus heading towards them.

"Lois, darling, go and keep an eye on Josh for me, will you?" Marcus said and rubbed her head.

"Bye," she said as she skipped off.

"I take it that you both know that she has gone again," Marcus said as he leaned down to talk to them.

"Er, no. We were in the area and thought we would come by and see how you are all doing," Em said nervously.

"When did she go?" Ronnie asked.

"Yesterday, she left a note," Marcus said.

"And...?" Ronnie waited for a response.

"Said that she had met someone else, that he was the one. I mean the other three were the one until she became bored of them," he said.

"I'm sorry, Marcus, if there is anything we can do just give us a call," Em said as she jotted their home number down.

"Thanks," he said and walked off.

*

They decided not to say anything to Abs about Claire's disappearance; she looked so sad as she got off the train. Em ran over and threw her arms around her. Abs burst into tears. They got to the house and Em gave Abs a grand tour. Ronnie put her case in the guest room and went to finish off cooking dinner. They came out of Ronnie and Em's room and Em felt a draught. She looked around. It seemed to be coming from above. She looked up. The attic hatch was open. "Ronnie," Em called downstairs.

"Yeah?"

"Have you been up in the attic today?"

"No, sweetheart, why?"

"Oh, the hatch is open."

"Do you want me to come and close it?" he called up.

"No, sweetheart, I'll do it," Em called back. She pulled the loop on the folding ladder.

"Are you going up there?" Abs asked.

"Well, I had better go and check it out, it's not like it can open itself," Em said as she started to climb the ladder. "You stay there, I won't be long," she added.

"No way! I'm coming up too," Abs said as she started to climb the ladder. "I just won't look down," she said. Em laughed.

"You're not climbing Mount Everest," Em chuckled.

*

Em looked around. Abs stood up and wiped her brow. Em smiled; it was good to have her around again. There was a crashing noise. Abs jumped up in the air. It came from one of the eaves. Em slowly walked over, and gasped.

"Oh my god, what's wrong?" Abs was trembling with fear.

"It's my dad's memory chest. It just threw itself open," Em said breathlessly. Abs walked over to Em. The chest was a big wooden box, with a lid. The lid was wide open, and the padlock was on the floor next to it still closed. "Can you call Ronnie for me, Abs?" Em asked as she was looking through bits in the chest. Abs walked over to the opening, called Ronnie and walked back to Em.

"Everything alright?" Ronnie said as he stood up. He had to stoop as he was taller than the sloping roof.

"Sweetheart, can you help me to carry this down?" Em asked as she was trying to move the heavy chest.

"Sure, where are we going with it?" he asked.

"Our bedroom?" Em looked at him for approval. Ronnie nodded and the three of them pushed the chest to the opening.

After a lot of pushing, pulling and swearing they finally managed to manoeuvre the chest down and it was put in the bedroom. Ronnie went back to the kitchen, while Em showed Abs the garden, wood and her workshop.

"Wow, Em, I had no idea," Abs said with wide eyes. She was looking at all the glass jars and bottles. All the herbs growing and the many books that were scattered about everywhere. Abs picked up a book that was open on the worktop. "Medicinal herbs and their properties," she read out loud. "How long have you been doing this?"

"A long time. It was a nightmare when we first got back. I hadn't even give the herbs and plants a second thought while I was away. They hadn't been watered. Luckily, I managed to salvage most of them." Em sighed. "Right, I suppose we better go and see if Ronnie needs any help," Em said as they both walked towards the door. Em locked the door behind them. Abs heard a dog barking. "Have you got a dog?" She looked towards the woods. Em looked too.

"No, my dog went missing with my dad," Em said and walked towards the woods.

There he was. Butch. Standing by the opening. Em leant forward. "Butch, Butch! Here boy!" Em said gently. The dog looked at her and tilted his head. "Come on, sweetheart," Em said and tapped her leg. Slowly the dog walked towards her. As he got closer his tail began to wag. When he saw it was Em he ran and jumped at her, knocking her to the ground.

Abs ran as fast as she could back to house to get Ronnie. She flew in the kitchen door. "Ronnie, quick, Em is being attacked by a dog!" she shouted breathlessly. They both ran back to the opening. There, sitting on the grass was Em, being licked to death by the dog.

"BUTCH!" Ronnie shouted in surprise. The dog then ran at Ronnie, jumped up and was licking him furiously. He ran back to Em and sat beside her.

"Where have you been?" Em said as she was rubbing the dog's jowls. She held her hands up to show Ronnie and Abs the drool. They all laughed.

After dinner, they were sitting in the conservatory. The sun was still up, and it was lovely in there. Butch sat across Em's feet. "I still cannot believe he came back," Em said as she stroked the sleeping dog. "Anyway, Abs, you still haven't told us was has happened, with you and Adam," Em said. She thought it might be easier for Abs to talk about it if she was relaxed, so she plied her with wine at dinner.

"We were fine when we got back. Adam asked me to move in, so I was sorting all my things ready to go. The night before I was due to move in, Adam was really distant. He kept his phone in his pocket, which he never does. You know what he's like, he leaves it anywhere. He kept going to the loo. Then at around ten, he came into the lounge and said that I should spend my last night at my flat. When I asked him why, he said that he thought it would do us both good. I didn't want to, but to keep the peace, I did. The next morning I loaded my car with all my things and drove to Adam's apartment. I was so excited. I texted Adam in the morning, but he didn't reply. I thought that maybe he was busy with work." Tears filled her eyes.

"Do you want another drink?" Ronnie asked them both.

"Love one." Em handed him her glass and smiled.

"Abs." He nodded at her glass.

"Sorry Ronnie, yes please," Abs said, choking back tears.

"So, what was he like when you got there?" Em asked.

"He told me to put my things away, and that he would be a while as he was very busy with work. I thought that I would pop out and grab us something nice for dinner. I took the keys from the rack. When I got back, he was on the phone talking to someone. I walked into the lounge and he ended the call, then went ballistic! Accusing me of spying on him, said he needed some space. He stormed out. I kept trying to call him, but it went to voicemail. I cried myself to sleep. I woke up to a text from him saying that he needed space and that he was going away for a while, and I haven't heard from him or seen him since." Abs looked up. She was clearly now very angry. Butch started to bark and the fur on his back stood up.

"You have to tell her," Peggy said as Butch stood barking at her. She put her finger to her lips, and he stopped. Em clapped. Abs and Ronnie looked at her. She giggled.

"I don't think it's very funny, Em," Abs said.

"Sorry Abs, I wasn't laughing at that, I was laughing at Peggy trying to train Butch," Em said, trying to be serious. Abs got up and excused herself.

"You shouldn't have laughed," Ronnie whispered.

"I know but it is true what I said, about Peggy and the dog. Anyway, Peggy said that we should tell her," Em whispered.

"Maybe I should do it. Your diplomacy goes out of the window when you have had too much wine," he said in Em's ear. He kissed her on the head. "I'll go and make some coffee." He winked at Em as Abs walked back into the room.

"I must say, Abs, it really sounds odd that he would act like that. He adores you. What the hell has got into him?" Em said. She was getting angry now. "I'm going to give him a bloody slap when I find him," she added. Abs burst into tears. Ronnie brought the coffees in on a tray; Em was sat with her arm around Abs trying to comfort her.

"Abs, calm down," Ronnie said as he handed her a coffee. Abs sniffed, wiped her eyes and took the mug.

"Look, there is no easy way to say this, Abs, but you have got to trust us, something is not right," Ronnie said.

"OK, what is it?" Abs sniffed.

"Peggy told Em that Claire had been messaging Adam. We went to Claire's house. She has left Marcus again." Ronnie looked at Em as Abs started to wail.

"Abs, pull yourself together," Em said. "We think he has been enchanted; we think they are using him to get to Ronnie," Em said as she put her hand on Abs' hand. "We will find him, and I will reverse the enchantment, I promise," Em said.

Once Abs had calmed down they all went up to bed. Em made sure that Abs was comfortable, then climbed into bed next to Ronnie. Butch was lying at the bottom of the bed. "How are we going to find him?" Em asked.

"Well, I have had an idea," Ronnie replied.

"Go on."

"I thought that maybe I should call him and tell him that you have gone missing."

"Why me!" Em said.

"You are the only one that can give them what they want. If they think you have gone missing and it wasn't them, they will pay attention." Ronnie looked very smug.

"Aah, I see. Very clever," Em said as she snuggled into him.

She had something over her head; she was tied up. Em struggled but could not break free. The smell. It smelt like tar. She could hear water dripping. "Mum, Mum, are you here?" she cried out. Laughing, she could hear laughing. It didn't sound like Katarina, but it did sound familiar. "Is anyone there?" Em called out. The laughing became louder. "Please, please help me!" she cried out. Someone was there with her. "Who's there?" she called out.

"Poor, poor Emily," she heard.

"Take this off my head, let me see you!" Em screamed. She could feel it being pulled off. Her eyes adjusted to the dim light. "BITCH!" she screamed out when she realised that it was Claire who stood in front of her.

"Now I am going to tell you what is going to happen. I have been given YOUR Ronnie. As soon as I hand you over to Katarina, he is to become MY

Ronnie. What do you think about that, CHOSEN ONE?"

Claire was loving every minute of it! Em surged forward, desperately trying to break free. She was going to kill her. Claire slapped Em so hard that the chair that she was tied to tipped backwards.

"STOP! Don't you dare touch her again," she heard. Her chair was pushed back up then, Katarina walked over to Claire and slashed her across the face with something in her hand. "She is mine, do not ever forget that!"

Em woke with a jump when she heard the loud bang. Butch was barking. Ronnie sat bolt upright. "What the hell was that?" Ronnie said. Em climbed out of bed and put the light on.

"It's the chest, it has moved," Em said. Ronnie got out of bed and joined her.

"Maybe someone is trying to tell us something," Ronnie said as he looked at his watch. "Em, it's quarter to six, shall I go and make some coffee and bring it up?"

"Lovely," Em said and blew him a kiss.

"You need to look inside, lassie," Peggy said.

"Peggy, how am I going to stop them from taking Ronnie again?" Em was so fearful.

"Your strong will and your good soul will stop them. Maybe there is something inside the chest that will help you."

Em began taking things out of the chest. Lots of memorabilia from Dad's sporting days. Lots of photos of Mum. Buried beneath all that, were lots of very old books. They were covered in dust. Em blew the dust from one. It was a plain leather-bound book. She opened it; she didn't understand what it said. It looked like symbols. Ronnie came in with the tray of coffee. He opened the curtains and was looking through the things that Em had taken out. Em put the book to one side and grabbed the one beneath it. She felt a surge of energy run up her arm and fill her entire body. She blew the dust off and opened it. This one was handwritten in English. It was a grimoire. It was written by Abagail Walcott. There were many spells and incantations. "Look at this." She handed it to Ronnie.

"It's certainly ancient," he said as he gently looked through the pages. "What's happened to your face?" He said as he looked up at Em. She looked in the mirror and saw a massive bruise on her cheek. She had no choice, she had to tell him about the dream. "Maybe, it's playing on your mind. You know, what with Adam missing," he tried to reassure her.

"But what if it was a vision and not a dream?" She had tears in her eyes.

"I wouldn't go near that spiteful bitch with a ten-foot barge pole, Em. I love you and I'm not going anywhere." He wrapped his arms around her.

"But they could enchant you, like they have Adam." She was crying now. She felt so helpless.

"I'm going to call Adam now and start the ball rolling. Why don't you jump in the shower and then see if there is anything in those books that could help us?" He kissed her gently on the lips.

*

Em was in the shower, washing her hair. "In the grimoire, there is a section on enchantment."

"What, who said that?" Em rinsed the shampoo out of her eyes. No-one there.

CHAPTER 14

She wrapped her robe around her, dried her hands and picked up the grimoire. She gently turned the pages until she found it.

HOW TO PROTECT AGAINST AND REVERSE ENCHANTMENTS

She read on. "Brilliant!" she said.

She quickly got dressed, grabbed the book and headed downstairs. Abs was sitting at the breakfast bar eating toast. "Morning, Abs, have you seen Ronnie?" Em asked as she pinched some toast from Abs' plate.

"He was on the phone, then told me to tell you he was popping out and that you'd know why," Abs replied as she scrolled through her phone.

"SHIT!" Em started to panic. "What the fuck is he doing?" she yelled as she was calling his mobile.

"Em, what on earth is the matter?" Abs said.

"No fucking answer, that's what the matter is, Abs. I am not going to lose him again!" She slid to the floor and sobbed.

"Emily, stop." It was Carrie. "Calm down. You cannot think rationally in that state." Em wiped her eyes. "Now, take the grimoire to your place and work a spell to prevent the enchantment." Carrie smiled. "You can control this situation, but you need a level head. Hurry, child." Em nodded. She got up, grabbed the grimoire and walked out of the door.

"Em, where are you going?" Abs dropped her toast and ran to catch her up.

"Abs, go back to the house; in case he comes back. I won't be long. Get dressed because we need to go out," Em barked at Abs.

Em took deep breaths and started to prepare the spell. She needed something of Ronnie's. *Shit.* She would have to go back to the house. As she walked to the door she noticed Ronnie's head scarf on the side. He took it off when they were trying to save all the plants. She took some hair from inside. "Purest of heart," she heard. She nodded and worked the spell.

She checked her phone as soon as she got back to the house. Nothing. Abs came into the kitchen fully dressed. "Are you going to tell me what the hell is going on?" she said.

Over a coffee, Em told her about the dream and how Ronnie was going to get Adam back. "So what are we going to do?" Abs asked.

"Have you seen Butch?"

"Yeah, Ronnie took him with him," Abs said.

"Oh shit, that's three of them now," Em said despairingly as she put her head in her hands.

"I don't know what to suggest," Abs said. "It's hopeless. Why don't these people just fuck off!" she added as sat shaking her head. Em's phone pinged. She ran over to it.

Message from Ronnie.

I'M OK SWEETHEART, COULDN'T ANSWER, WAS WITH ADAM WILL BE HOME IN 20 XXXXXXXXX

"Thank the Goddess," Em sighed a huge sigh of relief. Abs' phone then pinged. Message from Adam.

DID YOU KNOW THAT EM IS MISSING?????

"Should I reply?" Abs asked.

"Maybe wait until Ronnie is back, see what he says."

The front door opened and Butch came bounding through the kitchen, heading straight for Em. She gave him a big hug. Ronnie followed and Em nearly knocked him backwards as she jumped at him. She looked at him, to make sure that he didn't have that distant look in his eyes. He seemed fine. "Firstly, mister, don't you ever bugger off like that again, you scared the crap out of me," she said as she planted a big kiss on his lips. "Secondly, how did you get on with Adam?" she said.

"Well, it was like talking to a stranger. I think he bought it though," Ronnie said as he filled the kettle.

"Where did you meet him?" Abs asked. Ronnie looked at her.

"He is staying in a house about a twenty-minute drive from here."

"Alone?" Her eyes were full of tears. Ronnie shook his head. Em walked over to Abs and hugged her.

"I will put a stop to this, I promise," Em said. She looked at Ronnie; he shook his head.

"Em, have you seen the time?" he asked. Em looked at her watch.

"Yeah, it's half ten." She looked at him.

"What time is your appointment?"

"Appointment? Oh, Sally, I completely forgot," she said.

The drive to Sally's was fraught. Both of them were very quiet. "So, you haven't told me what you said to Adam," Em said, looking out of the window. Ronnie said nothing. "Ronnie!" She looked at him. He was looking straight ahead. "Ronnie, why are you ignoring me?" Em raised her voice. Ronnie shot her a look, but still said nothing. He pulled up outside Sally's cottage. "Are you coming in with me?"

"No, it's probably better that you go by yourself," he said, still not looking at her.

"Right, fine!" Em grabbed her bag, got out of the car and slammed the door. She stomped up the path.

"I'll tell you about Adam when I pick you up. Text me when you are ready," Ronnie called out from the car as he spun it around. Em carried on walking and didn't acknowledge him. She'd give him a taste of his own medicine, she thought to herself.

She took some deep breaths and then rang the bell. The door opened and Sally's old husky dog Star came out. She was sniffing Em and wagging her tail. "Star," Sally called to the dog, and the dog ran in. "Come on in, Em," Sally called out.

Em spent an hour filling Sally in with all the details of what had been happening; she even took her notebook, in case she forgot something. "Oh, Em, I'm so sorry. I had no idea that any of this had happened." Sally looked truly shocked. Em shrugged. She didn't know what to say. "Look, there is something that I could do to help you, but I don't know if it is something that you would want to do," Sally said and looked over the top her glasses.

"What? What is it?" Em asked.

"Clearly, all of this stems from when you were a child and had the sleepwalking episodes. Something must have happened, or you must have been told something. As you were a child at the time, it wouldn't be something that you would necessarily remember."

"So?" Em looked worried.

"So, we can take you back, into your dreams," Sally said. "You know, similar to regression therapy," she added.

"Is it dangerous?" Em asked.

"There can be an element of risk, but I will be with you every step of the way, Em, and I'm sure that your mum and Peggy will be watching out for you." Sally put her hand on Em's. "Anyway, you don't have to give me answer straight away. Go home, discuss it with Ronnie and let me know in a few days."

Some chance of that, Em thought to herself. Sally went to make them both some tea and Em sent a text to Ronnie to tell him she was ready. Sally brought a tray of tea and biscuits in and put it on the coffee table. Em's phoned pinged. It was a message from Abs.

Hey, I am going to pick you up. Will be there in 10 minutes. Abs X.

Em drank her tea and then went to wait outside for Abs. Abs pulled up in Em's car. Em got in. "Where is Ronnie?" She looked at Abs.

"Er, I don't know. I thought that he was with you, but then he called the house phone and asked me to pick you up," Abs said.

"Well did he say where he was, or why he couldn't pick me up?"

"No, that was all he said."

"Shit! What the hell is wrong with him!" Em was seething.

The journey back was then in complete silence. They got in and Em went straight to the house phone to see if there were any messages. None. For an hour she was constantly checking her phone. Nothing.

"Hey, shall I cook tonight? I'd like to." Abs smiled.

"That would be great, Abs," Em said. She got up and put her coat on.

"Where are you going?" Abs asked.

"I can't sit around waiting for him to contact me, I'm going to take Butch for a walk," Em said as she put Butch's new lead on.

Em walked down the garden and through the wood. It was a beautiful day, and the birds were in full song. At the back of the woods was a gate that led out towards the village. Em and Butch walked up to the village shop, to get something for dessert. She tied Butch up outside. Mr Brock, the shopkeeper, was stacking some shelves and seemed overjoyed to see Em. He asked her about her mum and dad; he was truly shaken when she told him about her mum.

She untied Butch and decided to walk the long way back. They went along the lane. Butch stopped. The fur on his back stood and he began to growl. Em looked all around her. She pulled on the lead, but Butch refused to move. "Come on, Butch," she said as she pulled harder. Then he started to wag his tail. Em looked up and her mum was standing in front of them. "MUM!" Em squealed. Her eyes filled with tears; how she longed to hug her!

"Em, my sweet Em, always know that I am with you, and I will do my very best to protect you." Em nodded, choking back sobs. "You need to do this alone, Em, it all rests on your shoulders, and only you can put an end to it all." Em nodded. She looked in her pocket for some tissue and when she looked up her mum had gone. "Be brave, my Em," she heard in the wind.

She started to run; Butch was running too. She needed to get back and call Sally. She arranged to go to Sally the following day.

Abs was busy in the kitchen. Em walked in. "Abs, I'm sorry I have been such a cow lately," she said.

"I have hardly been pleasant, Em." Abs walked over and put her arms around her. "Why don't you lay the table and pour us both a huge glass of wine? Dinner will be ready in about five minutes," she said as she turned back to the cooker.

After a lovely spaghetti Bolognese and a few glasses of wine both of them began to relax. "What are we going to do, Em?"

"Absolutely nothing!" Em laughed.

"Has he contacted you?"

"Nope. Has Adam contacted you?"

"Nope."

"Well, cheers to us then," Em said as she raised her glass and clinked it against Abs'.

"Have you contacted the police, about Ronnie?"

"No, what's the point? He is obviously with them. The protection against enchantment must have been too late," Em said as she looked at the bottom of her glass, noticing that it was empty. "Another?" She shook her glass at Abs.

"Please." Abs passed her the empty glass. Butch started barking at front window. Abs got up to look out. "Em, quick!" she called. Em joined her at the window; there was a black car parked on the drive. "Are there two people in it?" Abs asked. Em turned the light off.

"Yes, it looks like it," Em said as she headed in the direction of the front door. Abs ran behind her. Em marched out of the door, towards the car, but before she got to it, the engine started, and they drove off. "I bet that was something to do with them!" Em shouted.

*

She checked her phone. Nothing. She turned off the light and sobbed into her pillow. She had only just got him back. She was so angry. "Em, you need to lose the negative energy," Peggy said, perched on the bottom of Em's bed next to Butch.

"Peggy, I'm so angry. I can't believe that they have taken him from me again," Em said as she punched her pillow.

"Lassie, you are playing into their hands. They need you to be negative."

"Why?"

"Because your strength comes from your positive energy. When you are negative you weaken. If they wear you down enough, it will be easier for them to manipulate you. After all, it is you, that Katarina wants. Not Adam, your dad or Ronnie," Peggy said.

Em was disappointed that she had slept all night without a dream or vision. She showered, crept downstairs, left Abs a note and got in her car. When she reached Sally's she heard a voice. "This will be hard for you. Keep your will strong." She nodded and got out of the car.

She was lying on a meditation mat, while Sally was talking her through the steps. "Keep talking to me, Em, then I won't lose you." Em nodded.

She was walking down the stairs. She walked into the living room. Mum, Dad and Billy were there. A shadow walked over to where Billy was sitting. It said as it pointed at him, "Beware of him." Now she was walking out of the back door. She walked with the shadow to the base of a large hill. The shadow led the way up the hill. Halfway up, the shadow turned into a woman. A beautiful woman with long blonde hair.

"Are you still with me, Em?" Sally said.

"Yes," Em replied.

The woman stood beside Em and waved her hands over the hill. A vision appeared of water. Water coursing beneath the hill. The water had a brightness to it. It was almost white. Em looked at the woman. In her hand she had a metal cannister. She opened it and pulled out what looked like a page from a book. She placed the paper back inside the cannister, put the lid on and threw it into the bright water. "Seven different pages, seven different ley lines, and only those worthy will discover them," the woman said as she took Em's hand and led her back to her house. As they got to the front door the woman turned to Em and put her finger to her lips. Then she became a shadow again.

"Em, Em, come on, come back now. Ten, nine, eight…" Em sat up.

"Wow, that was amazing," she said.

"Do you understand it? You need to study the ley lines. Find the significance with the seven and read the grimoire," Sally said. Em nodded.

Em got in her car. She felt so uplifted, so full of energy. Her phone rang. It was a number she didn't recognise. "Hello?"

"Emily, it's Charlotte. I need your help; can you meet me?"

"And why would I do that?" Em sighed.

"Because I can tell you where your dad is," Charlotte said.

"Right, I am going to trust you because…?" Em waited.

"Look, Billy has shacked up with that bitch Katarina. The only way that I can get him back is to help you to stop her," she said. Em thought about for a moment.

"I need to think about this. I will call you back." Em ended the call.

CHAPTER 15

She told Abs about the call. "Don't dare meet up with her. It will most definitely be a trap." Abs had her hands on her hips.

"I know you're right, Abs. I won't, I promise," Em said as she crossed her fingers behind her back. "Right, I have some things to do in the workshop. Do you fancy nipping to the supermarket and grabbing something for dinner? Please." Em gave Abs her sweetest look.

"OK, but you had better not do anything stupid," Abs said.

*

Em went to the workshop, opened the grimoire and began by finding all the bits she needed. She worked a spell for herself, for protection, and one to block powerful magic. Then she called Charlotte. They arranged to meet up at a coffee shop in the nearby town. Em thought it would be the safest option, in case of an ambush. She popped her things in her bag.

Shit. Abs had taken her car. She looked online at the bus times and hurried to the bus stop; she had five minutes.

She walked to the coffee shop, constantly looking all around her. Charlotte was sitting in the window and began waving at Em. Em walked over to Charlotte. "I haven't ordered you anything. I wasn't sure what you would like," she said as she cradled a huge cup in her hands.

Em walked over to the counter and ordered a small coffee. "A small one. You on a budget?" Charlotte cackled as Em sat in the seat opposite her.

"So, what do you want?" Em looked over her coffee cup.

"So how are you, Charlotte? I cannot believe that my devious git of a brother has dumped you, Charlotte," she said in a squeaky voice.

"Quite frankly, I couldn't care less. I mean the last time that we crossed paths, you were going to smack me with a metal bar," Em replied.

"Er, if my memory serves me well, it was in fact you that attacked me with said bar," she said matter-of-factly. "Anyhow, that is neither here nor there." Em raised her eyebrows. "I know for a fact that they are all relocating as we speak." She sat back and folded her arms.

"Where?"

"Well, that information is dependent on whether you are going to help me."

"Help you do what exactly?"

"Get your stupid brother away from that awful bloody woman! I do not have a penny, they have it all!" she shouted.

"Keep your voice down, you don't know who might be listening," Em said. Charlotte laughed.

"They are on their way to Norfolk."

"Norfolk, why there?"

"Something to do with Katarina's family. They have property there."

"So, write the address down and I will sort it," Em said.

"No way! If you are going, I am coming with you. I know these people, and I know what you are up against. There is no way that you can do this alone, Emily."

"I have to do this alone," Em said.

"No address then." Charlotte stood up and began putting her coat on.

"Right! You win. We can leave tomorrow first thing. I will drive. Where do you want me to pick you up?" Em said.

"This is slightly awkward, but I have been staying in a B&B, but I only had enough money for three nights. Would I be able to stay with you tonight? We are family," Charlotte said. The door of the coffee shop opened and in walked Abs. She stormed over to the table.

"What the hell, Em? You promised!" she shouted. Em stood up and beckoned to Charlotte.

"I know, I'm sorry. I will fill you in when we get home. Sorry." Em smiled her best 'I'm sorry' smile.

"Where are you parked?" Charlotte asked.

"You have got to be kidding me. She's not coming is she?" Abs said, wide eyed and angry. Em nodded.

"Unbelievable." Abs shook her head.

"Excuse me, dear, but I didn't realise that you had shares in the house. Are you a family member that I have not yet been acquainted with?" Charlotte said, looking Abs up and down.

"Sarcastic bitch," Abs mumbled under her breath.

*

Back at the house, it was decided that Abs would move into Em's room and Charlotte would have the guest room. "So Charlotte, we need a location, I am booking the accommodation," Abs said looking up from her phone.

"Er, somewhere near Great Yarmouth will be fine." She looked awkward. Em looked at Abs and discreetly shook her head no.

"OK, thanks," Abs said and winked at Em.

It was just before nine. Em got up from the cuddle chair and called Butch. "I think we should all turn in now, I'm looking to be on the road by 6am," Em said and yawned. Charlotte took herself up the stairs, Abs put some milk on to boil and Em took Butch out onto the drive for a wee.

Sitting up in bed with a hot chocolate each, Butch snuggled between them. "So where have you booked?" Em said in a low voice.

"I have booked us a family room in a chain hotel in Thetford, it's about an hour's drive from Great Yarmouth," Abs whispered. "I thought we should have her in with us, so that we can watch her," she added.

"Good thinking," Em said and sipped her hot chocolate. Em finished her drink, checked her phone, just in case and snuggled down.

*

They were on the road by 6:30am. Charlotte was late getting ready. They stopped for coffees just outside Basildon. They decided to come off the motorway and drive the A roads instead. Abs took over driving and Em sat in the back because, for the entire journey so far, Charlotte had done nothing but moan about Butch in the back so Em swapped seats with her.

When they arrived they found the hotel, even though they were way too early to book in. They left the cases in the car and decided to walk around and find somewhere to have lunch.

Over lunch Charlotte looked up and said, "Why are we staying here? This is nowhere near Great Yarmouth." She looked at her watch. "If you'll both excuse me, I need the ladies'," she added as she walked inside.

"Go and sneak into the loo, see if she is on the phone," Em said to Abs. Abs giggled and tiptoed inside. Em laughed. A few minutes later Abs came bounding out with Charlotte hot on her heels. "Give it back!" Charlotte screamed at Abs. Abs held the phone above her head as Charlotte was trying to take it from her. "For goodness' sake, you two, everyone is looking. Pack it in," Em said.

"If you have nothing to hide, why won't you let me see who you were on the phone to?" Abs said, laughing.

"Because it is none of your business, now GIVE IT BACK!" Charlotte yelled. Em went inside and paid the bill. They were still arguing when she came back outside.

"Abs, for goodness' sake, give her the bloody phone," Em said as she grabbed Butch's lead and started to walk away from them. Abs caught Em up, but Charlotte stomped off in the opposite direction.

"Shit, what if she doesn't come back? We'll never find them," Abs said.

"Oh, she'll be back, there is too much at stake," Em said.

They took a walk around the park and Abs told Em what had happened. Charlotte wasn't in the ladies'; she was standing outside, at the back of the kitchen, talking on her phone. She tried to hear what Charlotte was saying, but Charlotte saw her. She ended the call and started to rant at Abs, waving her phone about, so Abs took it from her.

Em looked at her watch. "It's check-in time, shall we go and unpack?" Abs nodded. The room was OK, not great, but it was the only one that would accept dogs.

"I think we should take the double and Lady Muck can have the sofa bed," Abs said as she bounced on the bed. Em laughed.

"Do you fancy fish and chips tonight? I noticed a takeaway just down the road," Em asked Abs.

"Oooh, yeah. Shouldn't we wait and see if *she* wants some?"

"I suppose so, she had better hurry up though, I'm starving and Butch needs a walk," Em said as she looked at her watch.

It got to 7pm. "Right, I'm going now. Butch needs to go out. Cod and chips, Abs?" Em said. Abs nodded.

"I'll come with you." Abs got up off the bed.

"No, you had better wait here, just in case she comes back," Em said as she walked out.

It was getting dark. Em tied Butch to some railings outside the fish and chip shop, and went in to order. She came out with the warm paper bag, untied the dog and started walking towards the hotel. A white van pulled up beside her. The man in the passenger seat was saying something to her. She walked over to the van and the door opened really hard and knocked her to the ground. The van pulled forward and the back doors opened. Another man, who was already out of the van, dragged her into the back. The doors closed, she went to get up, but something hit her over the head. Darkness.

*

She came to. She was in a room, but she wasn't tied up. Shit, her head hurt. There was no sound; it was silent. There was a window. The glass had been painted on the outside. She tried to open it, but it was stuck. She looked around the room. The floral wallpaper was peeling away. There was a single bed, it looked quite old. It was metal painted white. It had a bedspread on it which was dusty. *I suppose many years ago, this would have been a pretty room,* she thought to herself. There was an old writing desk with a chair in the corner. There was also a wooden wardrobe, painted white, a chest of drawers, which were the same and a sink.

Em walked over to the sink to splash some water on her face. She looked in the mirror above; she had a split lip and a bruise on her face. She splashed her face and then put her mouth to the tap, she was so thirsty. She heard a car engine. She hid behind the door, with the chair beside her. The door opened and a man walked in. Em smashed him with the chair and he fell to the ground. She jumped on his back and dug her nails into his face. He was screaming. She was punching him in the head, but he managed to get up and throw her off him, sending her flying through the air and she landed with a thud against the bed. The man turned and faced her. "BASTARD!" she screamed when she saw his face.

"Now, now, sister dear, there is no need for name calling." He had such a smug look on his scratched and bleeding face.

"Piss off, Billy, or should I call you Will?" Em laughed. "So, I take it that Charlotte told you that I had come here," she added.

"Good old Charlotte, always dependable when there is money involved. Mind you, she did well. We thought that you would smell a rat. She must have been *very* convincing."

Em laughed. "I knew it was a trap, maybe I wanted to come." She looked him straight in the eye; he looked away.

"Oh, do tell, Chosen One, are you ready to join the dark side?" he laughed.

"That was the worst Darth Vader impression I have ever heard. Idiot!" Em muttered. The door opened and in walked Adam.

"Ah, here he is, Golden Boy. Isn't he wonderful? I wish I had got to know him better years ago," Billy said as he stroked Adam's hair. It made Em shudder. "Now Emily, we need you to be a willing participant, you will be paid well," Billy smiled.

"You can shove your money, and your weird cult up your arse, Billy. I am having no part in it." Em looked at Adam, who looked down at the floor.

"Adam, give me the poppet," Billy commanded. Adam handed Billy a wax poppet. Billy held it up, took a penknife out of his pocket and sliced down the face of the poppet. Em had already prepared herself for the pain when she saw the poppet. Nothing. Adam yelped. Em looked and Adam had blood running down his face.

"Now then, Emily, maybe you ought to reconsider," Billy said as he laughed. Em spat in his face and then lunged at him and stuck her knee into his man parts. Billy bent over double in pain. Adam ran over to Em and grabbed her arms.

"What the fuck are you doing?" she screamed at him. Billy walked over to her and backhanded her across the face, knocking her backwards. It felt like her cheekbone had exploded. He walked towards her and hit her again. "Adam, please help me," Em begged. Adam laughed.

"Now if you insist on behaving like a wild animal, I will have to treat you like one. Adam, tie her up," he ordered.

"Please no, I will behave," Em pleaded, but Adam carried on tying her hands together.

"We shall leave you now, let you think about it," Billy said as he and Adam left the room and locked the door.

Em was sat on the floor; her lip was bleeding, and she was sobbing, her tears stung the cuts on her face. She was so hungry and thirsty. The room started to spin. Darkness.

She awoke to the sound of voices and the door being unlocked. The door opened and someone landed on the floor next to her face down. Em moved closer. It was Charlotte, and she had been badly beaten.

"Shit," Em said through her very swollen lip.

"Bastards," Charlotte said as she struggled to pull herself up. "Are you tied up?" she asked Em. Em nodded. "Here, I'll untie you." She tried but she couldn't do it.

"Look in those drawers." Em nodded with her head in the

direction of the desk. Charlotte opened the drawer.

"The only thing in here is an old screw."

"That will do, maybe you can cut through the rope with that. Does it feel sharp?" Charlotte nodded. It took what felt like forever to cut through a small piece. Em pulled and pulled; the rope was cutting into her skin. She pulled again with as much strength that she could summon, and the rope snapped.

"You need to run your wrists under the tap." Charlotte helped her to the sink.

"Shit, that stings," Em yelped as Charlotte placed her wrists under the water.

"It's better that than a nasty infection," Charlotte nodded. Em nodded and carried on.

They both sat on the bed. "How did you end up here?" Charlotte asked.

"As if you didn't know." Em was now angry.

"You can think what you like, believe who you want, but I did not tell them anything!" Charlotte replied.

"So how did they know where to find me?"

"They had me followed. When I disappeared they sent two of the henchmen to follow me. Do you honestly think I would have been beaten, if I had deliberately led you to them?" Charlotte said, tears forming in her eyes.

"Wow, she does have feelings." Em looked at Charlotte.

"Oh, shut up," Charlotte laughed as she wiped the tears away. "So, how did you end up here?" she asked again.

"I went out for fish and chips. They pulled up beside me in a van and threw me in the back. Shit! What about Butch and Abs?" Em put her head in her hands.

"Abs has Butch with her. When I went back to the hotel, she was beside herself. Butch had come back on his own. She wanted to go and look for you, but she was too scared. I went instead and they did the same thing to me as they did to you. I take it that the van was white." Charlotte put her hand on Em's and smiled. "We can beat these bastards," she added.

*

They both must have fallen asleep. The door opened and Adam walked into the room. "WAKE UP!" he bellowed. "Em get up, you are wanted," he said as he nudged her leg. Em got up and he pushed her in front of him and out of the room.

They walked down a long hallway, until they reached a room at the end. Adam knocked on the door. "Bring her in," a woman's voice said. He pushed Em into the room. Sitting at a huge oak desk was Billy. Katarina was sitting in an armchair.

There was another person in the other armchair. Em couldn't see who it was. *If it's that bitch Claire, I'm going to beat the living daylights out of her,* Em thought to herself.

"Emily! So nice of you to join us." Katarina stood and pointed to a sofa. "Please take a seat." Em sat. She still couldn't make out who the other person was. "Now, Will has told me of your reluctance to assist us," she said as she sat back in the chair. Em said nothing, she just glared at her. "Which is rather a shame. So many people, so much pain." Her eyes were screwed up. "Now, to avoid any more of your loved ones being hurt, I suggest that you agree to help, so that we can get on with the matter at hand!" She was becoming impatient. Em stood up.

"I will not help or join your evil little cult. I will not give you anything. I would rather die!" Em said as she stood tall.

"SIT DOWN!" Katarina screamed. Em shook her head in defiance. Katarina lifted her hand and pointed it at Em. An invisible force pushed her back onto the sofa. "I do not wish it to be like this, Emily. We could form a most excellent alliance, you and I. Together, we could be the most powerful of mages."

Em looked directly at her. Her red hair was changing colour and she was ageing rapidly. "I Will not form an alliance with an evil sorceress like you. Never in a million fucking years!" Em shouted. Katarina looked at the person in the other armchair.

"Get up," she ordered. Tears immediately filled Em's eyes when she saw who it was. Ronnie. He wouldn't look at Em; he looked at the floor.

"So, now what is going to happen, Emily, is…" She held up a poppet, took a knife to it and swiped it across the poppet's face. Em looked at Ronnie. Blood was spilling out of a massive gash across his face. Em's mouth filled with vomit.

"POCKETS, POCKETS!" Em heard. That's when she remembered. She had emptied the contents of the spells into her pockets when she went to get the fish and chips.

"I will carve this pretty face beyond recognition!" Katarina yelled.

"OK, YOU WIN. STOP, PLEASE DON'T HURT HIM!" Em screamed.

"That's much better." Katarina sighed. "Go and clean yourself up," she said to Ronnie, who then headed towards the door. When he was beside Em, he looked down at her and then looked away. *I have lost him,* she thought to herself.

"I take it that you are now aware of what we are seeking." She looked at Em; her hair had now turned a dark grey colour. Em nodded. "The first ley line is around here, so today you can get yourself cleaned up, have a decent meal and plenty of rest. Tomorrow, we will travel to the ley line. Off you go," she ordered.

Adam was waiting outside the door for her. She glared at him; he looked at the floor. Em started to walk back to the room that she came from.

"No, this way," Adam said as he pointed to a huge sweeping staircase. He led the way down. They took the left hallway, which had doors on either side. He opened one and ushered Em in. It was a lovely room with a huge window that looked out on a beautiful, landscaped garden. Em gasped. "There is a bathroom through there," Adam said and pointed to a door. "I'll show you the dining room and kitchen," he said as he headed out of the room.

Once she had been shown, he led her back to her room. "All of the doors are locked, so I wouldn't attempt to leave," he said as he turned and disappeared up the hallway.

"Arsehole!" Em said under her breath.

Em went into the bathroom. There was a huge free-standing bath, which she began to run. She opened the wardrobe and nearly fell backwards when she saw all of her clothes hanging inside. She went to the drawers and opened them. They were filled with all her things.

*

She was lying in the hot, foamy water and almost forgot where she was, and what was happening. "You should play along with her," Peggy said as she perched herself on the edge of the bath.

"Peggy!" Em said as she covered up her lady bits. Peggy laughed.

"It's nothing I haven't seen before, lassie."

"Really?" Em blushed.

"Tomorrow, go along with them, until you get to the ley line. Then you will know what to do." She put her finger aside her nose, winked and then disappeared.

*

Em sat on the edge of the bed, brushing her hair. The door knocked and then opened. Billy walked in. "Nice to see you have made yourself at home." He smiled.

"I must say that it was very thoughtful of you to have all my things brought here," Em said. She tried to smile.

"That was all Katarina. She wants you to stay, and you never know, if you are a good girl and help her, she may even let you have Ronnie back."

Shit, he is so condescending, Em thought to herself. "Thanks for the advice." She gave him a sickly-sweet smile.

"Now make yourself presentable. Dinner will be served at 6:30 in the dining room. I take it that you know the way," he said as he headed to the door and closed it behind him.

"ARSEHOLE!" Em shouted as she threw her brush at the door.

Em emptied her pockets and wrapped the spell ingredients in pieces of paper. She then hid them in her walking boots.

To say that dinner was awkward would be an understatement. Katarina and Billy were at either end of the huge table. A very bruised Charlotte was sitting next to a very large and quite smelly man. Em was opposite Charlotte, and either side of her were Ronnie and Adam. There was one empty place next to Charlotte.

"Isn't this nice?" Katarina said and smiled. They all nodded, except for Billy.

"Yes, it's rather lovely to all be back together again," he sneered. A woman walked into the room and whispered something to Billy; he nodded and shooed her out.

"Please everyone, eat," Katarina said. Em was starving and as much as she hated to admit it the food looked and smelled delicious. As they all tucked in, the woman came back in with someone else. Ronnie pushed Em's foot with his. Em looked at him, and he looked over to where the woman was.

"DAD!" Em screamed. She jumped up and ran over and threw

her arms around him. He didn't hug her back, just looked puzzled. "Dad, it's me, Em," she said through the tears.

"Emily, be a dear and sit down," Katarina said. "He doesn't recognise you because he is enchanted. I will remove it when we have completed the works," she said and lifted her glass in Em's direction.

Shit. She wanted so much to get up and rip her hair out. Em was watching her dad throughout the meal. He had lost so much weight and seemed so frail. He didn't speak to anybody. He never looked up from his food.

After the meal Em was the first to stand up. "I'm off to bed now, big day tomorrow," she said as she yawned.

"Oh really? I thought that you might join us in the drawing room for a brandy," Billy said. Katarina nodded in agreement.

"That's very kind of you both, but I'm absolutely shattered," Em replied as the woman returned to take Dad back. Em waited and as they left, she followed. They were walking towards the right hallway. Em made a mental note and went to her room.

She was sitting in bed trying to come to terms with recent events when she heard a tapping on the window. She got up and opened the curtain. Ronnie was standing on the outside of the window looking straight at her. "Open the window," he said through the glass. Em was unsure. Was this another trap? Were they testing her? She shook her head. "Em, for fuck's sake it's cold out here. Open the window," he said. The deep gash across his face looked so painful. Reluctantly she tried to open the window.

"It's locked," she said.

"Use your energy, both hands," Ronnie said. She put both hands on the lock and drew on her energy. There was a click and it opened. Ronnie climbed through, closed the curtain and threw his arms around her. Em took a step back. "What is it? Oh shit, they haven't enchanted you too?" he said.

"What the hell is going on? I thought that you had been enchanted," she said. She was confused.

"They all think that I'm enchanted, but the enchantment that Claire did, didn't work. I thought that the only way to find out what is really going on, was to get close, so I played along with them. A bit like what you are doing." He smiled. "Argh." He grimaced.

"Maybe don't smile for a bit," Em said as she gently touched his face. "I would do some healing on it, but they will know," she said.

"Em, you need to reverse the enchantment on Adam," Ronnie said.

"How the hell am I supposed to do that, when all eyes are on me?"

CHAPTER 16

They sat together on the bed. Em rested her head on Ronnie's shoulder. "You didn't... you know... do anything with Claire, did you?" She looked up at him. She always knew when he wasn't telling the truth, he would flare his nostrils.

"No I bloody well didn't, Em, I can't believe that you thought I might have!" Ronnie looked at her in disgust.

"I thought that, maybe they made you, and you went along with it... you know, because of the enchantment," Em said. She could see by his face that she had upset him. "I'm sorry Ronnie." She grabbed his chin and turned his face toward her. "Look, you can't blame me for wondering... With everything that has happened."

"No, I don't blame you. I blame THEM, and I will promise you this, the minute we get your dad away from here, I will make each and every one of them pay."

"Shh, someone might hear you. I expect that they have put Adam on guard duty outside my door." Ronnie shook his head.

"He is in the library with Bonnie and Clyde, looking at the maps. I was excused," he said as he kissed Em on the forehead. "That's nasty bruising on your face, how did that happen?"

"Billy. I punched him, so he gave me a couple of backhanders," Em said as she felt the pain again.

"Man, I am so going to hurt that fucker." Ronnie's eyes were red with anger. He was stroking Em's hair and she drifted off to sleep.

She was walking through a beautiful meadow, so many wildflowers blowing in the gentle breeze. She could smell salt in the air but could hear no waves. She walked until she came to a small stone bridge, over a stream. There was a woman on the bridge, looking at the stream. She recognised her; she was the woman that took her sleepwalking. As she approached she asked, "Who are you?"

The woman smiled. "I am Abagail Walcott."

"So you are my ancestor." The woman nodded.

"Tomorrow she will take you to the ley line. If you do not give her what she seeks, your father will be in great danger. Emily, you must find the cannister and give it to her," Abagail said graciously.

"But… she will use it, to hurt and manipulate people," Em said.

"She needs all seven of them. Without them all she cannot further her magic or power in any way. Let her have it. Emily, you must reverse the enchantment on Adam. She knows that he too has the ability to find the cannisters."

"How? They watch me all of the time," Em said.

"Tomorrow morning when he comes to your room. He will be alone, be ready," she said as she faded away.

Em woke up with a jump. It was dark. Where was Ronnie? She got up, put on her walking clothes and into her trouser pocket, slipped the reversal spell. She drank some water and climbed back into bed.

She awoke again to knocking on her door. "Em, you have five minutes." It was Adam. She leapt out of bed and dragged the brush through her hair.

"Adam, wait!" she called out.

"What?"

"Can you help me with this? It's stuck." Adam walked into her room, still wearing the same expressionless face. Em was at the window, messing with the lock.

"Don't!" he shouted. "You are not allowed to open the window." He scowled.

"But I need fresh air to build my energy up, you know that," Em said. Adam walked over to the window. He was trying to unlock it. "Adam," Em called from behind him. As he turned she blew the spell into his face. He put his hands over his eyes and dropped to the floor. He rubbed his eyes and looked up at Em.

"What the... Oh my god, Em, I'm so sorry," he said as he rubbed his eyes, then jumped up and hugged her.

"Shh, we have to pretend you are still enchanted. Once we have found the cannister, we need to find a way of getting Dad out of here." She smiled. He smiled. He had his twinkle back!

"You need to reverse Ronnie's enchantment," he whispered.

"He never was, he just pretended to be." Em winked. "Now go, or they will become suspicious," she said.

They were being shoved into the back of the same white van that took her. Adam and the large smelly henchman were on guard. It was so hard not to speak to Ronnie or Adam, so Em just kept her head down. After about ten minutes she asked, "Where is Charlotte?" Ronnie shrugged his shoulders.

"She is not needed today," Adam said sternly. Em wanted to laugh. Although Ronnie had his head down, she could see a smirk forming. The van carried on for about twenty minutes then braked hard. Em went flying into Ronnie. She looked at him, their faces so close. She so wanted to kiss him. She moved back to her space.

The back doors opened, and they were greeted by Katarina, Billy and another person who had their back to them. *If that is Claire, I will not be held responsible for what I might do,* Em thought to herself.

They piled out of the van. Em looked at Katarina; her hair was deep red, and her eyes were the greenest green. "Do you think she's a vampire?" she whispered to Ronnie and giggled.

The other person turned around. "What's so funny, Emily?"

"Lovely to see you, dearest sister," Em said and smiled a sickly smile.

"Still bloody sarcastic. You should have knocked that out of her, Will," Jade said and they both laughed.

"HOW DARE YOU!" Katarina glared at them both. "Do not ever insult my guest again. Do you both understand me?" she shouted. They both nodded. "APOLOGISE!" she roared at them.

"Sorry," they both said in unison.

"PATHETIC!" Katarina said as she stormed towards Em. "Emily, do you have any idea which direction the ley line is?"

"I need to gather energy and be close to the earth," Em said meekly.

"Very well, you do what you need to do." She touched Em's shoulder. It was like an electric shock. "Adam, go with Emily; Ronnie, come with me and keep an eye on Billy and the other one," she called.

Em sat on the grass. She was running her fingers through the blades. She could hear water. She crawled in the direction of the sound. She began to smell salt. She carried on. The sound of the water, which began as a trickle, now sounded like gushing. Em stopped and looked at Adam. He nodded. She turned and carried on moving. The sound became a hum, then it was as though a thousand birds were singing. "It's here," she said to Adam. Adam signalled to the others and they all followed Katarina.

"How do you know?" she asked Em. Em lifted her hands; they were dripping with water, yet the grass was bone dry.

"Excellent!" Katarina shouted. She looked at Jade. "Start digging," she commanded.

"Darling, you cannot expect Jade to dig," Billy said.

"Why can't I? She stands to gain a great deal from it."

"Yes, I know but... she is quite fragile," Billy whispered.

"OK then, you can do it," she said as she thrust a shovel into his hand.

"Er, sorry to interrupt, but Billy has no idea where to dig, or how delicate this is. If you don't mind, I would like to dig," Em said as she looked at Katarina.

"You see? What a star. You two should let your sister be an example to you both," she said, smiling. Em swapped the shovel for a small trowel when she had dug about a foot down. She could hear the water cascading, and knew she was close. Very gently she was drawing out the earth and then she felt water. It was flowing, she could feel the energy, then she heard a ting. She put the trowel down and began digging with her hands. Everyone had gathered around as they watched in awe. She could feel the energy as she wrapped her hand around the cannister. It pulsated through her body like a lightning bolt. She held it up in the air.

Katarina pushed past everybody and ran to Em. She took the cannister and fumbled to open it. She handed it back to Em. "As you did all the hard work, I think it is only right that you open the cannister," Katarina said proudly. Em knew exactly what she was doing. Katarina couldn't physically open the cannister, and she knew that Em could.

"No really, Katarina, I'm sure that my ancestors would be

honoured that you do it," Em said as she crossed her fingers behind her back and pushed the cannister back towards Katarina.

"Oh, if you insist," Katarina said and laughed nervously. As she tried to force the cannister lid, there was a loud bang and Katarina flew backwards, dropping it. Em walked over, picked up the cannister and held her hand out to help Katarina up. Once she was on her feet, Em gently turned the lid and it came off. She put her fingers inside and pulled out the page. She handed it to Katarina, who snatched it out of Em's hand and walked off with it.

"Rude," Em said under her breath.

"Watch her now," Peggy said as she stood beside her. Em and Adam both looked at Peggy and then at Katarina storming towards them.

"WHAT THE FUCK IS THIS?" she screamed as she shoved the page into Em's hand. Em looked at it.

"I'm confused. What is wrong with it?" Em asked.

"IT'S A FUCKING BLANK PIECE OF PAPER!" she yelled. Billy walked over and looked over Em's shoulder.

"Well, I can see lots of writing and symbols," Em said.

"Adam!" Billy shouted. He handed the page to Adam. "What do you see?"

"I can see writing and symbols," Adam said and gave the page back.

"She cannot see it because her intentions are bad. Tell her that it is only the bloodline of Abagail that can see it," Peggy said.

Em told Katarina.

"Well, it looks like you are with us for the long haul then, Emily!" She stormed off to the 4x4 with Billy and Jade running behind her.

*

Back at the house – well, more mansion than house – Adam escorted Em back to her room. "Lunch in one hour," he said and winked before he closed the door. Em went into the bathroom and turned the shower on. She rummaged through the wardrobe for some clean clothes, then wrapped the reversal spell back in the paper and hid it.

She was sitting on the bed in her robe, drying off, when there was a *tap, tap* on her door. She opened the door slightly and was surprised to see Charlotte the other side. "Quick, let me in," she said. Em opened the door and Charlotte ran inside.

"How did you escape the dungeon?" Em asked her.

"After they took you yesterday, that big smelly man came and got me. I am in a room two doors up. I must say yours is a lot nicer," she said as she was looking around the room. "Anyway, the reason I'm here, is to tell you that while you were busy digging, they moved your dad."

"Moved him where? Wait… how did you know I was digging?" Em said suspiciously.

"I… er… I overheard the big smelly man tell the cook," Charlotte said awkwardly.

"Get out!" Em looked at Charlotte, who was so red she looked like she was going to explode.

"But—"

"OUT NOW!" Em yelled. Charlotte slammed the door behind her.

*

Lunch was the same as dinner the night before, except there were two places missing. The henchman was opposite Em. No Charlotte, no Dad. "Emily, after lunch, maybe you would be so kind as to join me in the library, so that we can make a start on the translation?" Katarina said. Her hair colour was very dull and dark circles had appeared under her eyes.

179

"That depends," Em said, not looking up from her food. Adam kicked her under the table.

"I'm sorry, I don't understand. Depends on what?" Katarina screwed her eyes up.

"Well, my dad has now gone again, according to Charlotte." Em looked up. Billy looked at Katarina and raised his eyebrows. "And I am staying in the same house as my boyfriend, yet I cannot go anywhere near him. I really do not see how it benefits me to help you," Em said. She could see the rage building inside Katarina.

"You seem to forget, my dear, that I brought you here. You will do as I say, or your loved ones will suffer the consequences," Katarina said matter-of-factly.

"But that will not affect me if I'm DEAD. Will it!" Em was about to boil over. Ronnie discreetly put his hand on her leg, under the table.

"WHAT?" Katarina roared.

"I have had enough of this bullshit. All the pain and suffering, for what, Katarina? It sure isn't for the money. Your eternal youth, maybe. Like I said, I have had it and I would happily take my own life just to spite you!" Em said as she stood up and moved her chair back.

"SIT!" roared Katarina. "Everyone except for Emily, I want you to leave, NOW!" she shouted. They all got up and left the room. Ronnie winked at Em as he walked past her. Katarina moved her place up the table next to Em.

"Emily, dear Emily, I do not wish to cross swords with you. I want us to be friends," she said, her hair almost white now.

"I'm sorry, how could I possibly be friends with someone who had my mum killed, and held my dad and the love of my life against their will? Do you have any idea of the amount of pain you have caused me and those I love?" Em felt tears sting, but she fought them back.

"That is all in the past. We can make a fresh start, and I promise you that when all of the works have been completed I will let you be with Ronnie and your father." Katarina tapped the back of Em's hand and, again, it felt like an electric shock.

"That could take years. I cannot live without them any longer. I was not joking when I said I would happily take my own life. You have everything I love, and I no longer have anything to live for," Em said. She stood up and left the room.

"Great performance," Peggy said and clapped, back in Em's room.

Em was lying on her bed wondering what the hell she was going to do to get them all out of the situation. She needed to know where Dad was. She got off the bed and walked over to the window. She heard voices. Katarina and Billy were in the garden, not far from Em's window. Very gently and quietly Em held the lock in her hands and it clicked. She opened the window just enough so that she could hear what they were saying. "Why did you send him there?" Billy said.

"Because, my dear, it is close to the next ley line location."

"What if she does... you know... kill herself?" he said.

"We can use Adam instead."

"He has nowhere near the same power as Emily. You are taking a big chance there."

"Hmm, maybe we should allow her to be with Ronnie, that should keep her happy for a while. They will have to be watched though," Katarina said. "I shall go and share the good news with her," she said as she turned towards the house.

Em quickly and quietly closed the window and jumped back on the bed. After a few minutes, the door knocked. "Who is it?" Em called out.

"Emily, it's Katarina. May I come in? Only I would like to

apologise," she said. Em got up and opened the door. Katarina walked in followed by Ronnie.

"I have come to offer my apologies; I was perhaps a little harsh," Katarina said. Em looked at Ronnie; he winked. Em nodded. "I have removed the enchantment from Ronnie, and he is to move into this room with you. This does not mean that you can leave the house unescorted, and you must both stay with us until the works are complete. Is that understood?" she added. Em nodded. "Now Emily, if you would come to the library in five minutes, Ronnie can move his things in here." She turned and walked away without waiting for a reply.

Ronnie wrapped his arms around Em. She leant back and looked at him. "What... what's wrong?" Em put her hand into her pocket, held it in front of his face and blew. "Argh!" he said as he rubbed his eyes. "What the bloody hell are you doing?" His eyes were watering.

"Just double checking," she said as she handed him a tissue. He wiped his eyes and laughed.

*

Em tapped on the library door. "Enter." She opened the door and walked in to find Katarina sitting at the large oak desk. There didn't appear to be anybody else in there. Katarina gestured to Em to come over. "Take a seat, Emily," she said without looking up from her paperwork. After a few moments she looked up and passed the paper to Em. "What do you make of that?" she asked. Em scrolled through the paper.

"It's written in Theban," Em said as she pushed the paper to Katarina.

"Excellent!" She smiled at Em, and Em noticed that her hair was becoming redder. "Now then, Emily, if you could write out exactly what is written on that page in Theban for me." She passed the cannister to Em.

"OK, no problem," Em said. Em felt the energy charge through her when she touched the cannister. It took Em about an hour to translate Abagail's words into Theban. "Here you are," she called out to Katarina, who was sitting in the armchair.

"Bring it over!" she commanded.

"Yes ma'am," Em muttered under her breath. She passed the paper to Katarina. Katarina read it and then looked up.

"And this exactly what is written on the page, yes?" Em nodded.

"Word for word," Em said.

"Because Emily, if you have deliberately made mistakes and it is not correct, someone will pay," she said.

"I understand that perfectly, Katarina, which is why I translated it word for word. I am not a fool," Em said.

Katarina nodded. "Very well, Emily, the next ley line is in Devon. I'm sure that after living there for a year, you will have no problem in locating it."

"I'm sure I will be able to find it. Katarina, could I ask for one more thing?" Em asked meekly.

Katarina sighed. "What now?"

"Well, as we are all in the house together, would it be possible to reverse the enchantment on Adam? It's only... I need him on side to assist me. The enchantment blocks his energy," Em said.

Katarina sat in deep thought for a while.

"I see. You must understand, there is to be no plotting, no escape plans hatched. I have your father, and... oh yes, you are not aware, I have your friend too." Katarina bent down and picked up a red handbag. Abs' handbag. "So they will remain unharmed, so long as you all behave yourselves and do as I bid!" she said.

CHAPTER 17

Back in their room, Em was furious. She told Ronnie what had happened. There was a knock on the door. Ronnie opened the door and Adam walked in. "She reversed, the already reversed enchantment." He grinned. Em walked over to him and blew from her hand into his face. "Shit, Em, why do you keep doing that?" he said as he was rubbing his eyes. Ronnie was laughing.

"Does that mean that we are allowed to spend time with you now?" Ronnie asked him.

"Yep, although she did say that someone close would suffer the consequences, if we all plotted, and that I was to ask you about it, Em."

"Shit!" Em sighed.

"What's wrong?" Adam asked.

"They have Abs, Adam, she showed me her handbag."

"What, the red one?"

"Yep."

"I'm going to fucking kill the lot of them," he said through gritted teeth. Adam walked towards the door; Ronnie blocked his way.

"Listen, Adam, we just have to keep our heads down for a few days. They are going to be watching us three like hawks. We just have to play the game. We need to stay level-headed. We must find out where Em's dad and Abs are being kept. We don't want anyone else being hurt," Ronnie said. Adam was sobbing.

"I need to tell her I'm sorry, Ronnie. I don't think that she will ever forgive me," he sobbed. Em walked over to where he was curled up on the floor. She moved his hands away from his face and held them.

"Adam, look at me," she said. He looked up. "Of course she will forgive you. She knows that you were enchanted, and she loves your very existence. She told me so," Em said sternly. "For Abs' sake, we all need to be strong, and think about what we do. OK?" Adam nodded and wiped the tears away.

"I think for a few days we should play at being the compliant disciples, then we may be able to find her," Ronnie said. There was a knock on the door. The three of them looked at one another. Em opened the door. It was Billy. He pushed past Em and sat in a chair. "How very lovely… the three musketeers, together again," he sneered.

"To what do we owe the pleasure?" Em asked in her sweetest voice. Ronnie choked.

"You may have fooled Katarina, but I know you better," he said, looking at Em.

"I have no idea what you are talking about," Em said defiantly.

"You are well aware what I am talking about… Oh Chosen One. I wanted to kill the lot of you but unfortunately Madame can only get her eternal youth through you, Emily, and I can only get the money and power when you have delivered the goods."

"And…" Em said.

"You all need to behave yourselves. There is much at stake, especially for you, Adam. I take it you know that we now have dear sweet Abbie, in our possession. What a positively charming, beautiful creature she is," he said as he licked his lips.

Adam lunged towards Billy. "You harm a single hair on her head, and I will end the fucking lot of you. DO YOU UNDERSTAND ME?" he screamed. Ronnie held Adam back. Billy laughed.

"I think you should leave," Em said and touched Billy's shoulder. She felt a bolt of energy run through her hands and Billy went flying forwards. He pulled his hand back to hit her but as his hand got to her face it stopped. He tried again, but it was almost if an invisible wall were between them.

"Witch!" he yelled at her as he walked towards the door. As he was walking through the door he turned to Adam and said, "I have no intention of hurting her. Well, not unless she likes to play rough." He slammed the door behind him. Adam roared as he tried to break free from Ronnie.

"ADAM, LISTEN TO ME!" Peggy shouted as she stood between Adam and Ronnie. "He is doing this to make you fail. He wants an excuse to hurt people. Do you wish Abbie to be harmed?" Peggy said. Adam shook his head. "You need to keep a level head, be clever and outwit them all," Peggy said as she turned and looked at Em. Em nodded and she disappeared.

Ronnie talked Adam into having a nap before they were all called for dinner. He walked him back to his room, while Em ran herself a bath. Ronnie came back in and sat on the chair in the bathroom, while Em was in the bath. "What happened back there?" Ronnie screwed his eyes up.

"Oh… you mean when he tried to hit me?"

"It's lucky that it did happen, because if he had hit you, both Adam and I would have killed him with our bare hands!" Ronnie said. He was red with anger.

"I felt it when I first held the cannister, it's like an electrical charge running through me. I only touched his shoulder," Em said.

"Might come in handy," Ronnie said and smiled his beautiful smile.

"Anyway, you, come over here, so that I can heal your face, and then you can scrub my back."

*

The knock on the door for dinner came. It was 6:25. Ronnie and Em were suited and booted, even though Em had to make sure that everything that she wore had pockets, just in case. As she closed the door Ronnie said, "You go ahead, and I'll go and grab Adam." She blew him a kiss and walked towards the dining room.

She sat down. "You are looking radiant," Katarina said. Billy scowled.

"Why thank you. So are you," Em replied.

Charlotte walked in with even more bruises. She sat opposite Em and smiled. Em smiled back. She secretly felt sorry for her, even if she was a scheming cow. Charlotte nodded at Katarina but completely ignored Billy. The henchman came in after and sat next to Charlotte. A few moments later Ronnie walked in alone. Em looked at him as he sat next to her. He shrugged his shoulders. *Shit!* Em thought.

The staff began to bring the food in. "Where is Adam? Was he not called for dinner?" Katarina asked.

"I called him before I called the other two," the henchman said as he looked in Em and Ronnie's direction.

"Well… What are you waiting for? Go and get him!" Billy bellowed at the man.

They had finished the starter and the staff were bringing in the main course when the henchman returned with Adam. Adam sat the other side of Em, and the henchman walked over and whispered in Billy's ear. Billy then whispered in Katarina's ear and they both looked at Adam. Em was wondering what the hell was going on. "Where have you been?" she asked Adam.

"I… Er… I needed a walk." He wouldn't look at her. Em looked at Katarina and she smiled.

After all of the courses had been served and cleared Katarina stood. "If you would all excuse us both for a moment, the staff will serve you all coffees and brandies. We will return in a short while as there is something we wish to discuss with you all." They both left the room. Em was desperate to ask Adam where he had been, but Charlotte was sitting with her ears pricked.

They all sat in silence, drinking their coffees, when Katarina came in. "If you would all be so kind as to join us in the library." She gestured towards the door. They all stood up and followed. Em, Ronnie and Adam were sitting on the sofa. Katarina was in her armchair. Charlotte went to sit in the other one. "What do you think you are doing?" Katarina yelled. "Floor." She pointed to the floor and Charlotte sat, like a dog. There was no sign of Billy or his henchman.

"Now then, if you are all sitting comfortably," Katarina said as she looked around the room at them all. "It has been brought to my attention, that somebody in this room, tried out something of, what shall we say, an investigation." She looked straight at Adam.

"Here we go," Ronnie said under his breath.

"Now, my instructions were quite clear. Were they not?" Katarina looked at Em. "WELL!" She roared in Em's face.

"Yes… yes they were," Em said.

"Good, so you will all be aware that someone will now have to suffer the consequences." Katarina smiled at Adam. The door opened and Billy walked in followed by the henchman, who was dragging Abs.

Adam went to jump up, but Ronnie grabbed hold of him. "Wait," he whispered to Adam.

Katarina walked over to Abs. "Such a shame, such a pretty face," she said as she ran her hand over Abs' cheek.

Em couldn't stand it anymore. She stood up. "STOP!" she shouted. Katarina held her hand to Em to push her down, but it didn't work. Em's energy blocked it.

"SIT DOWN NOW!" Katarina screamed at Em. Em shook her head. Katarina took something in her hand and swiped it over Abs' face. Blood started to seep out of the gaping wound. Adam roared and jumped up, but Katarina pushed him back in the seat with her electrical charge. Em jumped at Katarina, but Katarina's charge would not let her get close. Abs was sobbing, begging Katarina to leave her alone.

Katarina had her hands around Abs' throat. Again Em lunged at her and again she was blocked. Abs was gasping for breath. "IF YOU WISH FOR HER TO LIVE, THEN YOU WILL ALL SIT AND BEHAVE!" she screamed. They all sat, and she dropped Abs to the floor, choking and gasping for breath.

"Now, this is what happens when people don't do as they are told," Billy said smugly as he ran his hand through Abs' hair. Adam went to get up, but Ronnie pushed him back.

"Now, Adam, I need your solemn promise that this will not happen again." Katarina looked at Adam. He had his head down.

"I'm so sorry, Abs… for everything," he sobbed.

"ADAM, I AM SPEAKING TO YOU!" Katarina yelled. He looked at her and nodded. "Good, now we have an understanding, but let it be known that if anything of this kind happens again, I will allow Billy to deal with her. Understood?" She looked at Adam and again he nodded.

*

Ronnie thought that it would be a good idea to make Adam a bed up in their bedroom. There was no saying what he might do. The stress must have drained him because he fell asleep straight away. Ronnie and Em were sitting up in bed. "We need to be clever about this," Em said.

"Hmm… if Billy gets his hands on her, I dread to think what would happen. He is pure evil."

They both fell sound asleep in each other's arms.

She was back in the tunnel; she recognised it because of the cobbles and the gas lights. As she came through the other side it was the same as before. She walked along the streets and the same old pedlar woman approached her. She led her up the same alley and through the door. She felt happy. A young Carrie was sitting at the table before her. "Too many innocent people are being hurt, Emily," she said with a sorrowful look. "Darkness will be your friend. Find a way to get out. When the hound barks you must follow the sound. There is little time. You must hurry."

Em woke up to the sound of voices. There was light creeping through the curtains. She looked at the clock on the wall. It was 7am. She walked over to the window and pulled the curtains back. Katarina was talking to Jade in the garden. Em opened the window slightly. "How did he seem?" Katarina asked Jade.

"He is still weak. If she finds out, she may give up," Jade said.

"I am aware of this. My aunt, has she called the doctor in to have him checked over?"

"I told Mrs Dawkins that you wanted him to be looked at, but she said that she knew how to take care of him," Jade said.

"Stupid bloody woman! I knew it was a mistake to send your father to her. I'm sure she is going senile," Katarina said. "Anyway, not a word of this to Will, he will tell Emily for certain, you know how he likes to torment her." Jade nodded and they both walked back towards the house.

"Mrs fucking Dawkins!" Em shouted, waking both Ronnie and Adam.

"I told you to watch her, I knew she was trouble," Peggy said, looking very pleased with herself.

"Peggy, Dad must be unwell, we need to get out of here," Em said as she started to panic.

"Em, at least now, you know where he is," Peggy said. "That's how they drew you in, they used her. That was no coincidence that she mentioned Tintagel, and that's how they knew that you would be in the Lake District," Peggy said. "I will go and see your dad, now that I know where he is," Peggy said and disappeared.

"Em, what's happened?" Ronnie asked as he rubbed his eyes. Em told him about the conversation and the dream.

Over breakfast Katarina demanded that Em was to be in the library by 9:30am. Nobody else spoke. They all ate in complete silence. Ronnie and Adam went back to the room and Em went to the library.

Katarina was sitting behind the desk and Jade was sitting opposite. "Good morning," Katarina said as Em walked in.

"Morning," Em murmured back.

Jade stood up and nodded to Katarina. "Hello sister," she said as she walked past Em.

"Where have you been hiding?" Em replied.

"Busy, busy, you know me," Jade said as she closed the door

behind her. Katarina gestured to Em to sit.

"Tomorrow we will travel to the next location. You must all be up and ready to leave by 4am. Is that understood?" Katarina looked at Em. Em stood up to leave. "I did not hear a reply," Katarina said.

"Understood. Would it be possible to spend some time in the garden today? It's the only way I can build my energy levels," Em asked, not holding out much hope.

"I don't see why not; you are aware that there is electric fencing all around the grounds," Katarina said.

"Yes, thank you," Em said. "Was there anything else?"

"No, you may go," Katarina said.

As Em was walking down the hallway, she heard a *pssst*. She looked around. Charlotte was standing in a doorway. "Come here." She beckoned to Em.

"What?" Em said as she approached her. Charlotte handed her a key. It looked like a car key. Em looked at her in bewilderment. "Outside of the grounds, about twenty metres up the lane. It's a red 4x4," Charlotte whispered. Em shrugged.

"What about it?" Em whispered.

"Just in case you need to get out," Charlotte whispered.

"OK, I get it. It's another trap. Right?" Em said.

"No... No, I want to help you."

"Really?" Em smirked. "Meet me in the garden, by the big oak tree in an hour," Em whispered and walked towards her room.

"Where is Adam?" she asked as she kissed Ronnie's cheek.

"He's gone to have a shower."

"Shit. Will he be alright? You don't think he'll try anything. Do you?"

"No, we had a heart to heart. Last night truly terrified him." Ronnie smiled.

"I hope not. Anyway, follow me," Em said as she beckoned Ronnie into the bathroom. He followed and shut the door. "It's safer if we talk in here," Ronnie nodded. "I have a plan." Em handed the car key to Ronnie.

"Eh... Where the hell did you get this?" He looked confused.

"OK, so Charlotte gave it to me."

"So it's a trap then," he interrupted.

"That's exactly what I said, but... I think that she was enchanted a long time ago, and the effects are wearing off. They are so obsessed with us that they must have forgotten to top it up."

"Right. And...?"

"I am going to meet her in the garden in forty-five minutes. I am going to try and reverse the enchantment." Em looked very pleased with herself as she stood back and crossed her arms.

"I still don't understand." Ronnie was frowning.

"So, if I reverse the enchantment, we may be able to locate Abs. I will fill you in with the rest later. She blew him a kiss and walked back into the bedroom and opened the wardrobe. Adam walked in looking very sorry for himself.

"Hey Adam. You OK?" Em asked, with her head still in the wardrobe.

"Nope," was the answer that she got. She took the paper, with the spell in, and emptied it into her pocket. She then emptied the second one into her other pocket.

"Right, I will leave Ronnie to enlighten you." She smiled as she headed for the door.

"Em... What if this is a trap?" Ronnie said.

"I am meeting her at the big oak tree, you can see it from the window. I won't move from there. Love you," she called as she closed the door.

CHAPTER 18

E m sat herself at the base of the tree in line with their bedroom. She sat and meditated for a while. She saw Charlotte coming towards her and looked all around to see if anyone else was about. Charlotte sat down beside her. "Charlotte," Em said and as she turned Em blew into her face.

"What the bloody hell do you think you are doing?" Charlotte said as she rubbed her eyes. Em waited.

"What has happened to me?" Charlotte said. Em didn't know if it was the spell or emotion that was making her eyes run.

"What do you mean?" Em said. Charlotte looked around her.

"I feel different," Charlotte said.

"I'm not sure, but it think that you had been enchanted a while ago, and it was wearing off. I reversed it," Em replied.

"Thank you," Charlotte said and then sobbed.

They had been talking for about an hour when Charlotte looked at her watch. "Crikey, I had better go. Geoff will be waiting for me," she said as she stood up.

"Geoff? Who the hell is Geoff?" Em asked.

"You know, the big guy that always escorts me." Charlotte

blushed.

"Oh… Oddbod," Em said. That was the name that she and Ronnie had come up with for him.

"Hey, he is a good guy, and I persuaded him to bathe!" Charlotte said and laughed.

*

Em knew that she had about twenty minutes to tell Ronnie and Adam the plan before lunch. She rushed back to the room. Ronnie was lying on the bed and Adam was sitting in the chair, staring into space. She beckoned them both into the bathroom.

"OK, Charlotte is no longer enchanted. I have found out where they are keeping Abs," Em whispered.

"Let's go then," Adam said as he turned to walk out of the door.

"Wait, Adam." He turned and sat on the edge of the bath. "Bonnie and Clyde are leaving after dinner tonight to get to Devon before us. We are supposed to be leaving here at 4am. They are leaving us in the care of Geoff and Charlotte, until we leave."

"Who the hell is Geoff?" Ronnie asked.

"Oddbod! Charlotte has shown me which of the electric fences she will turn off. Once it gets dark we go and get Abs, go through the fence and up the road to the 4x4. Then we race to Devon and get Dad before they get there."

"Wow! Seems like you have it sussed," Ronnie said, as he rolled his eyes.

"Well, we are going to come up against a small hitch," Em winced.

"Go on… What small hitch?" Ronnie smiled.

"Claire is guarding Abs," Em said.

"So, easy. I will quite happily knock that bitch out!" Adam snorted.

"Yes, but what I haven't told you is, that she is Katarina's sister, and she too has magic in her veins." Em looked perplexed.

"Em, I'm sure you can handle her," Ronnie said and winked.

*

They were all seated in the dining room eating lunch. "I must say, it is lovely to see that you have settled now. It makes life much more pleasurable; don't you think?" Katarina said. They all nodded. Not one of them lifted their heads or made eye contact.

"My dear, I have to disagree. I enjoy the punishment side of things. Makes life more interesting. Don't you agree?" Billy said to Katarina. She laughed an overexaggerated laugh. Em looked up slightly and caught Charlotte's eye. She could see the hatred in Charlotte when she looked at Katarina.

When lunch was over, and everyone was leaving, Katarina grabbed Em's arm. "What are your plans for this afternoon, Emily?" she asked her.

"Oh, I thought I would take a walk around your beautiful grounds and then sit and meditate, bring my energy levels up," Em replied.

"Wonderful. May I join you?" Katarina asked.

"Of course!" Em said, trying her hardest to sound convincingly pleased about it.

"Super! Shall we say in one hour? We should meet at the main entrance," Katarina said and then floated off.

Em turned to Ronnie. "Great! Can't wait!" Ronnie and Adam both laughed.

Back in the room, Em was leaving Ronnie in charge of the packing. "Ronnie, make sure that the clothes you leave out for tonight are all black."

"Yes."

"Oh, and don't forget it's just the rucksacks," she added.

"Yes, Em, I know what I'm doing." Ronnie rolled his eyes.

"And Adam, can you scratch around to see if you can find a torch?" She looked at Adam; he saluted. "Discreetly," she added, and they all laughed.

*

She made sure that she was early to meet Katarina. They walked around the garden and Katarina told Em how her father had completely transformed the garden, that her grandfather had left it overgrown and unkempt. She told Em stories of how she and her sister would pretend to be princesses captured by invaders, when they were children. Em wondered how, after what seemed to be a perfect upbringing, they turned into complete monsters. Em realised it was quite easy to become captivated by Katarina, although she was most certainly not captivated. She despised this woman. This woman walking beside her had haunted her dreams, had her mum killed, was holding her dad hostage and hurt Ronnie, Adam and Abs.

"Emily, Emily," Katarina said.

"Oh, sorry, I was admiring your beautiful garden, I didn't hear what you said."

"I said, we both come from incredibly magical bloodlines. Between us we could be so strong. We could manipulate and influence everything and everyone in our favour," she said as she smiled. Em tried to smile. "So what do you say?" Katarina's eyes were wide and scarier that Em had ever seen them.

"I cannot commit to anything right now. I just want to focus on finding the cannisters and having my dad and our lives back," she said.

"I admire your honesty." Katarina looked to the sky. "I see a storm rolling in, I think we should go back now. Busy day tomorrow," she said.

Em went to their room. The rucksacks were packed and hidden in the wardrobe and Ronnie was running her a bath. The door knocked. Adam opened the door; it was Billy. He barged past Adam. "Where is the chosen one?" he asked.

"If you mean Em, she is just about to have a bath," Adam said, not making eye contact.

"Well go and get her," Billy commanded.

"Yes sir!" Adam saluted him. Em came out of the bathroom in her robe.

"How can I help you?" she said.

"Did, er… Katarina say anything about me, on your little bonding session?"

"Not that I can remember, no. Why?" Em said.

"Well, what DID YOU TALK ABOUT THEN?" he roared.

"Oh, this and that." Em laughed.

"Don't push it, sister." He got up and walked over to Em. He tried to push his face into hers, but the barrier was back. "I am telling you now if you and her are plotting against me, you will both pay. DO YOU UNDERSTAND ME!" he yelled.

"Oooh, someone is paranoid." Em laughed. Billy stormed out of the room and slammed the door.

*

Back in the room after dinner they were fully dressed, waiting for Katarina and Billy to leave. They sat at the window with the light off. A while later they heard the car start and watched as Billy and Katarina drove away.

There was a knock at the door. Em answered. It was Charlotte. She handed Em a piece of paper and the cannister. Em looked at Charlotte; the cannister was pulsating in her hand. "I have made a map of the basement where Abbie is. Be careful down there – it is dark and smelly. I waited for them to leave and took the cannister out of the library safe; the idiots didn't change the combination." She laughed. Em threw her arms around her.

"I don't know how to thank you," Em said as she squeezed Charlotte.

"I should be thanking you. You have freed me from this chaos and for the first time in years I feel like me again," Charlotte said. "Anyway, I had better go. Good luck, all of you," she said and left.

The three of them studied the map and then made a plan of action.

They found the door that led to the basement. It was dark and damp. Luckily, Adam had asked Charlotte if she could source a torch earlier in the day, and she brought him three. They checked the map. They were about two minutes away. Charlotte had given Ronnie a spare key to the room. The wind was howling through the building. Ronnie crouched and then crawled. He reached a corner and tilted his head around. No sign of Claire. Charlotte had told Em that although she was told to sit outside the room and keep watch, she would often go back to her own room, usually to entertain one of the many henchmen.

Ronnie crawled to the door first, followed by Em with Adam at the back. Ronnie put his ear to the door, looked at Em and shook his head. They both stood back, and Adam opened the door. They all rushed in and closed the door.

Poor Abs was badly beaten and tied to a chair. Em could see that Adam was going to lose it. She moved him out of the way and gave him the 'sort it out' look. She knelt and looked Abs in the eye. She moved her finger to her lips and then cut the rope that bound her. Ronnie opened the door and peered around. He beckoned with his head that it was all clear. Ronnie first, then Em, Adam followed carrying Abs. They managed to get outside without being noticed. The rain was pouring, and the wind was howling. Ronnie and Adam went to find the part of the fence which Charlotte had deactivated. Em held Abs up as they fought through the wind and rain.

Em heard a dog barking. *When the dog barks, follow it.* Em grabbed Abs' hand and moved in the direction of the dog. Abs screamed. Em turned and Claire was pulling Abs away. "You lot must think that I am bloody stupid! After what Adam attempted the other night, I knew that all of you would be scheming." She pressed a knife against Abs' throat.

Em put her hand in her pocket and grabbed the cannister; instinctively she pointed the cannister at Claire and felt the energy flow through. A lightning bolt hit Claire and sent her flying. "RUN, ABS!" Em shouted. Abs got up and ran in the direction of the dog. Em felt something heavy on her back. She managed to fight it off. She slipped in the mud and then Claire was above her with the knife. Em held the cannister in her hand, using the energy to stop Claire's hand.

Something hit Claire around the head, and she fell to the ground. It was Charlotte. Em breathed a brief sigh of relief as Charlotte helped her up. Charlotte fell forward as Claire plunged the knife into her back. "NOOOO!" Em screamed. She held the cannister and pointed it at Claire, with so much energy, Claire lifted up into the air and landed against the electric fence. The charge held her, her body jerking. Then she was still and dropped to the ground.

Em ran over to Charlotte, who was alive. "HELP, HELP!" she screamed out. Ronnie came running over. He looked all around him. Em was sobbing. Someone grabbed Ronnie's shoulder. It was Geoff. "I'll carry her, you sort that one out," he said as she swooped Charlotte up and carried her. Ronnie did the same to Em.

"Follow the dog," Em whispered in Ronnie's ear. He did and they found the opening. Adam and Abs came through and then Geoff, carrying Charlotte. "She is losing a lot of blood. We need to find shelter, so that I can try to stop it," Em said to Geoff. Em felt something warm around her leg. She looked down and was completely blown away, to see Butch standing beside her wagging his tail. She crouched down and threw her arms around him, tears streaming down her face.

"There is an unused barn, about five minutes' drive from here," Geoff said. "I'll take Charlotte in the van with me, you lot follow in the car," he said as he hurried towards the white van. Ronnie followed the rear lights of the van. The weather had got worse, and he could barely see through the windscreen with the wipers on full. They pulled into a yard, Geoff jumped out of the van and opened the barn door. He ran back to the van and grabbed Charlotte, running back to the barn with her in his arms.

The others followed. Em laid out all of their coats and told Geoff to lay Charlotte on them. She turned Charlotte, who was only just conscious, onto her front, so that she could locate the wound. She found it. It was so deep.

Em was praying to the Goddess that the knife hadn't hit any major organs. She held the cannister, drawing energy from it, and then held her hands over the wound. Very slowly the wound got smaller and the blood flow stopped. Em sighed. She was exhausted. She turned Charlotte around and made her comfortable. Charlotte soon fell asleep.

Everyone in the barn began to clap, except for Geoff, who walked over to Em and threw his arms around her. "Thank you," he said quietly when he let go.

Em walked over to where Adam and Abs were sitting. "Your turn," she said to Abs.

"I've already done it!" Adam said and beamed. Em held Abs' face up and noticed that the deep cut on her face had more or less disappeared.

"Well done you!" Em winked at Adam. He had such a huge smile on his face as he cradled Abs in his arms. She glanced in Ronnie's direction and he beckoned her over. He tapped his leg and she sat herself on it.

"My amazing Em," he said as he curled his arms around her.

"I don't mean to be a party pooper, but don't you think that we ought to get the fuck out of here?" Adam stood up. Everyone agreed.

"But where are we going to go?" Geoff asked.

"Do not go to Devon." Em turned and looked at Peggy, who was now sitting beside her.

"Oh, Peggy!" Em said relieved to see her.

"Your dad is fine. I don't know what Jade was talking about. Mrs Dawkins is doing an excellent job of looking after him. She has even taught him to play chess." Peggy smiled.

The tears ran down Em's face. "Thank the Goddess," she said and leant her head on Ronnie's shoulder.

"They are heading to Devon and expect to see you there in a few hours. Mrs Dawkins is moving your dad as we speak. Em, you need to go home and get the grimoire, and then you all need to hide for a wee while," Peggy said.

"Who is she talking to?" Geoff asked. They all laughed.

"I need a phone," Ronnie said.

"Why?" Em asked.

"I could call Ray, he has holiday lets in Scotland, maybe we could all go there," Ronnie said.

"Here." Geoff passed Ronnie his mobile. Ronnie took it outside and made the call.

"Who's Ray?" Adam asked Em.

"His older brother," she answered.

"Geoff, could you come here?" Em called. Geoff bent down in front of Em and she blew the spell into his face.

"Hey," he said and rubbed his eyes.

"Better safe than sorry," Em said and laughed.

*

So it was all sorted. Geoff would drive Charlotte, Adam, Abs and Butch to Scotland, stopping somewhere near Manchester to get rid of the van and hire a car. Ronnie and Em were driving to Kent in the 4x4, grabbing the grimoire and other bits, dumping the car and leasing a different one to meet the others in Scotland.

*

They were on the motorway just outside of Watford when the fuel light started flashing. "Shit, we don't have any money, they took my purse when they threw me in the van," Em said.

"I do," Ronnie said as he pulled his wallet out of his pocket.

"Thank goodness for that," Em said. They stopped at the services. Em had to eat; she was starving. They grabbed food and coffees to go, then brought two cheap pay-as-you-go mobile phones. Em had written Geoff's number down so that they could all stay in touch. They filled up with fuel and were soon back on the road. Em called Geoff's phone, and Charlotte told her that they were near Manchester, and that she would call as soon as they were sorted and back on the road. Because of her trust issues, Em made Charlotte put Adam and Abs on the phone, just to put her mind at rest.

"I don't think that we should park near the house, especially not in this!" Ronnie said, as they got close to home. They parked in a cul-de-sac, a ten-minute walk from the house. They went through the back door. Ronnie went upstairs to grab clothes and other personal things while Em rushed to the workshop. The lock on the door had been broken. She pushed the door with her foot and slowly walked inside. The place had been ransacked. They had gone through everything. Luckily Em had the foresight to hide the grimoire well. She had a tray of sage plants growing. She had wrapped the grimoire in plastic and buried it beneath. She dug in until she found the book. She ran back to the house and told Ronnie about the workshop. He looked at his watch. "We had better make a move," he said. They locked up and ran back to the 4x4.

They parked the car and walked to the train station. They decided it was probably safer to hire a car in London, so they were on the train heading to the 'big smoke' when Em's mobile rang. The others were all on their way to Scotland and all sounded in high spirits.

Once in London, they took a tube train to Lambeth and leased a car. They stopped at a supermarket and got food and drinks for the journey, and soon they were on their way. They took turns driving. They had no music, so they sang songs, and talked; it was just like their old road trips.

"They know that you have all disappeared and that Claire is dead," Peggy said from the back.

"Shit!" Em said.

"What's wrong?" Ronnie asked.

"They know, Peggy has just told me," Em said.

"Well, we knew it was coming. I think we should just stop for fuel and toilet. Let's get away as fast as we can," Ronnie said nervously. Em agreed. She called Charlotte to tell her, but they already knew. Geoff's phone had been ringing constantly.

"Shit, call them back and tell them to buy and new phones and to get rid of that one," Ronnie said as Em relayed the conversation.

CHAPTER 19

They had lost daylight by the time they were passing Manchester. Both of them were on edge. "Why don't you have a nap, sweetheart?" Ronnie said. Em shook her head.

"No, I'm too wired." She smiled. She was thinking about Billy and Jade. How could they both behave the way they had? Mum and Dad were such good parents, who gave them everything they could possibly want.

"Penny for them?" Ronnie smiled.

"Oh, I was just thinking about how Billy and Jade have turned out. I don't understand it. Do you think that they have been enchanted?"

"Sometimes, sweetheart, people are born bad. I mean I have been part of the family for God knows how many years, and I have never liked either of them."

"Yeah, true," Em said as she thought about a specific memory, one she had never forgotten.

Billy had just passed his driving test and he and Jade asked Mum if they could take Em out for a drive. Em wasn't very outgoing and spent most of her time at college, work or at home with Mum and Dad.

Mum asked Em if she wanted to go. Billy and Jade glared at her. She nodded her head yes because she couldn't stand any more taunting from either of them. They either referred to her as *weirdo* or *chosen one*.

Billy was driving really fast and Em's hand was clenched around the back seat. She was petrified. He drove to Canterbury which was about twenty-five miles from home. They parked up and decided to have a walk around. As usual, Billy and Jade raced off ahead of Em and she struggled to keep up. Someone banged into Em. As she looked up, Billy and Jade had disappeared. Em quickened her pace and was becoming panicky. She had only ever been to Canterbury with Mum and Dad, before now. She looked everywhere. She walked up and down the high street, no sign of them.

Finally she walked back to the car park and was relieved to see that the car was still there. As she approached the car, she could see that Billy and Jade were already inside. She walked over, and Billy rolled his window down. "Hop in," he said. Em grabbed the door handle.

"It's locked," she said.

Billy and Jade burst out laughing and then just drove off. They just drove off, leaving their very nervous, not very confident or streetwise seventeen-year-old sister, in a place that she wasn't very familiar with.

Em began to cry. Should she wait, to see if they came back for her? After twenty minutes, Em's first thought was to call Dad. Then she remembered that he had gone to watch the football with Pete. She looked in her purse. Luckily she had been paid and had enough money to get the bus back. She cried the entire journey back. When she walked in her front door, she ran into the kitchen where Mum was; she was hysterical. Mum was furious. Bastards!

It was around 2am when they finally arrived at the house. It was pitch black. The house was in complete darkness. They both looked at one another. "Do we have a key?" Em asked. Ronnie shook his head.

"I told Adam to leave it somewhere on the doorstep." They both got out of the car and closed the doors quietly. Em's heart felt as though it was going to beat out of her chest. Ronnie put the torch on low beam and was searching for the key. He looked under the mat, under the plant pot and even under a peeing garden gnome but couldn't find it.

"I know this might sound a bit obvious, but have you looked in the key safe?" Em whispered. They both giggled when Ronnie put his hand in and found the key. They both crept in, trying not to make any noise. All of a sudden they heard thudding coming down the stairs. They both stood against the wall holding their breath. Butch came rushing through and jumped up at Ronnie. They both sighed a huge sigh of relief and then laughed a lot! Then there were more footsteps from upstairs, and then coming down the stairs. Adam walked along the hallway, his hair was messy, his eyes wide. "Boo!" Ronnie jumped out on him.

Adam, who went into karate chop mode, nearly had a panic attack and Em and Ronnie creased up with laughter. "I could have bloody hurt you then, you stupid idiot," he said. When Ronnie finally stopped laughing he apologised.

Adam showed them around, although there seemed little point as they were moving on the next day. This house was just a stopover, just outside of Edinburgh. They were heading to the highlands. They thought that it would be the safest option, for a few weeks anyway.

*

Em woke up to the sound of plates clattering. She looked at her watch; it was only quarter to six! She climbed out of the really comfy bed and headed down the stairs. "Wow, you look tired," Abs said, she ran over and threw her arms around her.

"Is there any coffee on the go? It's the least that you two can do after waking me up," Em said as she yawned.

"I could say the same to you," Adam said as he then hugged her. They all laughed. Em propped herself up on a stool at the huge kitchen island cradling a cup of coffee when Ronnie came downstairs. Adam passed him a cup and he kissed the top of Em's head and perched himself next to her.

"I take it that Charlotte and Geoff are still here." Ronnie looked at Adam. He nodded.

"Are they coming with us today?" Adam asked. They all shrugged their shoulders.

"Don't you think that someone should go and ask them?" Em said sarcastically. They all looked at one another.

"Fine, I'll do it," Abs said with a sigh. They all clapped. Abs stuck her fingers up at them and left the kitchen.

A few minutes later she came back into the kitchen. "They've gone," she said.

"What? When?" Em said.

"Was the car parked outside when you guys arrived last night?" Adam asked. They both nodded yes.

"Well, we have been awake since five, and haven't heard a thing, have we Adam?" Abs said.

"Are all their things here?" Em asked Abs.

"Nope, the room is how it was when we arrived, how weird," Abs said.

Ronnie took out his phone and called Geoff's number. "The number that you have dialled has not been recognised," the woman said.

"What the hell?" Ronnie said as he put it on loudspeaker.

"Did they know that we were only stopping here for one night?" Em looked at Adam.

"Yeah, I told them that we were moving on today."

"But did you tell them where we were going?" Ronnie asked. Adam shook his head.

"No, I only said that we were moving on."

"Phew!" Em sighed.

"I think that we had better clear out quickly then," Ronnie said as he jumped off the stool.

*

They were all on the road by 8am and were hoping to be in the highlands by lunchtime. They had stopped at a supermarket and bought enough groceries to feed an entire army! Abs kept asking if there was a freezer at the accommodation.

The higher they drove the more stunning the landscape became. There were lots of oohs and wows coming from the girls in the back. They finally pulled up outside the beautiful wooden lodge, nestled in the mountainside, at 11am.

It was impressive from the outside, but the inside was truly stunning. The girls were running around checking it all out, while the boys brought the cases in and unpacked the shopping. There was a veranda outside overlooking the mountains. Em stood there taking deep breaths, filling her lungs with fresh mountain air. Ronnie came out and wrapped his arms around her. "Stunning, isn't it?" he said as he muzzled her neck. Em laughed and Butch barked.

"Yes, we can go for a walk," Em said. Butch barked again. Abs came out to the veranda carrying two mugs of coffee.

"I can't believe there is still snow on the mountains," she said as she handed them the drinks.

"You can take a girl out of the city," Ronnie said, and they both laughed.

"What?" Abs said, looking confused. She walked back inside.

*

The walk was beautiful; Em had never experienced anything like it. It was lovely, just her, Ronnie and Butch. They walked for miles. There were brooks, mountains, heather and wildflowers everywhere. "Now I know why Peggy couldn't leave this place." She beamed at Ronnie. She had fallen in love!

When they got back to the lodge the temperature had dropped rapidly. They opened the door to the most wonderful aroma of one of Adam's famous curries. The fire was roaring. It was gorgeous. Abs walked through. "We managed to get the hot tub going. Go and get yourselves sorted and jump in, it's amazing. We didn't want to get out." She laughed.

They went upstairs and put their swimming gear on and their robes. On their way out Abs handed Em a wine and Ronnie a beer. "Enjoy," she said as she went through to the kitchen area.

*

"It almost feels too good to be true," Em said as she sat in the hot tub, sipping wine, enjoying the stunning view of the mountains. "I'm scared, of what is going to happen next." She looked fraught with worry.

"Babe, just enjoy the here and now. We can worry about that, whenever it happens," Ronnie said as he drank his beer. Em leant back and sighed.

*

They were sitting enjoying their meal. Both the girls were in their pyjamas; both girls were in awe of their surroundings. "What do think happened to Geoff and Charlotte?" Em asked the others.

"Maybe they went back to Bonnie and Clyde, maybe they were scared," Abs said.

Adam shook his head. "No, from what Geoff was telling me, he was sick to death of them both. He hated them, especially the way that they treated Charlotte," he said.

"Well, I hope that they are both OK," Em said, looking into her wine glass. Ronnie took the glass from her and filled it up.

"Em, will you please, just for one night, chill out, woman!" he said as he handed her the full glass of wine.

Of course she took those words to the extreme and had drunk so much wine, Ronnie thought that he might have to carry her to bed. "I'm fine," she said, staggering all over the place.

"Night, you two," Ronnie shouted as he closed the bedroom door and tucked Em into bed.

She was in the meadow. There in the distance, she could see the bridge. She hoped that Abagail would be there, but she was alone. She stood on the bridge and looked into the brook. She felt uneasy. "Peggy, are you with me?" she called out. No reply. There was a fierce gust of wind. It almost knocked her off her feet. This isn't right, she thought to herself. It's supposed to be a gentle breeze. She turned to walk from the bridge, then from out of the water appeared a giant horrific version of Katarina, screaming. Her eyes were red with fury. Her huge hands lunged forward to grab Em, but something unseen stopped her. "YOU WILL NEVER BE FREE OF ME. I WILL FIND YOU!" she screamed and disappeared.

Em was running back to the meadow, as fast as her legs could carry her. "Emily, wait!" she heard. She was too afraid to look back. "Emily please, it is I, Abagail!" Em turned and was relieved to see that it was in fact, Abagail before her. "She cannot hurt you here." She smiled.

"I am so afraid of her," Em said, trembling with fear.

"Child, your power is so much stronger than hers, even now. The only way to put an end to all of this, is to collect all seven cannisters. When you have possession of them all, you can destroy her power." Abagail smiled and disappeared into the wildflowers.

Em woke with a jump. She sat bolt upright. Where was Ronnie? "RONNIE!" she cried out.

He walked through from the bathroom. "Hey, whatever's wrong?" he asked as Em ran to him sobbing. She told him about the vision. "I think that tomorrow, you and I should drive to Fort Augustus and you can build up some much needed energy from Loch Ness," Ronnie said as they sat on the edge of the bed. He was stroking Em's hair.

"Em, he is safe and happy," Peggy said as she appeared.

"Where have they moved him to? Do you know, Peggy?" Em asked as she wiped the tears from her face.

"It wasnee them that moved him." Peggy winked.

"Eh, I don't understand." Em was confused.

"I have managed to get through to your dad spiritually. He can hear me, and he can speak to me. I think that Mrs Dawkins, or Sandra as she likes him to call her, has a wee crush on your dad. I told him to convince her to get him away. I told him to go to our cottage," Peggy said.

"What, yours and Uncle Bill's cottage?"

"Aye, lassie, so you can stop your fretting about him. Get on with the job at hand!" Em blew her a kiss and she disappeared.

Em and Ronnie were up before Adam and Abs, so they went downstairs and prepared breakfast. Em made the pancakes, while Ronnie laid the table and made the coffees. Abs came down first. "That was the best night's sleep, I think that I have ever had!" she said with a beaming smile. "And those pancakes smell amazing, Em."

She sniffed in hard. Adam came down the stairs, eyes half shut, and his hair all tousled.

As they sat round the table eating, Adam asked, "What is the plan of action today then?"

"Well I thought that I would drive Em to Fort Augustus," Ronnie said.

"Isn't that where Loch Ness is?" Adam asked. Ronnie nodded.

"Ooh! I have always wanted to see Loch Ness," Abs said. "Isn't it where that giant snake lives?" she added. Em burst out laughing.

"Well, you are more than welcome to join us," Ronnie said. "It's about an hour and a half drive from here, so we will have to make a move soon." Adam looked at Abs; she was furiously nodding her head.

"As long as you guys don't mind." Adam looked at Em.

"Of course not! I will have to spend some time re-energising, but I'm sure that there are plenty of things to keep you both amused." Em smiled.

*

Em couldn't believe how beautiful it was. Adam and Abs had gone off to do their own thing, and Ronnie found a quiet spot on the shoreline. He had packed them a picnic, so they sat on a blanket and enjoyed the views. Adam had taken Butch with him, to give Em some time to re-energise.

After food, Em sat herself on the shoreline and put her hands in the loch. She felt the power running through her veins. It felt wonderful. She had her eyes closed and could hear the water gently lapping. She could hear the birds singing. She could hear the gentle hum of the boats as they cruised up and down the loch. The water began to bubble and then to Em's amazement, it parted. There in front of Em stood a woman with long golden hair, dressed in flowers. She was beautiful and Em felt no fear. She sat on the shore next to Em. She smiled a most radiant smile.

"Begin the search where your life form began, it will aid you greatly in your search," she said to Em.

"Thank you," Em whispered and bowed. She looked up and the woman had gone. Em felt something on her shoulder. She jumped and turned and was relieved to see it was Ronnie.

"Are you alright, sweetheart?" he asked as Em was holding on to her chest.

"I don't know... I have just had the most unbelievable experience," she said.

"Try me." Ronnie smiled. She told him about what had just happened.

"That, my wee darling, was the Goddess Brigantia," Peggy said in her ear.

"Wow!" Em murmured under her breath.

*

Adam, Abs and Butch had now re-joined the group, so they walked back to the car park. Em told Abs about her experience while Adam and Ronnie were chatting about fishing; Butch was sniffing everything! They had a walk around the Fort Augustus ruins, but had to leave as both Em and Adam were picking up on a lot of negative energy, probably because of the history of the Fort.

They were back at the lodge. Tonight it was Em and Ronnie's turn to cook, so Adam and Abs took Butch for a walk. They prepared the food, put it in the oven and then had half an hour in the hot tub. Em had never felt so relaxed.

Adam and Abs came back with the dog and they had their turn in the hot tub. They all sat eating lasagne with salad and garlic bread. Ronnie's mobile rang. He answered it and walked out onto the veranda. Adam looked at Em. Em shrugged.

"Ronnie came back in; his face was ashen. Em stood up. "What's wrong, babe?" She began to shake.

"That was Geoff."

"And?" Adam said, beckoning Ronnie to speak.

"The reason that he and Charlotte disappeared was... well... she started to bleed heavily in the night. Geoff took her to the hospital."

"And?" Em said impatiently.

"She died this morning from a massive internal haemorrhage," Ronnie said sadly.

"Fuck!" Adam said. Em and Abs just sat looking at the floor.

"Is he going to come here?" Adam asked. Ronnie shook his head.

"No, he is going to spend some time with his family in Yorkshire. He said he wants to meet up when we begin the search, if that's OK with you, Em?" Ronnie said.

"Of course it's OK," Em said as she wiped the tears from her face.

CHAPTER 20

So for the next two weeks they all did research on the ley lines, enjoyed their surroundings and built up as much natural energy as they could. The ley line that they needed to find, ran from Coldrum Long Barrow in Kent to Holyhead in Wales. It was where to start, that was the problem. Adam thought London, Ronnie thought Wales, Em thought Kent and Abs didn't have a clue!

They all finally came to a decision. On the journey back, they would stop off in Wales for a few days, and would then make their way to Kent. Ronnie phoned an old friend of theirs who rented holiday cottages and luckily there was a vacant one for four nights.

It was the last night at the lodge and they all felt sad; even Butch looked sad. "One day, Ronnie, I think that we should live here, it's so peaceful and beautiful," Em said as she looked around at the mountains surrounding them.

"I'd love to," he said and sighed.

*

The car had just about made it; the rented cottage was halfway up a mountain!. They went inside, unpacked and decided to have a twilight walk before dinner. It was beautiful. There were so many sheep with their lambs, and many trickling waterfalls. When the light began to fade they decided to head back to the cottage. Em ran a bath, Ronnie lit the fire while Adam and Abs drove to the village to pick up fish and chips.

"Well, I don't know about anyone else, but I am full up and knackered!" Em said as she stretched and yawned. The others nodded in agreement. Ronnie got up from the sofa and tapped Em's leg. "I'll take the dog out; you make us a cuppa to take up," he said.

They sat in bed. Butch was lying across their feet, and they looked at an ancient map of ley lines that Ronnie had ordered from the internet, trying to work out the best place to begin. They thought about starting somewhere near Caernarfon Castle.

When they could no longer keep their eyes open, they nestled down under the thick duvet. Em wrapped herself around Ronnie and they both drifted to sleep.

She was walking a mountain path; there was someone in the distance. She did not feel afraid. She walked towards the figure. As she got closer, she saw that it was her mum. Her mum pointed to the summit of the mountain. "You will find the cannister near the cairn, Em, feel for the water. Stay safe," her mum said, then disappeared.

Adam and Ronnie were busy getting the walking gear ready; Em and Abs were in the kitchen, preparing food to take with them. Em put Butch's lead on and they all got in the car. "So, which mountain?" Ronnie said as he pointed to all the mountains on the map.

"I don't know why, but I have the name Llewelyn running around in my head," Adam said. Em pointed to it on the map.

"Well, I hope you guys are fit, it's just over 1,000 metres high, and we have to go to the summit. Yes?" Ronnie said as he looked at Em.

She nodded. "Also there isn't a route, so to speak. Adam, did you pack the map and compass?"

"I most certainly did," Adam said.

They found a parking space next to a lake.

So while the boys had the map spread across the bonnet of the car, Em boiled some water in the jet boils and made them all a coffee. "I think we should all have something to eat, before we walk," Em said as she handed each of them a bag of food.

Ronnie had mapped out the route up. It took them three hours; Abs and Em collapsed when they reached the summit. There was low cloud so there were no views, and it was so cold! Once Em had got her breath back, she walked in the direction of the cairn in the thick cloud. She located the cairn and as she placed her hands on it, she felt the water beneath the ground. It was moving towards the north-west. She got on her hands and knees and followed it. Luckily, they were the only people up there. Other ramblers would think that she had lost the plot!

She felt a rumble below her. She called to Ronnie and Adam who joined her. Adam passed her a hand trowel, and she began to dig. The ground was pretty soft and soon she could hear the water. She carried on until she felt the energy and then the water gushed through her fingers. Very gently she carried on until she felt the tip of the trowel hit metal. She put the trowel down and dug with her hands. She felt the same bolt of energy the moment that she grabbed it. Slowly and carefully she removed the cannister.

She opened the cannister and pulled out the spell page; the energy shot through her and almost lifted her from the ground. She put the spell page back inside the cannister and put the cannister in her pocket and zipped it up.

It was an arduous trek back down the mountain and both the girls were moaning that the descent was harder on the knees than the ascent!

Back at the cottage in front of the fire, Em and Abs were sitting on the rug. The boys were on the sofa, Em took out Abagail's grimoire and the two cannisters. She found where the first missing page should go and carefully slid it in. Em jumped back; the page had moulded back into the book. The others looked on as she did the same to the second page and again it moulded back in. "Wow," Abs gasped.

All of a sudden the fire roared and huge flames rose. Within the flames was the horrific image of Katarina, the same image that Em had seen on the bridge. Abs screamed and jumped up. Em held onto the grimoire for dear life!

"Do you think she knows where we are?" Abs was still trembling.

"No idea. Look, I know we have paid for another two days, but I think that we all need to get out of here as soon as we can. You can't be too careful," Em said nervously.

*

Em tossed and turned all night. She couldn't settle. She thought that she would sleep for Britain after the day's climb, but after the fire episode, she felt very unnerved. Ronnie on the other hand was out for the count and snoring for England! By 4am she had had enough. She got up and went to the kitchen and made herself a coffee. She spied Ronnie's coat on the hook. She looked in his inside pocket and found his secret stash of tobacco. They both decided to give up a few years back, but both of them had a secret stash. Trouble was, Em's was in her car and the Goddess only knows where that was.

She rolled herself a cigarette, unlocked the back door and stood in the small porch. Everything was so quiet, even the wind, which was a first. Every time they had climbed a mountain, the wind had felt like it was hurricane force.

Em heard footsteps coming towards the cottage. She quickly stubbed out the cigarette. "Only me," said a voice in a strong Welsh accent. It was Howard! The guy that owned the farm and rented them the cottage.

"Crikey, you scared the hell out of me!" Em said, still trying to catch her breath.

"Very sorry, I've got a ewe up there." He pointed up the mountain. "She's having a bit of trouble giving birth, see," he said, as he tipped his hat and carried on up the mountain.

Em decided it was probably a good idea to finish her coffee inside. By the time everyone else was up, Em had packed everything, made breakfast and prepared food for the journey.

*

Adam was driving, while Em, Ronnie and Butch were in the back. They must have only been driving for twenty minutes before Em fell fast asleep. Ronnie had decided that Kent wasn't the safest place for them to stay, but they needed to be within driving distance. Adam had a friend that owned a few properties in Surrey, so he called in a favour and got them somewhere to stay in the Surrey countryside.

When they were just outside Oxford Ronnie's phone rang, which woke Em up. When he had finished his conversation he looked at Em. "Something is not right," he said. Em rubbed her eyes. Adam turned the music off.

"There is a services two miles away. Shall we have a break there?" Adam asked. They nodded.

"I'll fill you all in over a coffee." Ronnie looked worried.

*

"It was Geoff," Ronnie said as they sat around a small table. "He wanted to know where we were starting the search."

"So? I thought that we had all agreed that he would help us," Em said.

"Yeah we did, but something inside me told me not to tell him. So I said that we hadn't worked it out yet," Ronnie said.

"Right, so what do you think is wrong?" Adam asked.

"He was very insistent that I told him exactly where we were staying. I just found that odd."

"So, did you give him the address?" Em asked as she started to panic.

"What do you think, Em? Honestly... I told him that we were going back to our house." Ronnie shook his head at Em.

Em nudged him with her elbow. 'Sorry,' she mouthed and smiled.

*

They pulled up outside the house. It was very lovely. It was a suburban executive house. Em didn't want to touch anything. It was all so shiny. Once unpacked, Em decided to jump in the shower. When she came downstairs, they were all in the kitchen and immediately stopped talking when she walked into the room. They all looked at her. "What?" They then looked at one another. "Bloody hell! What is it?" she said.

"Adam and I are going to drive to the house. Just to see if there is anything suspicious," Ronnie said.

"NO BLOODY WAY!" Em shouted.

"Em, sweetheart, you need to chill. It will only take us a couple of hours, and you and Abs can cook us something delicious for dinner," he said and smiled.

"No, if you two are going then we can all go. What if they get you both again? I can't cope with that." Em wanted to cry.

"I think that both Adam and I know them well enough now, not to be fooled by them. We just want to have a look, that's all," he said as he kissed the top of her head and put his coat on. Adam stood up and put his coat on. He walked over to Abs to give her a kiss, but she turned her head away. Then they both left.

"Bloody hell. What are we going to do while they are gone? I can't just sit around waiting for them to call," Abs said frantically.

"Right, first we go and get some shopping, then we can go to a nature reserve, not far from here," Em said.

"One problem with that," Abs sighed.

"What?"

"They have taken the only car."

"Shit! OK, I have a better idea." Em smiled.

*

They took a bus to the supermarket but got a taxi back. Whilst in the shop they bought food, lots of wine and two swimming costumes. Abs didn't realise that there was a swimming pool at the house. Em hadn't mentioned it as they had no swimming gear. They unpacked the shopping, put their phones in their rooms, got changed, grabbed the wine and headed to the pool.

They swam, they drank, they laughed. They had gone through two and a half bottles and were both collapsed on the loungers next to the pool, when Ronnie and Adam got back.

"Oi!" Adam kicked the lounger that Abs was on. She looked up and laughed. "We have been trying to call both of you. What the fuck? We thought that something had happened to you." Adam was angry. Abs laughed.

"I think that Abs and... er, I know them well enough," Em slurred and they both burst out laughing. Ronnie shook his head and walked out of the pool room, with Adam in quick succession.

*

Em walked down the stairs the next morning with the mother of all headaches. Abs was already in the kitchen. They both looked at one another, knowing that they were in for a royal rollicking. They sat quietly at the island, drinking coffee, when Ronnie appeared. "Morning," Em said very quietly.

"Good morning!" Ronnie bellowed in her ear. Em threw him a look. Then Adam walked in. Abs didn't look up from her coffee. After what seemed an eternity of silence Em plucked up the courage to speak.

"So, had they been there?"

"Like either of you two give a toss," Adam huffed.

"She was only asking. There was no need to be rude." Abs stood up. Adam opened his mouth to say something. "NO, we were expected to be the obedient housewives, sitting here cooking and worrying while the gallant knights ride out to save the day. I'm sorry that we got drunk and had a laugh. I'm sorry that there was no meal laid out for you on your return, but there is only so much worry that either of us can take. Now piss off and leave me alone!" Abs shouted as she stormed up the stairs.

"That went well then," Adam said as he looked down at the floor.

"Ah…hem." Ronnie looked at Adam, and then at Em.

"Sorry Em, it's just that we both panicked when neither of you answered your phones." He gave her a sweet smile.

"Well, at least now, you know how it feels," Em said as she stood up and walked out of the room.

*

It was the smell of food that tempted Em downstairs. She was starving. Ronnie was cooking one of his famous fry-ups and Adam was washing the dishes. "Still no sign of Abs then?" Em asked as she kissed Ronnie's cheek.

"She's locked the bedroom door," Adam said miserably.

Em went back up the stairs; two minutes later she was back down with Abs behind her.

Adam grabbed hold of Abs. "I'm so sorry, babe, it's just the thought of losing you." Abs gave him the biggest kiss. That was that. All was forgiven!

After they had eaten and cleared the dishes Ronnie spread out the map of the ley lines on the table. "I think that this one is important to get next. I don't know if you guys agree," he said as he looked up and over the top of his glasses. Em smiled. She loved him so much.

"You still haven't said what happened at the house." Em smiled.

"Absolutely nothing," Adam said and blushed. Abs rubbed his hair and smiled.

"Yes, I think we all agree that the sooner we find this one, the better," Em said.

"Have you had any visions, you know, to guide you to where it is?" Abs asked.

"No, but I have a feeling, if I touch the long barrow, it will point me in the right direction," Em said.

"When did you want to do it?" Ronnie asked.

"No time like the present." Em stood up.

*

Luckily, the weather was on their side; it was a beautiful sunny day with just a gentle breeze. They parked in a car park and followed a route through a woodland, which was stunning, and up to Holly Hill. As it was quite late in the afternoon, there weren't many other people about. The hill was 300 metres high, not too bad, and Em headed straight for the Barrow. She sat on the grass next to it and felt the hum of the earth beneath her. She drew the energy up towards her. She stood and put her hands on the stone. It was warm and she could feel energy pulsating through it.

She knelt down and could just about hear the distant trickling of water. She followed the sound getting louder and louder and when she heard it cascading she stopped. She took the trowel out of her rucksack and started to dig. It didn't take long before she felt the water running through her fingers. She started to dig with her hands; she felt the energy of the cannister before she felt the metal. She gently pulled it from the earth.

She took the top off and as she did the energy sent her hurling through the air. She landed in a heap. Ronnie ran over to her. "Em, are you OK?" he said as he lifted her up.

Em was laughing. "My darling, I have never felt so alive," she said as she stroked his face.

Adam had picked up the lid, which had shot out of Em's hand. Ronnie and Em sat on the grass, watching the sunset. Abs walked over to the brow of the hill; Adam followed her. "Where the hell did you get those?" Adam asked as he watched Abs looking through a pair of binoculars.

"I found them in a drawer at the house." She smiled. "Hey, I... don't believe it!" she called out.

"What?"

"Take a look." She handed the binoculars to Adam. He looked through them and then looked through them again.

"Go and grab those two," he said, still looking.

Within a few seconds Ronnie and Em were standing beside them. Adam passed the binoculars to Em; she looked and then passed them to Ronnie. "Unfuckingbelievable!" Ronnie said as he moved them away from his eyes.

"Lying bastards!" Em said.

CHAPTER 21

Geoff and Charlotte were looking through the windows of the car. There was only one other car in the vicinity, which was parked a little way up a country lane. Abs was keeping watch, while Adam ran down to the car parked in the lane. He looked through the window and spied Geoff's bomber jacket and Charlotte's handbag. He tried the driver's door. They had left it open. He gestured to Ronnie, who had already opened the five-bar gate that led into a nearby field. Adam got into the driver's seat and let the handbrake off, while Ronnie pushed the car into the field.

Adam steered the car close to the hedge, so that it couldn't be seen from the road. Then they both ran back up the hill to join Abs. Meanwhile Em began the walk down to the car park. Charlotte saw her when she was halfway down. She alerted Geoff and they both ran in the direction of where they had parked their car.

Adam, Abs and Ronnie, then ran as fast as they could to join Em. She was panicking. "Hurry up!" she shouted out to them. They all bundled into the car, and Ronnie pulled away at high speed. "What if they have already found the car?" Em said nervously.

"I wouldn't worry about that," Ronnie said and winked. "I cut the fuel pipe!"

They laughed the entire journey back. "Hey, why don't we all get dressed up and go to that lovely restaurant? You know, Em, the one we passed on the bus yesterday," Abs said.

They got back to the house and were all showered and dressed. Em fed Butch and let him out to the toilet. "Now you be a good boy, look after the house. We won't be too long," Em said as she kissed him on the head.

"The dog gets more of her affection than me," Ronnie said and dropped his lip.

"Nonsense," Em said as she smacked his bum.

"Cab's here," Adam called out as he walked from the window.

It seemed like a million years had passed since Em had had such a civilised evening. The food was delicious, and the restaurant was pretty quiet. They had all had quite a bit to drink and were feeling fuzzy. Adam called a cab which they waited outside for.

"Make me a roll-up, babe," Em said to Ronnie. He looked at her in bewilderment. "I found your secret stash in your pocket. Don't worry, mine was in the car." She laughed.

Adam had put the lights on timer. Of course he had, how boys love their gadgets! It was lovely not to pull up outside a house that was in complete darkness. Em paid the taxi driver while Ronnie and Adam did their ninja checks. All seemed well.

As soon as she got inside Em kicked her shoes off. She hated wearing heels! The underfloor heating was on and it felt so warm beneath her feet. Butch came running through to greet her and nearly knocked her flying. "Who's for a nightcap?" Ronnie asked.

They all sat in the lounge, on the extremely comfortable sofas, with their drinks. Butch started to bark at the window. "Adam, turn the lights off quickly," Ronnie said quietly. He slowly walked over and slightly moved the curtain back. Ronnie turned and shook his head. "I can't see anything or anyone," he said.

CRASH! It sounded as if it came from the kitchen. They all jumped up. They could hear clattering. Em grabbed the cannister from her handbag. "I'll go first, I'm armed," she said as she moved in front of everyone. She peered through the gap in the door. Geoff was pulling everything out of the cupboards.

"You distract him, Em," Ronnie whispered.

"WHAT THE FUCK DO YOU THINK YOU ARE DOING?" Em screamed, pointing the cannister at Geoff and closing the open back door with her foot. Geoff began laughing and then walked towards Em; she shot her energy into the cannister and it blew him across the kitchen. Abs grabbed a knife and held it to his throat as he lay on the kitchen floor. Em looked at Abs in disbelief and shook her head. The back door flew open and in walked Ronnie with Charlotte.

Adam had been to check the rest of the house and made sure that all doors and windows were locked.

Ronnie and Adam then tied Geoff and Charlotte to chairs. "I knew I should never have trusted you. Was this the plan all along? You help us to escape, we find the cannisters and you take them to the master?" Em said as she looked on both of them with disgust.

"WE HAD NO CHOICE!" Charlotte screamed out.

"YES YOU DID!" Em yelled in her face.

"They said that they would turn us over to the police. They have put me in the frame for your mum's murder," Geoff said. Em walked over to him and slapped him as hard as she could across the face.

"I didn't do it. I swear to you, Em. It was that other nasty bastard Joel," Geoff said.

"I don't trust either of them," Ronnie said and looked at Em.

"What are we going to do with them?" Em asked.

There was a bedroom upstairs that they weren't using, so they decided to lock them in there for the night. Em knew that she couldn't possibly sleep, knowing that they were in the house. She sat up in bed next to a very loudly snoring Ronnie. They had to leave, but where could they go? Katarina would not rest until she had Em and the cannisters in her possession. She finally dropped off to sleep.

She was walking through the tunnel, the same tunnel that led to Carrie. She came through the other side. This time instead of an old pedlar woman, an old man with a staff took her by the arm. He gestured towards a building. They walked inside. It was like Aladdin's cave. So many artifacts and antiques. He pointed to a chair and she sat. "You must seek out Cedric Trowbury, he is a gifted metal smith. He can recreate the cannisters. She will never know."

"Where will I find him?" she asked.

"You must travel to a small town in Staffordshire. It is called Leek. He lives nearby," he said, then disappeared into thin air.

She left the building and walked back onto the cobbled streets. Carrie was walking beside her. "You are in great danger, Emily, so too is your father. They have located him. Give her the cannisters."

Em woke with a jump to loud voices on the landing outside her room. She opened the door to Adam and Ronnie both shouting at Geoff.

"What on earth is going on?" she said, still half asleep.

"He was trying to get out. He picked the lock!" Adam said.

"Really, and where were you going?" Em asked Geoff. He shrugged his shoulders. "Where is Charlotte?" She looked at Ronnie.

"Downstairs with Abs," Ronnie said.

Em went to the kitchen and poured herself a cup of coffee.

Charlotte was a pitiful sight, sat at the island sniffling and sobbing.

"Pull yourself together, woman," Em snapped at her. Abs looked at Em in shock.

"I didn't want to go, but Geoff is petrified that they will turn him into the police. He is wanted for quite a few things." Charlotte sniffed.

"Yeah, and it will be a few more if he continues to work for Bonnie and Clyde," Abs said.

"Em, can you come here?" Ronnie called as he walked through the kitchen and out of the back door. Em followed Ronnie into the garden. "I don't know what you're thinking, but I think that we should keep them close," Ronnie whispered.

"I agree, but I don't think that we should stay here, we need to go to Staffordshire," Em said.

"Why?" Ronnie looked confused. Em went on to tell him about the vision. One by one they told Adam and Abs the plan, after Ronnie had made his phone calls.

They were going to lease a different vehicle, drive Geoff and Charlotte to Ronnie's brother Ray's house. Then the four of them were going to try and find this Cedric guy.

*

They pulled up outside an absolutely beautiful house in Buxton. Ray met them as they pulled up. Ronnie and Adam took Charlotte and Geoff to one of the many outbuildings. Ronnie had a quick chat with Ray and then they left for the town Leek. Ronnie was quite familiar with the place and knew a few people there. After about an hour of asking around he had managed to locate him.

They travelled to a village called Gratton and found his workshop. They parked up and went to the door. Ronnie knocked. Em nearly fell over when he opened the door. He looked identical to the man in her vision. He looked at Ronnie and then at Em. "I've been expecting you," he said to Em. "Do come in." They both followed him. Adam and Abs stayed in the car with Butch.

They walked through one workshop, and then through a door that led to a stairway. When they got to the bottom of the staircase, they reached a double padlocked door. They looked at one another and then at Cedric. "This is where I do my magical workings," he said as he unlocked the padlocks. They walked in. Em was amazed. It was an exact replica of the Aladdin's cave that she went to in her vision.

"Now, if you would be so kind as to give me the cannisters," the old man said.

"But... but how did you know?" Em asked.

"I have been waiting for this day for a very long time, my dear," Cedric said. Em took out the three cannisters and handed them to Cedric. He examined them. "Hmm, very powerful indeed, just like the woman that created them." He smiled. "Now then, if the two of you would take a seat over there." He pointed to a very regal sofa. "I have some pewter from this era, I think it's in here," he mumbled to himself as he rummaged through one of his many cupboards.

He was humming, as he was tapping and banging for about twenty minutes. "I say!" he gasped. Em stood up.

"What's wrong?" she called over to him.

"It has just occurred to me that I haven't offered you refreshments. How very rude of me!" he exclaimed.

"Really, it's fine, we had just had a cuppa in Leek," Ronnie said.

"Oh, a local man! I didn't realise," he said as he carried on tapping and banging. After another twenty minutes he walked over to them and handed Em six cannisters. Em looked at him in bewilderment.

"But how will I..."

"You will feel, my dear, go on," he said as she took them from him. Sure enough she could feel the power in the real cannisters, but the others looked identical.

"But surely Katarina will know," Em said.

"Alas, only folk from Abagail's direct bloodline can feel it. You try," he gestured to Ronnie.

Ronnie took the cannisters. "They all feel the same to me," he said.

They gave their thanks and said their goodbyes and headed straight back to Buxton. They collected Geoff and Charlotte and were heading towards Norfolk. As they passed the sign for Norfolk Geoff turned and looked at Charlotte in horror. "What the hell are you doing? If you go back there they will kill you," he said to Ronnie.

"We're not going back there. You are, Geoff," Em said. "Charlotte will stay with us; you know, just to ensure that you deliver the goods," she added.

They stopped just outside Cambridge. Em sorted the cannisters and put them in a chest that Cedric had given her. "Why can't Charlotte come with me?" Geoff moaned as he got back into the car.

"She will be perfectly fine with us. Once you have given Katarina the goods, we will contact you and tell you where we are," Adam said.

*

They dropped Geoff off about a mile from the house and then headed in the direction of Skegness. They found an old pub which offered accommodation. Ronnie went in to see if they allowed dogs. He came back out and called to them, nodding. They all clambered out of the car. Ronnie and Adam went inside, while Em, Abs and Charlotte walked Butch around the car park and Em had a sneaky cigarette.

It was olde worlde inside; it oozed character. Ronnie showed them where their rooms were, and they all went to get showered before dinner. Adam and Abs had drawn the short straw and had Charlotte in with them!

*

They all went downstairs and ordered food. They had been on the road all day and were shattered. After the food Em and Ronnie took Butch outside, and the others went off to their room. Once they were settled in bed with Butch lying over their legs Ronnie looked at Em. "What did you write in the note?" he asked.

"I told her that I was happy to find the remaining cannisters and translate them for her, on the understanding that she left us to do things our way, and that I wanted my dad back," Em said sleepily.

"And how are you going to know if she agrees?" asked Ronnie.

"Oh she'll agree, I know it," Em said as her eyes were closing. Ronnie kissed her on the head and turned out the light.

*

"What's that bloody noise and what time is it?" Ronnie shouted as he sat up in bed.

"What, oh, it must be Charlotte's phone. I took it off her, just to be safe," Em said as she clambered out of bed and was rummaging through her bag. "It's four thirty," Em said as she looked at the time on Charlotte's phone.

"Who were the calls from?" Ronnie scratched the top of his head.

"Who do you think?" She handed him the phone. Ronnie was still holding the phone when it began to ring for the umpteenth time.

"Yeah?" Ronnie answered it. He passed the phone to Em.

"Emily, it's Katarina, I am most pleased that you have decided to comply."

"Katarina, I will not look for another cannister until you have removed the enchantment from my dad, and I have him back with me," Em said. She was shaking like a leaf.

"Yes, understood. I will send him back to you with Geoff, tomorrow morning. Is that acceptable?" she asked.

"Yes, that would be most agreeable," Em said and ended the call. Ronnie raised his eyebrows.

"Well, what do you think?"

"I think it's another bloody trap," she said as she snuggled back under the duvet.

The phone was ringing again, and there was someone knocking on their door. "Shit, it's like Clapham bloody junction," Em said as she fell out of bed. While Ronnie answered the phone, Em opened the door. Abs walked in followed by Charlotte.

"Em, please give her the phone, she is driving us bloody mad!" Abs said.

"Two seconds, I think Ronnie is talking to Geoff," Em said and gestured to them to be quiet. Ronnie ended the call and gave the phone to Charlotte. "No need for any funny business, you will be reunited by this afternoon." Ronnie laughed.

"Thank goodness for that! We'll meet you for breakfast in half an hour," Abs said as they both left the room.

"Well, what's the trap... er, I mean plan?" Em chuckled.

"I have told Geoff to meet us at ours," Ronnie replied. "It seemed silly, him driving all the way here to then drive back down." Em nodded.

*

Em took Butch out for a walk around the car park and then met the others for breakfast. She was so excited that she was going to see her dad, but she was also so scared.

They packed up and were on the road for 8:30. Em was very quiet during the journey. Abs was very excited to be staying with Em and Ronnie. They had all agreed that it would be safer for them if they all stayed together for a while.

They pulled up at the house. There was a car on the drive. Em took a deep breath and got out of the car. Butch jumped out and bound past her, running straight for the front door. It made Em smile. Em put the key in the door, but it opened without her turning the key. Her dad stood there with his arms wide open. Em fell into him, in floods of tears. Butch was going barmy jumping up, waiting for her dad to make a fuss. Em didn't want to let go. Finally, after Butch nearly pulled her trousers down she let go. Dad made a huge fuss of Butch, then hugged Ronnie who was directly behind Em.

They all went through to the kitchen. It was emotional, even Abs and Charlotte were crying. A tray of coffees landed on the kitchen table. Em looked up. "Mrs Dawkins!" she shouted.

"Well, I weren't going to leave him, was I?" She smiled at Em. "And I would prefer it if you called me Sandra," she added. Em introduced her to the others. Dad winked at Em.

Em put her hand in her pocket and walked over to her dad. "Dad," she said. He looked up and Em blew from her hand into his face.

"Arrgh!" he shouted as he put his hands over his eyes. Everyone laughed, well, everyone except Sandra!

"Just checking," Em said as her dad rubbed his eyes.

CHAPTER 22

Em had arranged to meet Katarina and Billy in Devon in a few days. Sandra said that they could stay at her cottage. At least they had a few days to reacquaint themselves before the hell began again. Geoff and Charlotte had left, they were going to stay with Charlotte's parents.

Ronnie and Adam brought all the things from the car and were sorting things out. Abs was in the kitchen, checking what groceries were needed. Dad was showing Sandra the garden, specifically his roses. Em went to the workshop, to clear it up. So many of her plants had died! She had made a list of what needed replacing. She swept the floor and lit some incense. She looked around. *Much better!* she thought to herself. She was about to the lock the door when Dad walked over with Sandra. "I was just going to show Sandy your little miracle shop," Dad said and beamed.

Sandy! Really! Em thought.

"Oh, do you think that's wise? I didn't think she approved of such things," Em chuckled. Dad threw her a look.

"You know that was all for show, Em. I must have been good though, I had you fooled," Sandra said and winked at Em.

"Touché," Em chuckled.

Ronnie was walking towards them as the three of them left the workshop. He put his arm around Em, and they all walked back to the house. Adam had taken Abs to the local shops to get the shopping and to acquaint her with the locals. Em made the coffees and took them through to the conservatory, where they were all sitting. Butch had found his favourite ball which he was running around the garden with, so happy.

"So, who is cooking tonight?" Dad asked. Em looked at Sandra. Sandra looked at Em.

"Would you like to, Sandra?" Em asked.

"Ooh, I'd be honoured to cook for you all. Bob says that you are all very good cooks!" She beamed a huge smile. Ronnie nudged Em with his arm and when she looked at him he blew her a kiss. Adam and Abs came back with the groceries, Em and Ronnie went to the kitchen to help them unpack. "He hasn't mentioned Mum once. Do you think he knows?" Em said quietly to the others.

"Yes, he knows," Dad said as he stood in the kitchen doorway, tears in his eyes. Em ran over and threw her arms around him. They linked arms and walked out into the garden. "I knew before it happened," he said. "The moment she went missing, I knew that it had started." He had his head down looking at the ground.

"What had started?"

"I have had visions since I was a nipper, just like you, Em. The one thing though, that I never saw coming, was that your bloody brother and sister would be involved." His tears had turned to anger. "I will end the pair of them. So help me, I will," he said, his fists clenched and his eyes red.

"They will both get what's coming to them, don't you worry about that," Em said as she touched his hand. "I have Mum's ashes. What do you want to do with them?" Em asked.

"That's something I want to talk to all of you about," he said. Em nodded. It felt so good to have him back.

"I never stopped searching for you all," Em said, her eyes full of tears.

"My darling, I know that," he said as he held her face in his hands. "And I will never be able to thank you enough," he said.

"But Dad, I couldn't save her." She was sobbing.

"Em, that was not your fault, and no matter what you did, it was always meant to happen. Now, come on. Dry those tears, I feel a karaoke night in the air." He had a twinkle in his eye.

"Oh no!" Em laughed.

*

They were all sat around the dining table. Sandra had cooked a delicious roast dinner, and Abs had made a lemon meringue pie for dessert. Dad nodded to Ronnie who walked around the table filling everyone's glasses. Ronnie sat down next to Em and put his hand on hers. She looked at him and smiled. Dad stood up. Speech time! She knew it!

"I would just like to say a few words," he said, and everyone cheered. "Firstly, I can't tell you all how good it feels to be back with my wonderful family. I want to thank my surrogate son Adam and his gorgeous other half Abs, for helping Em and Ronnie, in these dark times." He lifted his glass. "To Adam and Abs." Everyone raised their glasses. "Next is to my Ron. I couldn't have wished for a better son-in-law. He loves my Em to bits, and he has always done me and Mags proud. To Ronnie." He raised his glass. "Now to Sandy, thank you for lifting me up when I was at my lowest. To Sandy." He raised his glass.

"And finally, to my Em. The moment that I looked at her as a babe in arms, I knew that she was special. She is the most honest, genuine, caring and brave person that I have ever known. There are not enough thanks in the universe to give to her. To Em." He raised his glass.

Everyone stood and clapped; Em was in floods of tears. "Right, if you could all sit your bums down, there is something I want to discuss with you," Dad said. Everyone sat.

Ronnie threw his arms around Em and gave her the biggest kiss. "Aww!" everyone called out.

"Now then, I had a chat with Ronnie earlier. My sister Peggy left us her cottage and some land when she died. I think that once this shit show is over, we could all do with a fresh start." He looked around the table. They all nodded their heads.

"Sandy and I have been looking into it, and the landowner who sold it to Peggy had many years ago applied for planning permission on some of the land, and it turns out that under old law, it still stands."

"And?" Em said impatiently.

"Alright, I'm getting to it!" Dad laughed. "Anyway, we thought it would be nice to build ourselves a small estate, so that we can all be in the same place." Em grinned.

"I'd love to." She looked at Ronnie who was nodding and smiling. Adam and Abs also agreed.

"Does that include me?" Sandra asked meekly.

"Of course it includes you! I thought that a nice two-bedroom bungalow, would be good for us. Strictly platonic, of course. We can keep each other company," he said, blushing slightly.

"Thank you," she said, blushing.

"So," Ronnie said, "the plan is, that after Devon, Adam, you put your apartment on the market, and we'll do the same here. Are you selling yours too, Sandra?" She nodded. "My brother has kindly given us free reign on the lodge in Scotland, and we can all use that as a base when the building works start. We contacted an architect this afternoon and they are making a start on the plans," Ronnie smiled.

"As for Mags' ashes, I think that we should make her a little garden on the estate, put her ashes beneath a rose bush. That way she will be a part of it too," Dad said bravely.

"Beautiful," Em said and blew him a kiss.

"Right then, I think we have cause for a celebration. Adam, get the karaoke set up," Dad said and burst into song. "Just warming the old vocal cords up," he said. Everyone laughed.

They had such a laugh that evening. Sandra and Em's dad had hogged the karaoke most of the evening, while the others joined in and consumed lots of alcohol. Butch was jumping at Em, so she opened the kitchen door; he bounded out. She poked her head out. It was a beautifully clear night, so many stars. She felt truly happy.

"I'm not trying to replace your mum, Em," Sandra said from behind her. Em jumped.

"The thought hadn't even crossed my mind." Em smiled.

"I need to apologise to you, dear. I am so very sorry for spying on you. I am not going to lie and tell you that she made me do it. I did it to give me something to do, but once I had got to know you, I told her that I wasn't going to do anymore. She went ballistic!" She looked worried.

"There is no need to apologise. If you hadn't led them to me, I would never have found Ronnie or Dad. So Sandra, it should be me thanking you," Em said.

"I do care an awful lot about him," she said as she watched him singing away to Dean Martin.

"I know." Em smiled.

"Oh, but I do have a favour to ask of you," Sandra said. Em nodded. "When you go back to Devon, would you pop to Mrs Greggs and pick up Jeremy for me?" she asked. Em looked puzzled.

"Jeremy?"

"My dog." She giggled. "Oh, I do believe I have had a bit too much wine."

"Coffee?" Em said, shaking the kettle at her.

"Oh, yes please, dear." She smiled.

"She's not that bad really," Peggy said, making Em jump. Em laughed.

*

It felt so good to be back in their own bed, with their duvet and their pillows. They were both sat up; Ronnie had a cup of tea, Em had a hot chocolate. They sat and chatted about the day. Em felt so happy. One thing she would always be grateful for, was having this day. It would always be a memory to treasure.

She was walking through the meadow, the sun was warm, the flowers were in full bloom. Abagail was on the bridge, waving at her. She hurried her pace. Abagail walked towards her and together they sat in the long grass. "The next cannister, it is amongst nine. Alas, do not touch any of them." She nodded. "Emily, the one after, poses the greatest danger. It is the most powerful. You must take great care. It is near the giant stones," she said and then disappeared into the meadow.

She got up and began to walk back. Something grabbed her ankle, pulling her to the ground. She was kicking to break free, but the grip tightened. Then she heard it. It was back. She looked down and the beautiful meadow grass had turned black and opened up. It was pulling her down. "NOOOOO!" she screamed at it. She gathered all her energy and blew as hard as she could at it. It let go. The hole closed.

"Come on, sleepy head, your coffee is getting cold," Ronnie said.

"What time is it?" she said, half asleep.

"Half nine!" Ronnie said, shaking his head.

*

Em had her list, and they were walking around the local plant nursery. "Is there any point in re-planting, if we are moving?"

She looked at Ronnie. "You can put them in a removals truck, you know." He laughed.

"Alright, no need for sarcasm." She nudged him and nearly sent him flying. "What the hell, Em?" he said.

"I hardly touched you!"

Ronnie was intrigued by this newfound strength that Em had. They stopped off at a sports shop. Ronnie came out with two bags of sports equipment. Em looked at him. "Taking up sports, are we?" she said.

"You'll see." He laughed.

They got home. Em took the plants to the workshop. While she was in there, she worked on a few different protection spells for the trip to Devon. The vision had made her feel on edge; she decided not to tell anyone about it. Not even Ronnie.

Abs came through the door. "Madame, you are wanted," she said in a posh voice. Em laughed and followed her outside. Ronnie and Adam were in the garden. The girls walked over to them.

Ronnie picked up a tennis racket and ball and handed them to Em. "What?" she said.

"See how far you can hit it." Ronnie said.

"I'm not a performing monkey!" she replied and passed it back to him.

"Fine," he huffed. He hit the tennis ball with the racket as hard as he could. Adam took out a tape measure and measured it. "Your turn." Ronnie passed them to Adam. He too hit the ball with all his might and Ronnie measured it. Adam was in the lead; he was a foot over Ronnie. Adam passed them to Em. She shrugged her shoulders. She pulled her arm back and hit the ball as hard as she possibly could. They all stood in astonishment as the ball flew past all of them and disappeared. The boys ran in the direction of the ball. The girls caught them up at the fence. The ball had gone straight through the wooden fence leaving a perfect circular hole in its place.

"What the hell?" Adam looked at Em.

"I told you," Ronnie beamed.

"Can we have lunch now?" Abs said.

*

They spent the next two days just enjoying being at home, in each other's company. Sandra had been baking non-stop. Dad had been on the phone to the architects and to Pete non-stop.

It was the night before they were travelling to Devon. Em took out the grimoire and was looking through it. There was a verse in it, on the page next to the missing page. It mentioned nine maidens dancing.

"That's it. I know where to start the search for the next cannister!" Em shouted. Ronnie came out of the bathroom, rubbing his face on a towel.

"Em, ring your dad, make sure they are OK," Ronnie said.

She called her dad's mobile. He was in high spirits. He was happy, due to the fact there was a pool table in the hotel, and he had beaten Sandra four times. Em ended the call and sighed.

They decided to be safe, they would book her dad and Sandra into a hotel in Surrey. Adam had hired a car to drive to Devon, so he took them to the hotel in the afternoon.

They left the house at 4:30am to give them plenty of time. They were to meet Katarina and Billy at Sandra's cottage at 11am. The night before, Em had taken the spare cannister that Cedric had made for her and put in the blank piece of paper. That man had everything in his workshop, even centuries-old parchment! This was the last of the fake cannisters, so before they searched anymore they would have to go back to Cedric.

They pulled up outside Sandra's cottage at 10:30 to see that Katarina and Billy were already there.

Em slid the cannister up her coat sleeve. She took a deep breath and got out of the car. The others followed. Abs was trembling with fear. It was so easy to forget about all of this when they were all at home together, and now they were back in the eye of the storm.

She opened the front door and could just about make out Billy's silhouette in the kitchen. "How lovely, the cavalry has arrived," he sneered as they walked through to the kitchen.

"Do you know where to begin the search, Emily?" Katarina asked. Her hair was the deepest red.

"Yes, it is about a twenty-minute drive from here," Em said.

"What are we waiting for?" Katarina said as she gestured to the door.

Billy and Katarina followed them in their own car. They parked in a village car park and began the trek up to the moors. They climbed a steep hill and then opened a five-bar gate and walked onto the moors. There were a few Dartmoor ponies grazing. When Katarina got close they all reared up and galloped off over the moors.

Em had walked this way before and she knew exactly where to go. They came to a small stone circle, hidden by the rough moorland. She had already warned Ronnie, Adam and Abs not to touch the stones. Em got on her knees and ran her fingers through the grass.

The water was already at gushing point. As she moved with the rhythm of the water, she heard the birdsong, ringing out. She stopped and Adam handed her the trowel. She began digging; she could feel the power beneath her. Then the water. She put the trowel down and began using her hands. She shook her arm, so that the cannister up her sleeve was at the rim. She felt the metal of the cannister in the ground. She put her arm in and pushed the cannister up her sleeve and released the other one into the hole. Once it was wet, Em pulled it out and held it up.

"Excellent work, Emily," Katarina shouted as she walked to Em.

"Do you want me to open it?" Em asked. Katarina nodded. Em opened the cannister and pretended that it knocked her back. She took out the paper and nervously handed it to Katarina.

"Wonderful!" she exclaimed as she examined it. Em silently sighed relief. "Back to the cottage now. You can translate it and then we can all be on our way," Katarina said. She passed the cannister to Em and then turned to the stones. "Not very clever maidens, are you?" she said as she ran her hands over the stones.

They began to walk back across the moors towards the car park. They heard a cry from behind. They turned to see Katarina being pulled into a bog, begging Billy to help her. Billy stood and laughed, shaking his head. Em walked over to her and put out her hand. She pulled Katarina out. "Thank you," she said quietly to Em. Then she turned to Billy and punched him as hard as she could in the face. They all grinned.

CHAPTER 23

They drove back to Sandra's cottage. Em was furiously scribbling the words written on the missing page onto her hand. It was the only way of translating the page, that Em could think of. They pulled up outside the cottage. Em was nervous. It only took Katarina or Billy to look at her hand and they would all be in big trouble.

Billy pulled up behind them. He got out of the car and walked over to the driver's side door of their car. Ronnie put the window down. "Katarina is feeling unwell. We are going to travel back. She will send Geoff to collect the page once you have translated it, Emily. Oh, and she said not to forget to translate into Theban. Call her when it is done," he said as he turned his back and walked to their car.

"Phew!" Em said as she breathed a sigh of relief.

They stopped at Mrs Greggs' house and collected Sandra's West Highland terrier, Jeremy. Em was a bit worried that he wouldn't get on with Butch, but after a lot of sniffing they got along fine.

Before they all headed back home, Em wanted to take them all to Boscastle. They drove there and parked up. Abs fell in love with the place, the minute she set eyes on it. They went into a café and ordered four coffees to go, and then went and sat on the rocks where

Em had first seen Carrie.

"So, what's the plan now?" Adam asked. Ronnie looked at Em.

"I think that we should head back to Kent today. I will do the translation as quickly as I can, and once it has been collected I think we should head up to Peggy's place and take a look around." She smiled.

"What about the next cannister? Do you know when or where?" Adam asked. Em shrugged.

"She hasn't said when, and as for where, I believe it is somewhere near Stonehenge," Em said as she blew on her hot coffee.

"Have you had any visions or dreams about the next one?" Adam screwed his eyes up. He was clearly troubled by something.

"No," she lied. "Have you?" Adam shook his head, but Em could tell he wasn't telling the truth.

As they walked back towards the car park, they walked past the Museum of Witchcraft. "Can we go in?" Adam asked. They all nodded. The place was amazing, it housed so many ancient artefacts. They were walking around chatting amongst each other about different exhibits. Abs and Em were looking at the ancient poppets. "They bring back painful memories," Abs said as she shivered.

"I know," Em agreed. Em turned and noticed Ronnie and Adam whispering in a corner. She walked over. "What are you two plotting?" she asked as she slid her hand into Ronnie's.

"Nothing, we were just admiring this impressive collection," Ronnie said and smiled. Em noticed that he flared his nostrils when he said it.

As they were about to leave, someone grabbed hold of Em's arm. It was an older man. "You must go to Tintagel and look for Willow. She owns a shop there. She has information for you," he whispered and then disappeared around a corner. Em didn't mention it to the others. When they got back to the car Em decided that before they left, they needed to go to Tintagel.

"Really, Em? We have got at least a five-hour drive, and then we have got to go and pick up Dad and Sandra!" Ronnie wasn't happy about the thought of another stop.

"It is three miles away. I have to go there," she said. She wasn't backing down on this one.

"Fine," Ronnie huffed as he started the engine.

They walked along the street. "Oh, I recognise this place," Abs said excitedly. Em nodded and smiled.

"Hey Em, look, isn't that the old woman, that gave you the scarf?" Abs said, and they all looked across the road in the direction that she was pointing. Ronnie and Adam looked at each other, neither having a clue what they were talking about.

"Yes, yes it is," Em said as she began to cross the road. The others followed her. She walked up to the woman, who was sitting outside the shop. "Willow?" Em asked.

"I've been expecting you. This way, dear," she said as she got up and led Em into the shop.

"How do you know who I am?" Em asked.

"It was written a very long time ago. We share the same bloodline – mine is not as strong as yours," she replied.

"What is the information that you have for me?"

"It is about the whereabouts of the next cannister," she whispered.

"And?" Em whispered.

"There is great danger, dear. This is the most sacred of places. You must be careful where you dig and what you unearth," Willow said.

"So do you have any idea where to begin?" Em asked. Willow sighed.

"You must go north of the stones. Head towards a place called Larkhill. That is as much as I know." Willow smiled.

"Thank you," Em said and smiled back.

"Take great care, Emily," Willow said and ushered Em out of the shop.

The others were waiting outside, adhering to Willow's instructions. "Well, are you going to tell us what the hell that was all about?" Ronnie was agitated. Em shot him a look and walked back in the direction of the car park, saying nothing.

They were back on the road, heading for home. Nobody spoke for hours. They stopped at a services to walk Butch and have a break. Adam and Abs had gone to grab the coffees, Ronnie had nipped to the loo and Em walked Butch and Jeremy around a grassy area. Ronnie walked towards her. "Sorry," he said.

"I have enough enemies to fight against. I don't need you to join in," she replied, still pretty angry with him. She hated the long silences, and he knew it.

"Sometimes, I feel that I am only here to carry the bags," he said, looking at the ground.

"Don't be bloody ridiculous!" Em raised her voice.

"Shh, everyone is looking," he said.

"I couldn't give a toss! You are not just here to carry the bags, Ronnie, but sometimes you and Adam hide things from me. I thought that I would give you a taste of your own medicine." She looked directly at him.

"Sorry," he said again. "Are you going to tell me what happened back there?" he asked.

"That depends, are you going to tell me what you and Adam are hiding from me?"

"He has had visions of the next search. In every vision, we are all surrounded by a red aura. He is just worried about it," he said.

"A man in the museum told me to go to Tintagel and search out that woman, Willow. She told me that there was danger on the next search, but she has given me directions of where to begin the search."

"Do you trust her?" he asked. Em nodded and told him about the scarf.

The rest of the journey was much better, they were all talking, sharing thoughts and worries. They dropped Adam, Abs and the dogs off at the house and then carried on to collect Em's dad and Sandra.

Em's dad was very excited. "The plans should be at the house when we get back. Pete collected them this morning," he said and rubbed his hands together. It made Em smile.

When they got back, they walked in to the smell of curry. Adam was cooking. It smelt delicious! Em's dad headed straight for the study. Em took the cannister and grimoire down to the workshop. She was busy translating or in fact not translating the page, when Adam came in.

"I'm sorry that I've been a bit edgy lately," he said as he put his hand on Em's shoulder.

"It's OK. Ronnie told me about the visions. Try not to worry too much. We just need to be incredibly careful," Em said as she put her hand on his and smiled. She tried to be as reassuring as she could but in all honesty, she was as worried about it as he was.

"Have you finished Cruella's work?" he said and laughed. Em laughed.

"Nearly done. Get back to that curry. I will be back in ten minutes." She smiled.

She had finished. She put it in the cannister and walked back to the house. Ronnie was in the study with her dad, looking through the plans. Sandra and Abs were in the kitchen preparing/arguing about the dessert. Em thought that it was best to let them get on with it. She walked into the study. Ronnie beamed at her. "Sweetheart, come and look at this," he said. Em looked. It was the first draft of the plans for their new home in Scotland. They had decided to go for a barn-like design.

"Wow." She kissed his cheek. "Isn't it exciting?" she gasped.

"Look at this, Em," her dad called out. She had a look at the plans for the bungalow.

"Very modern, Dad. Didn't think that was your thing." She smiled.

"A change is as good as a rest, girl." He grinned and winked.

Em went up to the bedroom and called Katarina. She told her that Geoff would be there in the morning to collect the cannister. Before she ended the call Katarina said, "Emily, there is a delicate matter that I need to speak to you about, are you alone?"

"Yes."

"I am concerned about Jade's influence on Will. She seems to bring out the worst in him," she almost whispered.

"I think that they are both as bad as each other, but if you are asking for my opinion, they are both much worse when they are together," Em said and smiled to herself.

"That was my thinking. Yes, I think that they must be separated. Thank you," Katarina said.

"No problem," Em replied.

"Another thing, Emily, I think that we should begin the next search in four weeks. When the moon is full. Is that agreeable?"

"Most definitely," Em said and ended the call.

Em jumped in the shower. She came out of the bathroom and her phone was ringing. She picked it up and sighed when she saw the number.

"What?" she said.

"You are a bloody scheming bitch. What did you say to her?" Jade screamed down the phone.

"Oh, have you had to leave? Poor you," Em chuckled.

"Laugh all you like, weirdo, but I am coming to stay with you." Jade then laughed.

"Er, I don't think you are," Em said.

"I have nowhere else to go."

"Grovel to your husband, Jade, beg his forgiveness, because I'm telling you now, if you step foot in this house, there will be a queue of people ready to floor you!" Em said and ended the call.

Em got dressed and went downstairs to tell everyone about the phone calls. They had all made a promise to one another. No secrets, no holding anything back. They were all to be kept in the loop.

*

The next morning Geoff and Charlotte arrived at 8:30. They took the cannister off to Katarina. There must have been twelve missed calls on Em's phone, all from Jade.

They were all having breakfast, talking about the trip to Scotland. Adam had taken the hire car back and swapped it for a minibus. Ronnie had drawn up a driving rota, but because it was a twelve-seater, only Ronnie and Adam had a licence to drive it, so they were doing two-and-a-half-hour stints of driving each.

Abs had booked two nights' accommodation and then they were heading up to the lodge. Em and Sandra had written lists and they were heading off to do the shopping that afternoon. There was a knock on the front door. They all looked at each other. "I'll go," Ronnie said as he stood up.

He came back in the room followed by Lewis. "What the bloody hell is that arsehole doing in my house?" Em's dad roared and stood up. Adam stood beside him.

"I think that we should hear him out," Ronnie said.

"Look, I just want to make it perfectly clear, that I was against the entire thing from the start," Lewis said.

"So what do you want? And if it's to ask if she can come and stay here, the answer is most definitely no!" Em shouted.

"No, I have told her that she can stay with me. The reason I am here, is that I know for a fact that her and Billy are plotting against that ghastly woman, but I am also led to believe that all of your lives are in danger," Lewis said.

"How?" Em asked.

"The next search. I know that they are planning something then. When I know, I will make you all aware."

"And why the hell should we trust you?" Adam said.

"Because Adam, I never wanted any of this to happen. When Mags died I was mortified."

"Murdered, you mean," Em's dad said through gritted teeth.

"Well, so long as you keep us all in the loop, we should be OK, yes." Em looked at Lewis. He nodded. "Should I make Katarina aware of this?"

"That is entirely up to you," he said and then turned and left.

"I still don't trust him," said a lovely Scottish accent.

"Peggy!" Em and Adam said at the same time.

"Hello, my lovelies, I shall be around a lot more. Need to keep you all safe," she said and smiled.

"Thank the Goddess for that!" Em said. Sandra was looking on in utter astonishment.

"Would someone mind telling me, who the hell they are talking to?" Em's dad laughed.

"Come with me, girl, and I'll fill you in," he said as he put his arm around her and led her into the garden.

*

It was chaos in the minibus. Butch couldn't make his mind up where he wanted to sit, so he jumped over everyone. Em's dad kept falling asleep and snoring so loud that they couldn't even hear the music that was playing. Everyone was relieved when it was the first stop.

Ronnie walked the dogs around, while Em, and Abs went to the loo. Em's dad and Sandra went to get the coffees and Adam went to get the food. They sat around a picnic table enjoying the sunshine.

By the time that they had arrived in Melrose, it was dark, and they were all tired and hungry, so they decided to head straight for the hotel.

It was a small boutique hotel, which allowed dogs. It had a bar and a restaurant. Once everyone had checked in and been shown to their rooms, they all met in the bar. Ronnie took Butch and Jeremy for a walk around the car park. They had a lovely dinner and then all disappeared up to their rooms. Em and Ronnie took Butch out again, so that they could have a sneaky cigarette.

Tucked up in bed Em and Ronnie were talking about how excited they were to go and see the place where one day they would be living. They also made a pact that, while they were away, they would not discuss the next search, Katarina, Billy or Jade.

Darkness, she was underground. She could smell the damp earth. Voices, she followed the sound. The ground beneath her feet was soft. She felt uneasy. "Peggy," she called out quietly.

"Right beside you, lassie," she sighed.

The voices were getting louder. There was light. She followed the light. It was an opening. She peered through. There was a large stone slab. Someone was bound to it. Bright red hair. It was Katarina. Laughing and taunting. It was Billy and Jade. Billy was reading from a book. Katarina was screaming. Her hair was losing its colour. Peggy nudged her. Jade, her hair had turned red. Billy slashed Katarina's arm with a long knife; the scream was piercing. Jade put Katarina's arm to her mouth and was taking the blood into her mouth. Billy was reciting from the book. Katarina fell silent. She stopped moving. Laughter, cackling. Jade had taken the form of Katarina. Billy was howling.

She jumped about a foot in the air. She was sweating. She opened her eyes, relieved to see Ronnie sitting beside her stroking her hair. "What happened, sweetheart?" he said. She told him.

*

The next morning at breakfast Em and Ronnie were both quiet. "Have you seen this? I do not bloody believe it," Em's dad said as he looked up from the newspaper. He turned it around, so that could all see it. There was a photo of Billy, dining with a government minister. They were all gobsmacked.

"So are either of you two going to tell us what is wrong?" Em's dad said, peering over the top of his glasses. "Remember, no secrets," he added.

Em went on to tell them all about the vision she had. They all looked at one another, wide-eyed.

"So, do you think that it has already happened?" Abs asked. Em shrugged.

"To be honest I really don't have a clue," Em said as she ate her toast.

"There is one person who could shed some light on it," her dad said. "We could call Lewis, see if she has been there."

"Hmm, but I don't really trust him, he could be in on it." Em was not convinced.

"It wouldn't hurt to try though, would it?" Ronnie said. Everyone nodded, except for Em, who still thought that it was a bad idea.

"Shall I give him a call?" Her dad looked at her with his phone in his hand.

"Call him, but after this I do not want to speak about it again. We are here to enjoy ourselves. Yes?" She looked around at everyone. Her dad got up and walked outside to make the call.

"Well, I don't know about anyone else, but I am very excited to see the land and to go to the lodge. I have never been to the highlands before," Sandra said and giggled. She was obviously trying to lighten the mood.

"It's beautiful, the lodge is gorgeous," Abs said and smiled.

Em looked out of the French doors that led into the garden. Her dad was gesturing her to go out to him.

"Excuse me," she said as she got up and walked to the garden. She walked over to her dad. He looked at her and shook his head. He covered the phone.

"I can't make out what he's going on about," he said as he passed the phone to Em.

"Hello Lewis, it's Em," she said.

"I only popped to the shops; I was no longer than ten minutes." He sounded frantic.

"OK, and what happened when you got back, Lewis?" Em asked.

"I only popped to the shops; I was no longer than ten minutes," he repeated.

"Lewis!" Em raised her voice. "Can I speak to Jade please?" she said.

"I only popped to the shops…" She ended the call.

"What's wrong with him? Why does he keep repeating himself?" her dad asked.

"He's been enchanted, Dad," Em said as she passed him back his phone.

"Poor sod," her dad mumbled as they joined the others in the dining room.

*

Ronnie had planned the route on Google Maps, to get to Peggy's cottage. As they pulled up Em was gobsmacked. It was absolutely gorgeous. The cottage was white with trailing roses, and there was so much land. They got out of the minibus and walked up the path to the front door. "Where's the key, Dad?" Em called over as he was inspecting the roses. He looked up, puzzled. He scratched his head.

"What happened to the key?" he asked Sandra. She scratched her head.

"Do you know, I don't have a clue. When that giant oaf turned up he just shoved us in the back of that van," she said.

"Great," Ronnie tutted.

"Em, look under the plant pot," Peggy whispered in her ear.

Em walked amongst them, lifted the plant up and picked up the spare key. She dangled it in the air. "Oh, well done Em!" Sandra shouted, and they all went inside.

They all went off in different directions. Em's dad and Sandra went straight outside to where they were going to build the bungalow. Adam and Abs were admiring the view from an upstairs window. Em was in the pretty kitchen, making drinks for everyone when Ronnie came in. she turned and smiled.

"What's wrong, sweetheart?" he said as he wrapped his arms around her. She sighed.

"I know that we agreed that we wanted to build, but—"

"You have fallen in love with this place, right?" Ronnie interrupted. Em nodded. Adam and Abs walked out into the kitchen.

"It's a bit poky in here, Adam. Can we knock this wall down?" Abs asked and tapped the wall.

"No you bloody well can't. It would break Peggy's heart!" Em shouted. Abs looked hurt. "Sorry, Abs." Em smiled and then hugged her.

"Listen, you two, it's obvious that you are both used to modern living, and Em and I are a bit quirky. Why don't we change it so that you have the new build, and we'll have the cottage?" Ronnie said.

"Really!" Abs squealed and looked at Adam. He nodded and she jumped at him.

"That makes me very happy," Peggy said, smiling.

"Me too," Em agreed as she put her arms around Ronnie and kissed him.

"What's all this then? Cor, you turn your back for five minutes." Em's dad tutted and laughed. Sandra giggled.

*

The journey to the highlands took about four hours. They left early so that they could spend the remainder of the day exploring. Adam took Abs into the town to do some shopping. Em's dad and Sandra took Butch and Jeremy for a walk. Em was unpacking and Ronnie started to prepare dinner. Ronnie made them both a coffee and they sat out on the veranda.

Em sighed a huge sigh. "It's so beautiful and peaceful here, isn't it?"

"It certainly is," Ronnie agreed. "I think that we are going to very happy living in this part of the world."

"Absolutely! To our new adventure." Em held her cup up against Ronnie's and they chinged.

They had an hour in the hot tub before the others came back, and then carried on with the food. Em's dad and Sandra were the first back. Sandra really wanted to go in the hot tub, but Em's dad point-blank refused. Said he would rather have a bath.

Adam and Abs came back an hour later and wasted no time in jumping in the hot tub.

Em's dad was sitting on the veranda reading the newspaper, Sandra was sitting beside him dozing off in the last of the day's sunshine. Between them they had prepared a lovely meal. Ronnie had made mulligatawny soup with fresh bread for starter, Em had made Mediterranean steak casserole with cheesy potatoes for the main meal and they both made syrup sponge pudding for dessert.

They sat around the table eating, drinking and laughing for a few hours, and then played cards. Em's dad wanted to watch News at Ten, so he and Sandra sat in front of the TV while the others carried on drinking. Adam went to get some more beer from the fridge and tripped as he was coming back. They all creased with laughter. "Shh, you lot, come over here!" Em's dad shouted.

It was a news report about a man's body being found at the bottom of some cliffs in Kent. They showed the man's car that was parked on the top. It belonged to Lewis. Em gasped and put her hand over her mouth.

"Shit!" Adam said under his breath.

CHAPTER 24

Em did some meditation before she got into bed; she really needed a good night's sleep. Ronnie had taken the dogs out for a wee and then took them both up a cup of hot chocolate. They sat in bed and chatted while they drank their drinks. Em snuggled under the warm duvet and within seconds she was sound asleep.

"Em, Em, follow me." She was back inside the place under the earth. She recognised the voice. It was Mum. She slowly walked forwards and then she saw her. She was waiting for her. "She doesn't have long," Mum said and pointed in the direction of the huge stone slab. She couldn't hear or see anybody else. As she approached the slab, the hairs stood up on her neck. She looked down. It wasn't Katarina, it was Jade lying there. Her skin had wrinkled, and her hair had turned grey and most of it had fallen out in clumps.

"What has happened?" she asked.

"This is yet to come. Just before the full moon. If you do not find her in time, she will die," Mum said.

Voices, becoming louder. She went back inside the tunnel and watched. Billy and Katarina walked towards the slab. She took out a long knife and cut Jade's arm, then they both took the blood into their mouths. They were laughing as the blood ran down their chins.

Em sat up; she was gagging. She thought she was going to be sick. Ronnie sat up. He guessed that she had had another vision and passed her a glass of water. She told him about it. Ronnie rubbed his chin. "Fuck! How the hell are we going to find her and the cannister?" he said.

"I think that she will be close to where we search for the cannister, but I'm not sure where," Em said.

"You will have an idea soon," Peggy said.

"Do you know where it will be?" Em asked her. She shook her head.

"I only know that you will be guided and that I will protect you," she replied. "This will be very dangerous, Em, build up as much energy as you possibly can," she said before she disappeared.

"Shit!" Em put her head in her hands.

*

After two wonderful weeks in the highlands, it was time to leave. Em was able to build upon her power, enjoying the most magnificent landscapes. The only thing that had marred the time, were the constant visions. Em was having them every night. They just replayed, over and over. Nothing had changed.

On the way home to Kent, they had to make a detour to Leek, to visit Cedric. Ronnie dropped the others off in Leek, to have a walk around and grab a cuppa, and then he and Em drove out to Grattan. They were downstairs in Cedric's magical workshop, drinking tea, which he insisted they had, while he worked away on the final cannisters.

He walked over with the cannisters and parchment and was carefully placing them in the magical box. "There is much danger surrounding your next search. Yes?" He looked directly at Em. She nodded.

"So I am told," she sighed.

"I have crafted for you a protection pendant, Emily. You should wear it at all times," he said as he handed her something wrapped in black cloth. Em opened the cloth. The necklace was beautiful, it was made with orange and black crystals, and the pendant was of a dragon wrapped around the earth, all crafted in silver.

"It's beautiful." Em looked at Cedric.

"The necklace is made from Baltic amber and Whitby jet. I crafted the pendant from ancient silver," Cedric said proudly.

"Thank you, Cedric," Em said as Ronnie fastened the necklace around her neck.

"As for your other problem," Cedric said. "You need to read through the grimoire; you will find how to reverse the transmutation. It will take much of your energy," he added. Em nodded. "Emily, it is most urgent that you build your energy levels daily, from now until the time." Cedric looked uneasy.

"I will," she said. They said their goodbyes and were walking through the upstairs workshop.

"Emily I send you with my blessings," Cedric said as he made a symbol on Em's forehead.

They met the others back in Leek, and then made the journey back to Kent. It was a long drive. It was dark when they got back, so they decided to order pizzas for dinner. They were all shattered.

Adam ordered the pizzas, Ronnie and Em's dad emptied the minibus, Abs and Sandra were sorting through the laundry and Em was putting everything away. Em's dad went into the study, Ronnie followed him. Em took all their things up to their room. She put the grimoire under her mattress and hid Cedric's box. She put her hand on the pendant. It began to tingle. She could feel the energy from it, flowing through her.

"That is beautiful," Peggy said, looking at it in adoration.

"I know. He is a wonderful man. Isn't he?" Em replied.

"He most certainly is, lassie." Peggy smiled.

Em went downstairs when she heard the doorbell. She was starving! The kitchen was a hive of activity and arguments. Sandra was insisting that everyone had plates and knives and forks. Ronnie and Adam were refusing, saying that the only way to eat pizza, was from the box with your hands.

Em took a plate, so did Abs and they sat at the table with Sandra to eat theirs, while the boys sat on the sofas in front of the TV.

Em grabbed all the empties and took them out to the kitchen. Abs grabbed the cheesecakes and bowls and Sandra made teas and coffees. Em cut Ronnie a slice of cheesecake and handed it to him. "Thank you, sweetheart." He smiled. She then handed her dad his plate. He winked at her. "Did you check the answerphone?" Ronnie asked him. He shook his head. "I'll do it when I have finished this," Ronnie said as he shovelled the cheesecake into his mouth.

Ronnie came out from the study. "Do you want the good news or the bad news?" he said.

"Go on, start bad and end on a high note," Em's dad said.

"We had a voice message from DI Strickland. We are going to get a telling off from him tomorrow for not informing him that we had found your dad."

"Shit! I completely forgot." Em put her head in her hands.

"Also, it was Lewis's body that was at the bottom of the cliffs. The DI is calling around tomorrow, as he needs to find Jade." Ronnie looked at Em, wide-eyed.

"What are we going to tell him?" she said.

"We say that we haven't seen her," Em's dad said.

"What do we say about you though, Uncle Bob?" Adam said.

"We say that I had a bit of a breakdown and went on a wander," he replied. Em shrugged. She didn't have a clue what to say.

"Was there any good news?" Abs sighed.

"Yes. Someone has made an offer on this place, full asking price, no chain." He smiled.

"Oh, that reminds me, I have sold the apartment, I forgot to tell you," Adam said.

"All we need now, is for you to sell yours then, Sandy." Em's dad beamed.

"I'm working on it, Bob, don't worry." She smiled.

She was walking through a field. The grass was short. She heard Ronnie calling her name. She ran to find him. Darkness. She saw his hand reaching out. She tried to grab. She reached it and then it was snatched away from her. She screamed.

"Em, it's OK," he said as he stroked her head. She was sobbing. Was she going to lose him again? She couldn't bear it. She didn't tell him; she said that it was the same as the others. "You should do a little more meditation before you go to sleep," Ronnie said as he handed her a glass of water. She nodded.

*

The kitchen was its usual morning chaos. Em poured herself a coffee and then called the dogs and took them in the garden. She needed some peace. Ronnie must have told them all that she had a bad night as they left her alone. She had just finished the last of her coffee when Sandra poked her head out of the door.

"Em, that policeman is here," she called.

"Coming," Em replied and walked slowly back to the house. She wasn't looking forward to this. As she walked through the kitchen her dad came through and gently grabbed her arm. "I've got this. Follow my lead," he whispered. Em nodded and followed him into the lounge.

The DI stood up and shook Em's hand. "It's been a while, Ms Wells," he said as he sat down. Ronnie tapped the seat next to him and Em sat.

"So, Mr Wells, could you tell me what happened?" he said.

"I went looking for Mags. I thought it would be better if I did it alone, no distractions you know. I covered most of the UK, you know," he lied.

"But what I don't understand is, why you didn't contact your family. They were extremely worried," the DI said.

"I understand that now, but you see Officer, at the time, I wasn't thinking straight. I just wanted Mags back," her dad said as tears formed and fell down his cheeks. Em touched his hand. The DI nodded his head.

"Well, we can close the case now. What about Jade? Does anyone here know of her whereabouts?" he asked.

"The last time I saw her, was when I was in Devon and she came to visit," Em said.

"And you haven't heard from her since then?"

"No, we rowed about Mum. I stopped speaking to her," Em said.

"And what about you Mr Wells?"

"The last time I saw her was the night I went off. I had a row with her too," Em's dad said as he wiped the tears away.

"OK, I will leave you good people in peace, but if any of you should hear from Jade or her whereabouts, if you could give me a call," he said as he stood. Ronnie stood up to show him out.

"We certainly will," Em's dad said as he stood and shook his hand.

"Thank you, goodbye." The DI nodded at Em. She smiled and put her head down. She hated herself for lying. When the front door closed, Em let out a huge sigh.

"Do you think he bought it?" Em's dad asked Ronnie. He nodded. Em wasn't convinced.

*

Later that day Em had taken herself down to the workshop. She was reading the grimoire. Every time she looked she could not find a thing about the transmutation reversal. "Maybe it's one of the hidden pages," she said out loud to herself as she closed the grimoire. She looked out of the window; it was a beautiful sunny day.

She grabbed the grimoire, locked the workshop, walked over to the big beech tree and sat down. She always went to the tree. She called him Alan. She grounded herself and began meditation.

She was walking through a field; it was a calm day. The wildflowers were dancing in the breeze. She could see something up ahead. It was a beautiful old well, dressed in flowers. She approached the well, something told her to look inside. She looked down, the water began churning and bubbling. Then something was coming through the water. The most beautiful woman rose from the well and stood beside her.

"You must look at it in a different way. It is not always black and white. There is a pattern you must find. Think of the energy lines," she said, smiled and then disappeared down the well.

"That's it!" she shouted as she sat upright. She counted seven words in on the first line, then seven words on the seventh line. It was starting to make sense. She hurried back to the workshop.

She wrote it all on the parchment that Cedric had given her, and then slid it inside the grimoire and headed back to the house.

Ronnie was in their room and he had started packing things up. "Blimey, you're eager," Em said and smiled as she walked into the room. She walked over and kissed Ronnie.

"You feeling better?" he asked.

"Sorry, I've just got a lot on my mind at the moment." Em smiled a sad smile.

"I know, sweetheart." He smiled. "Hey, why don't we book that lot downstairs a table at a restaurant, and then you and I can have one of our fine dining nights? It'll be fun," he beamed.

"Sounds like a wonderful idea, I'll go and book it now," she said as she skipped out of the door.

She told them all that they had booked it as a treat for them all to say thank you. Abs couldn't understand why Em and Ronnie weren't going. Em lied and said that she was still looking for the reversal spell.

"I think that they might need some alone time," Adam said and chuckled.

"Oh, why didn't you say that, Em?" Abs said and laughed.

Em went to their room to tell Ronnie the good news. "Right then," he said as he stood up. "I'll go to the shops, while you, my lovely, run yourself a bath and have a soak and a pamper." He kissed her and left. The door closed and her heart sank. The thought of losing him again was unbearable. Abs knocked on the door and poked her head around. Em wiped the tears from her eyes.

"Hey you, what's wrong?" Abs said as she put her arms around her. Em looked into Abs' big blue eyes; she knew she could trust her.

"I had a vision last night. Ronnie was taken again," Em sobbed.

"Maybe, you had that vision because it is the thing you are most afraid of, Em," Abs said, trying to reassure her. "You are not alone now. We will not let anything happen to any one of us," she added and wiped Em's tears. "Now, young lady, get yourself in that bath. I am going to get ready and then I will be back to give you a lovely makeover." Abs grinned.

"Thank you, what would I do without you? You are the best friend that anyone could ask for." Abs blew Em a kiss and left.

She felt like a million dollars when she walked down the stairs. Everyone complimented her on how beautiful she looked. Adam drove the others to the restaurant.

"You, my love, look stunning," Ronnie said as he put his arms around her. The evening was perfect!

*

The next morning she woke up in such a good mood. No visions or dreams. She felt great. The boys were going to a meeting with the architect, so the girls decided that a trip to the beach was on the cards. They put the dogs in the back of the car and were on their way.

Sandra had taken a parasol as she didn't want to burn. Abs was lying on a beach towel in the smallest bikini that Em had ever seen. Em was running in and out of the sea, playing with the dogs.

A while later when she was burying herself in the sand, she sighed. "What's wrong?" Sandra said as she looked up from her book.

"It's not the same here anymore," Em said sadly.

"Things change, Em. Just think, we'll have new beaches to explore when we move." Sandra smiled.

"Well, that's if it's not snowing all the time," Abs said, not moving. They all laughed.

*

It was one week until the search. Katarina had phoned to arrange times. Was it Katarina, was it Jade? Em didn't know anymore! She had spent every day building her energy. She swam in the sea when it was raining. She even sat beneath the beech tree during a thunderstorm!

CHAPTER 25

They had booked a farmhouse just outside of Larkhill. They thought that spending the week there would help them all to familiarise themselves with the place. The farmhouse was very homely. There was a big canopy attached to the back of the house and a large outdoor table and chairs. The table had a firepit built into the centre of it. Ronnie was in his element.

They first night Em spent an hour meditating before she went to bed.

Darkness, she could hear Dad calling her. She was crawling, pawing at the earth following her dad's voice. He sounded distraught. She had to help him. "Em. Em," he was calling.

"I'm coming," she called out. Lots of voices. Lots of shouting. "Shut up, I can't hear him!" she shouted.

A hand appeared out of the darkness; it was Dad's hand. She took hold and began to pull with all her strength. He lost his grip. He let go. Silence.

She looked at the clock – it was 4:45am. She got out of bed and looked out of the window. The light had started to creep up into the sky. The birds had begun their morning chorus and somewhere in the distance a cockerel was in the process of waking all those near him. Em felt suffocated. She needed to be outside. She crept out of the bedroom and went down to the kitchen. She took her coffee outside and sat at the table. It was beautiful. The sky had the most beautiful colours running through it; it gave a reflective hue all over the garden.

At the bottom of the garden was a big oak tree. She heard the sound of twigs breaking. She looked down at the tree to see a man standing beneath it. Her heart was in her mouth, and her first instinct was to run inside. He beckoned to her, gesturing her to go to him. As she stood he started to laugh. Not an ordinary funny laugh, a nasty sadistic, Billy sort of laugh. She jumped out of her seat, knocking her coffee cup flying, ran inside the house and locked the door.

She stood with her back against the door, trying to catch her breath. Ronnie walked into the kitchen. "Em, what the hell has happened?" he said as he walked over to her. She was still trying to catch her breath, so she pointed at the garden. Ronnie looked out of the window and shook his head. "There's nothing out there, sweetheart," he said. Em moved and opened the door.

"There was a man, beneath that oak tree at the bottom. He wanted me to go to him, but then he started laughing in an evil sadistic way, so I ran inside," Em said, her heart still racing. Ronnie walked out into the garden.

"He must have ran off. There is no sign of him now," he called to Em.

They all had breakfast. Em wanted to go to Glastonbury Tor, which was around an hour's drive. Dad and Sandra wanted to go off and do their own thing. Abs wanted to go to Glastonbury, but not up the Tor.

They parked in the town. Adam and Abs headed into the town,

while Em and Ronnie walked toward the Tor. The atmosphere was magical. Ronnie felt it too. They walked up hand in hand. It was quite busy at the top, so they sat on the grass, waiting until it was quiet before they went to the tower. They were chatting about anything and everything, when Em became aware that someone was watching them. She turned to her right and saw a man about thirty feet away, sitting on the grass, looking straight at her. "Ronnie," she said calmly, "look to my right. The man that was under the tree this morning is sitting on the grass over there," she said quietly. Ronnie looked.

"Em, there isn't anyone there," he said, looking puzzled. Em looked; he was still there and now he was laughing.

"What, you mean you can't see him!" she said. Ronnie shook his head as he looked over again. "That means he is not living. Shit, Ronnie, he is scaring me," she said, not taking her eyes off him. He got up and walked towards them. Em was almost sitting on Ronnie's lap.

"Almost time," he laughed. "You belong to me, tick tock," he laughed again.

"GET AWAY FROM US!" Em screamed then blew with all her power at him. He disappeared.

"What the fuck?" Ronnie looked shellshocked.

"Did you see him?" she asked Ronnie.

"No, but I fucking heard him!" he said. "Em, why did you breathe fire at him? How the hell did you do that?" He looked petrified.

"I didn't realise I had breathed fire. I was sending my power out to repel him, that's all," she said as tears streamed down her face. Ronnie put his arms around her. "Ronnie, what's happening to me?" she sobbed.

With all the commotion, all but one person had left the tower. They took a slow walk over. Em saw Peggy standing just inside the tower. They walked over to her. "What the hell was that?" Em asked her.

"Something not of this world, but incredibly dangerous," Peggy sighed. "As you are getting closer to the next cannister, you are drawing attention from everything arcane," Peggy said. "I see the pendant that Cedric made works," Peggy laughed.

"So that's where the fire came from," Em said with a huge sigh of relief and laughed. Peggy disappeared and Em turned to see where Ronnie was. He was standing with an elderly gentleman. Em walked over to them. "Michael, this is Emily," Ronnie said.

"My goodness, I have waited such a long time for this," he said as he took Em's hand in his. She felt his energy, good energy. Em looked at Ronnie in bewilderment.

"Er, I, er, I'm sorry but I have no idea who you are," she said, trying her hardest not to sound ignorant.

"I am guardian of this place and all that surrounds it. I have spent many years waiting for you to come. Their time is coming to an end and I for one will be relieved when you have rid us of them," he said.

"I'm sorry, I don't understand," Em said.

"Vultures, they are! All gathering, all waiting for *it* to be unearthed. They know the power it holds within," he said.

"Do… do you mean the cannister?" Em asked.

"Yes my dear, what else?" he smiled.

"So should I destroy it?"

"ABSOLUTELY NOT!" he roared. "Sorry, no. What it contains can destroy them all! The negative spiritual elements that breed on happiness and destroy it. No, my dear, it is your job to keep it safe, until you have found all of the missing pages. Then and only then can Abagail return and destroy them." Em turned to look at Ronnie. He smiled and when she turned back, Michael had gone.

They walked back to meet Adam and Abs and said very little; they were both dumbstruck. They found the café where they were to meet them. It was quirky to say the least. "Wow! It's cool in here," Em said as she sat down next to Abs. Abs nodded in agreement.

"No, Em, we are not moving here!" Ronnie said and laughed.

"So how did it go, up the Tor?" Adam asked. Secretly he wanted to go too but Abs was adamant that she wasn't climbing any bloody hills today! Ronnie and Em burst out laughing.

"Why don't you ask the dragon?" Ronnie said and they both howled with laughter. Adam looked at Abs, she shrugged her shoulders.

"It's a long story, mate, we'll tell you in the car," Ronnie said.

*

That night Em was sitting in bed reading the transmutation reversal from the grimoire. She closed the book and turned to Ronnie. "If I don't find Jade within the next two days I will not be able to do the reversal. It has to be done on the night of the full moon," she said despairingly. Finally after a few hours of tossing and turning, she managed to drift off to sleep.

She was in a huge field. There were mounds on it. She was alone and walking. She heard the awful growling. It was coming from all directions, but she could see nothing but grass. "Emily," she heard in a whisper. She walked towards it. In the distance beside the mound, she could see Carrie and Merlin. She ran over to them.

"Emily there is very little time, Katarina is preparing the spell to make the transmutation permanent. If you fail to do the reversal, Jade's soul will be trapped in Katarina's dead body for eternity," Carrie said sadly.

"I have no idea where to find her," she said desperately.

"You must find this place," she said as she waved her arms around, "in the waking hours. She is trapped below. You will hear her, Emily," she said, and then disappeared.

Everyone else was up and about when Em and Ronnie went down the stairs the following morning.

"Here you two are. Sit yourselves down. I have cooked bacon for breakfast," Sandra said. Em sat next to Abs.

"Are you alright, Em? You look like you have got the weight of the world on your shoulders," Abs said.

"What she needs is a good breakfast and plenty of fresh air. I have already prepared a picnic and I know a lovely spot, not far from here," Sandra said as she passed a plate of bacon sandwiches towards them.

"I'm not really in the mood, Sandra, but thanks anyway," Em said as she passed the plate to Ronnie.

"Em, Sandra has gone to a lot of trouble to plan this picnic," Em's dad said and gave her the look.

"Sorry." Em smiled. "A picnic sounds lovely, Sandra," she said and tried her hardest to look genuinely happy.

*

They parked in a layby and then climbed over a five-bar gate. "Are you sure that we are allowed in this field?" Abs said as she threw her leg over the gate. "I haven't seen any public access signs anywhere," she said as she jumped down.

"Aww, the city girl has turned all country bumpkin," Em said and laughed.

"Hey, I have been doing my homework like a good girl," Abs laughed.

Sandra led the group and found a spot. Em was thinking that it seemed familiar. It wasn't until she sat down and looked around to see the mounds that she realised that she was in the same field as her vision the night before. This aroused suspicion. *Why would Sandra randomly pick this place for a picnic?* Em thought to herself.

"Are you alright, love?" her dad asked as he passed her a tub of sandwiches to put on the blanket. She smiled at him.

"I'm fine, Dad."

"You look a million miles away," he said and rubbed the top of her head.

Ronnie sat down beside her and then Adam plonked himself the other side. Em's dad, Abs and Sandra had gone back to the minibus to get the dogs and another basket of food. "There is something bothering me," Em said to both of them.

"No shit, Sherlock," Adam said and smiled. Em nudged him with her elbow.

"It's Sandra. How did she know to come here? This is the field that was in my vision last night. Jade is below here somewhere, I know it, I can feel her," Em said.

"Well she is Cruella's aunt. Maybe she is spying for her," Ronnie said.

"Shit, we haven't told her about the fake cannisters, have we!" Em started to panic.

"No, we haven't even told your dad." Ronnie put his hand on hers and smiled.

"Phew. Right, I'm going for a little wander," Em said as she got up.

"Whoa, not on your own you're not! Wait until they get back and then we can come with," Ronnie said as he grabbed her hand.

So Em, Ronnie, Adam and Abs said that they were taking the dogs for walk around. Sandra seemed happy about this, Em's dad not so much. They walked behind one of the mounds, and that's when Em heard it. Crying. Adam heard it too. They walked around but couldn't see that there was any sort of entrance. Butch began to bark and then started to dig. Em ran over to him. There was something beneath the earth. It was a wooden board. Em was furiously moving the soil. Ronnie and Adam took either end and after a couple of attempts, moved it. There was a staircase carved out of the earth.

Em went first, closely followed by Ronnie and then Adam. Abs was staying above so that she could watch Em's dad. The smell was so familiar. She had most definitely been there before. Em was leading them through the earth tunnel. Adam had the torch from his phone on. Em could see the opening. As she got close, she poked her head around. Jade was tied to the slab. Em ran over to her. Jade began to sob. Em put her finger to her lips. Ronnie was cutting away at the ropes, while Adam kept watch. Then Ronnie picked up Jade's frail body and they went back through the tunnel. Adam was in front and Ronnie passed Jade to him as he got to the top of the steps. Ronnie grabbed hold of Em and they both came out. Em pushed the board back over and covered it with the earth that Butch had dug.

Adam carried Jade over to the picnic blanket and laid her down. "What the bloody hell has happened to her?" Em's dad said, tears filling his eyes.

"Her bloody aunt, that's what," Em said as she gestured at Sandra.

They got Jade in the minibus, packed the picnic things up and left. Back at the farmhouse Ronnie put Jade on the sofa; she was only semi-conscious. "Thank you. Em, I'm so sorry," she said and then closed her eyes.

Em walked out into the kitchen, where Sandra was. "Care to explain?" Em said. Sandra began to cry. "Look, the crocodile tears might work with Dad, but they don't wash with me, so either give me a really good explanation as to your part in all of this or get out!" Em said with her hands on her hips.

"Look, Em, the reason I took you there today was because I knew Jade was there. Katarina told me that if I told you, she would kill

Bob. I was scared, I didn't know what to do. I'm sorry. You have to believe that I wanted no part of this, and the sooner those two monsters are stopped the better," Sandra said, sobbing. Em didn't know what to think or who to trust. Her entire world had been turned on its head. "But I can tell you, that once you have found all the lost cannisters, they are planning to do to you, what they tried to do with Jade, and take all your power," Sandra said, wiping her eyes with a hanky.

"Why are they doing it, Sandra? What would drive them to be so evil?" Em asked.

"Katarina is not my niece through blood, in fact she was adopted by my great aunt when she was two years old, but she never aged. When my great aunt turned 80, she started to become very poorly. The sicker she became, the more Katarina aged. When my great aunt finally died five years later, Katarina was a teenager. She stayed that way and lived with my aunt until she turned 80 and then the same thing happened again. Exactly the same!" Sandra looked genuinely frightened.

"Shit, that would explain her hair changing colour every time she uses her power," Em said. Her head was spinning.

"So my aunt died at 85 and my sister took care of Katarina. She noticed a badness in her and once she became a woman, my sister sent her packing. She contacted me about five years ago, giving me a sob story that she had changed and was so lonely, and of course I fell for it. There are so many stories I could tell you about her that would make your hair curl," Sandra said and shuddered.

"So, how is it that she doesn't age, or only ages when she uses her power?" Em was intrigued.

"I was told by a seer, many years ago, that she dates back hundreds of years. She would fall pregnant and prepare the transmutation. As soon as the child was born, she would perform the spell and become an orphan. I believe that your ancestor, Abagail, put a binding on her, so that she could never age naturally, but once she had taken the blood from my great aunt, she realised that she had broken the binding. We are all in great danger, Em, she will want my blood for sure now!" She began sobbing again. Em put her arms around her.

"Now listen, I believe you, and there is no way on this earth that I will let her hurt any one of us. OK?" Em said, trying to sound reassuring, but secretly she was as afraid as Sandra.

Ronnie poked his head around the kitchen door and gestured to Em. She walked over to him. "Jade's not looking good," he whispered. Em walked over to her; she noticed that her breathing was very laboured.

Em went to the magic box and took out the grimoire. She needed to find something that would help Jade before she did the reversal. The moon wasn't full for 24 hours, so she had to buy some time. Em told Abs to sit with Jade and call her if there was any change. She took the grimoire outside and sat at the table.

There was a big gust of wind that flicked the pages of the grimoire. The page it opened to, happened to be a healing work. Em read through. There were a few bits that she didn't have, so she would have to send Adam to Glastonbury to grab them from a shop there.

Em put a piece of paper in the grimoire to mark the page. Honestly, the book was like a labyrinth; every time you found something in it, the next time you looked it had either disappeared or moved places. Em thought to herself. Then, she felt eyes on her. She was compelled to look at the oak tree, but she was terrified. She turned and looked. There he was. THAT man. Looking straight at her. It felt as though his eyes were burning through her. He began laughing and started to walk towards her. She grabbed all her things and turned to run. He was behind her. "You cannot keep running from me, little Em," he breathed down her neck.

She drew all the power up inside her and turned to blow at him. He was gone. She ran inside, straight into the arms of Ronnie. She was crying. "Hey," he said as he lifted her chin. "What has happened?" he asked.

"He was there again. He was right behind me." She was trembling.

"Sandra, can you make Em a strong cup of coffee?" Ronnie shouted out. He led her into the lounge and sat her on the armchair.

*

Em gave Adam the list and spent the rest of the afternoon sitting stroking Jade's head. They had a terrible relationship, but Em wouldn't wish this on her worst enemy. Well, there were a couple of people that she would, she thought to herself.

As they afternoon was drawing to a close, Jade's breathing became worse. Em kept looking at her watch. Then she heard the front door close; she jumped up and ran and grabbed the things from Adam.

In the lounge she had everything she needed laid out on a cloth. Everyone cleared out of the room. Em grounded herself and brought her power up. She began the healing work. After three attempts, she began to despair. "I think that they have caused too much damage, Em," Peggy said as she stood at Em's side.

"It must work, Peggy; I won't let them do it to her," Em said and began the healing again.

After ten minutes Peggy whispered in Em's ear, "She's gone."

"NOOOOOOO!" Em screamed and doing so released fire that singed the carpet. Everyone ran into the room. Em's dad's legs gave way and Adam caught him. Sandra was talking quietly to him through the tears. Everyone was distraught. There was a knock on the door.

They all looked at one another in horror. How were they going to explain this? Ronnie answered it. He walked back in the room followed by the elderly gentleman Michael. Em looked at Ronnie in disbelief.

"I am so sorry to intrude at this terrible time, but I am here to help," Michael said. Em looked at Ronnie; he nodded. "I was aware that this would happen. I have spoken to my very trusted guardians. We can lay her body to rest peacefully, without it ever being found," he added. Em stood and took his hand in hers, she could feel his energy pulsating.

"Thank you, Michael," she said as the tears streamed down her face.

"Do not punish yourself, Emily, or ever think that you failed her. You stopped her from being trapped in a dead body for eternity, and I am sure she will be eternally grateful to you." He smiled. "OK, I just need to make a phone call. Do you mind?" he said as he walked out into the kitchen.

Abs came through with a tray of hot drinks and put them on the table. Em's dad walked over to Jade's lifeless body. He bent over and kissed her forehead, and then collapsed in a heap. Ronnie and Adam picked him up and took him through to the kitchen, Adam opened the back door and they stood either side of him, just so that he could catch his breath.

"Ronnie," Adam said and gestured his head towards the oak tree. Ronnie frowned and shook his head. Then Adam started running towards the tree. "Adam, what the hell are you doing?" Ronnie shouted. Adam went down on the ground; it was as though an invisible force had knocked him down. Ronnie and Em's dad ran to him. He was on the ground and it seemed as though something, which they couldn't see was kicking the life out of him. "GET OFF

OF HIM!" Ronnie roared. Em's dad ran back to the house to get Em.

She and Michael ran to Ronnie. Well, Em ran, Michael in his twilight years hobbled down. THAT man had Adam on the ground and was choking him. She went into his face and roared as she drew her energy. He burst into flames and disappeared. Adam was on the ground, choking and struggling to breathe. Now Abs and Sandra had ran down to see what was happening. Abs screamed and became hysterical. Sandra was doing her level best to calm her down.

"What the bloody hell happened then? Em, since when have you learnt to breathe fire?" Em's dad said. Michael walked over to Em. He held the pendant in his hand. "Dearest Cedric," he said and smiled.

"You know Cedric?" Em asked.

Michael nodded. "We all know Cedric," he said. "I think that we all need to get back inside. There is great danger out here," Michael said, looking all around him.

Within a few minutes of being back inside the house, Michael's guardians had come to collect Jade. Michael promised them that as soon as the body was safe and secure he would take them to her. They sat in the lounge. Michael asked Ronnie and Adam to close all of the curtains, and lock all of the doors.

"Now then, Emily, you must search for the cannister tonight. Katarina and Billy have been to the chamber, they know that Jade is not there, and she is furious. That thing at the tree, that unworldly evil thing, is linked to her. They were together hundreds of years ago. Between them they created the transmutation spell. She used him to get what she wanted, and then cast him away as though he was nothing. He vowed revenge. He knows that she wants you for your magical energy, Emily, so he is hell bent on getting you first. I do not mean to frighten you, but the only thing that can help you now is that missing page," Michael said.

*

Em went up the stairs to prepare everything. She was shaking with fear. She had never been so afraid. Ronnie tried to comfort her. "Em, I owe you my life and I vow to you, that I will not let anything happen to you." He looked into her big brown eyes. She kissed him and as she did a determination started to grow inside of her.

"There is a job to get done," she said as she gathered her things together. Ronnie winked at her and then followed her down the stairs.

*

They all got in the minibus, even Michael. They drove back to the field where the chamber was. They walked past the chamber heading north. Ronnie, Adam and Em's dad all carried torches. Em noticed in the distance a freshly dug mound. She headed in its direction, ignoring the alarm bells that were ringing inside her head. She heard water, just a trickle. She got on her hands and knees and began to follow it. The closer she got to the mound the louder the water and right beside it she heard it cascading. She heard the birdsong. This was it. She took out her trowel and began digging. Deeper and deeper; she could feel the energy. "Did we bring a shovel? This one is deep," she said quietly.

Ronnie handed her the shovel. "Do you want me to do it?" he asked. Em shook her head.

She dug deeper and deeper. The water was close. She was inside the pit that she had dug. She started to use her hands. She could feel the water, she could feel the energy. Then she felt the cannister. She grabbed it and held it up. They all cheered. The ground beneath her started to shake, she started to scramble. Something had hold of her foot. She looked down. It was HIM, his black eyes burning through her. He was laughing. "Mine," he said.

"GET YOUR FUCKING HANDS OFF OF ME!" Em screamed. Ronnie and Em's dad grabbed her shoulders and started to pull her. He was too strong; no matter how hard they pulled, he pulled her down further. Then the earth around her caved in. She was buried. She held her breath. She could hear them above, all of them digging. There was light she could just about open her eyes to see it.

Above Ronnie, Adam and Em's dad were digging furiously. "I can see her!" Ronnie shouted.

She felt a hand; she could feel it was her dad's hand. She used all of her energy and managed to free her hand and grab it. "I've got her, everyone clear the earth away," her dad shouted. They pulled and pulled. The earth was cleared from her face. She took a deep breath and gasped for air.

"Stay with us, sweetheart," Ronnie said desperately. "Come on, you lot, hurry!" Ronnie shouted.

Her dad was pulling her hand. "Come on, Em, give it your all," he said as he pulled again.

DARKNESS.

"She's stopped breathing, get her out!" Ronnie screamed.

To be continued…

Find out what happens to Em in the next book,
Wild Mountain Thyme.

ABOUT THE AUTHOR

Louise lives in Devon, close to Dartmoor, with her husband and five children. She has had eleven children in total, but the others have flown the nest! When they are not teaching the children, Louise and her husband enjoy walking on the moors and the coastal path, and of course writing!

Printed in Great Britain
by Amazon

61857553R00169